THE MANHATTAN MATTER

Dick Jacobsen

ISBN: 0692783768
ISBN 13: 9780692783764

1

MELANY AND BRAD

His naked body, damp with perspiration, thrust into hers at a frantic, painful pace as he neared his climax. Seeming not to care, he roughly tore at her near-lifeless form laying beneath him. She had a slender dancers' body developed by some earlier dream, now quashed after several years of meth and prostitution.

"Oh God," Brad gasped with each shove as he neared the end. He knew she was oblivious to what was happening, and didn't care as long as he got what he wanted. In her meth-induced stupor, her eyes were rolled back in their sockets, beautiful face creased with pain; her natural blonde hair matted as her arm dropped off to the side of the bed and fluttered, like a helpless one-winged bird, to the rhythm of his constant pushing.

"Aaaaah!" He grunted finally, as every muscle in his body tightened from his release. He pulled out abruptly and fell to her side, breathing heavily and wiping his brow with the bed sheet. He lay there panting for several minutes and looked over at her with a blank stare. Brad got up and went directly to the shower; she didn't move.

When he got back to the room, she lay as he had left her, looking nearly dead. He shook his head in disgust and strolled naked to the kitchen. He found a Corona in the refrigerator and sat at the kitchen table, drinking and admiring his taut body, smiling as if he had just made a private conquest. *She's a great fuck,* he thought, *too bad she's a meth head. I can take it or leave it, but she's hopelessly hooked.*

He picked up his beer and went out onto the small fire escape landing to have a smoke. Leaning back on the window sill, he looked out at the surrounding buildings, flaunting his nakedness. Brad began stroking his modest genitals, not caring who might be looking or who might be offended. He had no concern for the *creeps* who lived in this run-down section of Brownsville-East New York City. *I'd give my left nut to get out of here,* he said to himself. *If that bitch had two pussies we'd be outta here in no time.* Inside, though, he knew that the cunt's meth habit was holding them down. They would never escape at this rate.

He had tried busting johns, street stickups, and drug dealing, but the only thing he was really good at was pimping, and as long as Melany held on to her figure and her looks they could eke out a living.

"For God's sake, what the hell did you do to me? I feel like I've been raped by a wire bottle brush!" Melanie snarled, appearing naked at the window. "For Christ's sake, can't you have sex without ripping me to pieces? Shit, I still have a shift to put in tonight." She stomped off to the bathroom and slammed the door.

She looked at herself and tears filled her mascara-stained eyes. *What happened to the graceful ballerina,* she thought to herself, doing a third position pose in front of the mirror. She got into the shower and tried to scrub the pain and sadness from her body. She was beautiful, smart, and sexy, and yet the wrong decisions she had made along the way threatened to take that all away. The drug dependency and the need to be with the so-called bad boy gripped her and would not let go.

She emerged from the bathroom and went straight to her dressing table. Tonight she had two school girl gigs with men over sixty years old. That means extra rosy cheeks, ringlet curls, and two pony tails, one on each side of her head. Satisfied with her hair and makeup, she went to her closet and selected the appropriate costume. Brief pink lace panties, pink lace demi cup bra, Tartan plaid miniskirt, long sleeve white shirt, matching plaid men's tie, thigh-high knit white stockings and six-inch spike black patent leather heels.

She took one last look at herself in the full length mirror and joined Brad in the living room for a last hit on the meth pipe. *If you could call this living,* she thought to herself. Melany knew that by the time Brad got her to the first john's location, she would be in the perfect mental state to deal with an overweight, 60-plus-year-old man with erectile dysfunction: oblivious and completely detached from her body. The first John was a nice sort of man who had recently lost his wife and needed to look at and touch young female bodies. He was always gentle, almost to the point of being creepy. The second one was not as nice, and insisted on rough sex. He paid well, but she insisted that Brad be in a nearby room in case things got too rough.

"Hi, Mr. Johnson," she said as she skipped bouncily into the first john's apartment. Brad did the usual five hundred dollar transaction and left to wait outside the apartment.

"Hi Melany," the old man smiled. "You look lovely tonight, would you please get me a drink?"

She walked, long legged, to the sideboard and poured him a neat two fingers of Scotch. She purposely dropped a cocktail napkin so she could bend over and tease him with a peek at her panties; by now, this was a customary ritual they had established.

"Come and sit on my lap," he asked, patting his pajama-clad thighs.

She handed him his Scotch, and straddled his legs as she sat facing him. He took a sip of his drink and leaned back in his easy chair to take in her beauty. He put his free hand on her upper thigh and stroked the bare skin above her stocking and below her hem. She smiled. Slowly, he moved his hand forward.

She playfully slapped his hand. "You naughty man," she squealed impishly.

He smiled and pulled back his hand to begin caressing her soft, supple thigh and she let out a soft moan. He put down his drink and caressed both thighs, and she moaned again. He quickly slid his hands under her skirt, behind her buttocks, and pulled her on top of his genitals.

"Let's play horsey," he begged.

She began slowly bouncing up and down, forward and back on his penis, with her hands on his shoulders and her legs curled up on either side of him. She was still sore from the rough sex with Brad, and cursed him under her breath. She felt Mr. Johnson's penis slowly swelling.

"Oh, Mr. Johnson, I think you are a nice horsey," she purred as he reacted to her rhythm.

"Take off your shirt and tie," he insisted, and she deftly complied, all the time rubbing and bouncing. He stared at her beautiful, bouncing, bra-clad breasts, her nipples hardening beneath the transparent pink lace. He leaned forward and kissed her cleavage. He pushed back her skirt to reveal her pink panties and to watch her move her pelvis, expertly rubbing him to hardness.

"Oh, Mr. Johnson, I think the saddle is getting harder and harder," she cooed.

He reached down, and with one hand pulled her panties aside and used the other to free himself and enter her. Thankfully, within eight to ten strokes he ejaculated and the encounter was over.

Slowly, she climbed off his lap and walked to the bathroom to clean up. When she returned, he was smiling and sipping his Scotch. Within minutes, there was a knock on the door as Brad came to escort her to her next gig.

Mr. Holloway was a completely different animal. He was obese, hairy, pasty-faced, and all business. He didn't much care for the niceties. Brad stayed in the apartment living room while Melany went into the bedroom with the john. Within minutes, things got rough and Brad burst into the room to find Melany on the floor with blood running from her nose, her skirt torn, and her blouse ripped open.

"Back away, asshole!" Brad shouted at the piggish man standing over Melany. "One more move from you and I'll slice your cock off," Brad said as he pulled his straight blade hunting knife from the sheath tucked under his jacket.

The man grunted, stood erect, and backed away. He scowled at Brad with a menacing look as Melany woozily got to her feet.

"Give me my money back and get that whore out of here," the john growled.

"Fuck you pig, she's not a punching bag and this is going to cost you," Brad took off his jacket and wrapped it around Melany's shoulders. "Put this on baby, we are out of here. Here are the keys. Go to the car and wait for me."

The fat man's scowl changed to fear as he watched Melany leave the apartment. He turned as Brad walked toward him. Brad suckerpunched him and he fell flat on his stomach, letting out a loud grunt as he hit the floor.

"Not so brave when it's a man you have to deal with, are ya, asshole?" Brad scoffed as he kicked the downed man several times in the ribs. "Where's your wallet, pig?" Brad shouted.

The fat man pointed to his dresser and Brad went to retrieve it. There were six one hundred dollar bills, two fifties, four twenties and some ones. Brad removed the bills and the driver's license and threw the wallet at the agonized man on the floor.

"If I ever hear of you doing what you just did again, I'll personally cut your balls off, you fat fuck. I've got your ID, I'll track you down," Brad threatened as he walked toward the door, "It's assholes like you that fuck it up for everyone."

Brad slammed the apartment door behind him, and took the stairs down to the street where Melany waited. She sat dejected and crying as he got in the driver's seat.

"Sorry babe, I knew the asshole had a rep, but I didn't think he'd try anything if I was in the apartment. He won't do it again, at least not in this town, and he thought you should have an eight hundred dollar tip."

"A tip?" She asked.

"Yeah," Brad said. "It took some persuasion, but he quickly saw the reasonableness of my request." He smiled at her and touched her bruised cheek. "I'm sorry babe, let's go home and get high."

When they got home, Melany went to the bathroom to shower away the events of the evening. The more she thought about the pig, the harder she scrubbed. She wanted the memory, the pain, the humiliation, and the shame to be gone. She couldn't stand the thought of that man touching her, let alone being inside her. She scrubbed and scrubbed until her entire body was a radiant pink. She dried off, wrapped her hair in a towel and rubbed her tingling skin with lotion before going to the bedroom to put on pajamas. When she emerged, she felt a little better. Brad was on the couch with the meth pipe and crystal ready to go. She sat down beside him and took a sip of his beer as he got the pipe going. She took the first hit, and within seconds her brain began to release the sweet dopamine she desperately needed. She fell back on the cushions, eyes rolling up in her head, as the chemically induced euphoria took over.

The next morning they awoke entwined on the couch. As Melany rose, the pain from the blow she took the night before hit her, and all of the memories flooded back. She got up and ran to the bathroom, nearly throwing up before she made it to the toilet. She washed her face, rinsed her mouth and returned to the living room.

She sat next to Brad, took his hand in hers and looked up at him with tears welling up in her eyes.

"Brad, I can't do this anymore. I can't deal with the pain and humiliation any longer. We have to find some other source of income," she began.

"Aw, don't jump to conclusions babe. It was a shitty deal last night, but I promise it won't happen again. I'll vet the johns better, you'll see. Calm down, baby."

"No, I won't calm down. I'm serious. It is getting harder and harder living with myself, and I need to get back some of my dignity and self-respect. Don't you see what this is doing to me? Doing to us?" she pleaded.

"What the fuck are we going to do for money?" Brad immediately demanded. He hadn't worked at a real job in years, and had no particular skills other than roughing people up.

"I still have my body, I still have my looks. I can still dance. I can work at a strip club, and you can be my bodyguard. It pays pretty well, and I won't have to fuck johns anymore," came Melany's conclusion.

"Most of the clubs demand that you lap dance between stage numbers. What will you do then?" he probed.

She thought for a moment, and knew he was right. She had seen the girls many times. Some of them appeared to enjoy it. In most places, the men were allowed to touch only their thighs, backs and stomachs. There were some places that didn't allow any touching.

"I don't think I'll have a problem with lap dancing, where touching is controlled. You would be there to make sure the johns played by the rules," she concluded. "Please Brad, I can't do this anymore."

Brad looked into Melany's pleading brown eyes and thought for several minutes before he spoke. "It'll mean that you will have to work longer shifts and more nights you know, to bring in the same amount of money as you do now. I know you want change, but I'm not lowering my lifestyle. You gotta produce," he finally said.

"I understand," she said meekly, looking down at her hands.

"Okay, get dressed and we'll go looking," he said.

"Okay, let's see what you've got," said the owner of the Pussy Cat Club.

Melany got off the bar stool and walked up onto the stage. The music came on and she began to slink and strut around the floor in time with the beat, gracefully removing her clothing. Her movements were sultry and her smile was seductive. The owner leaned forward on his bar stool and swiveled to get a better look. He seemed to be enjoying her efforts so far. She got down to her bra, panties, heels, and stockings and began to use the brass pole in the middle of the stage.

"We go all the way here," the owner called to her.

She smiled and kept on turning and writhing around the pole. Finally she stepped away from the pole and reached behind her back to unsnap her strapless bra, which she threw on the pile on the chair at the back of the stage. She deftly pulled down her panties and twirled them over her head on her index finger. She smiled and bowed as the music ended.

The owner stood and clapped as he walked over to the stage. "Come over here, baby, and let me have a closer look at you," he said.

She walked to the front of the stage and looked down at him, legs slightly apart, hands clasped behind her back.

"Beautiful," he said. "Turn slowly for me."

She slowly turned sideways, and then fully away from him, exposing her backside.

"Legs apart, bend over and touch your toes, baby," he directed. "Ummm, beautiful."

She stood erect again and turned her other side to him. He looked her up and down and was taken by her flawless taut skin, her trim muscular legs, flat stomach, perfect breasts, and beautiful smile. Brad was smiling smugly as if he had something to do with Melany's appearance.

"I can start you at a house fee of two hundred dollars a night. You keep everything you make. How does that sound to you?"

"One fifty," Brad said.

"One seventy five," the owner returned, "and you work six nights a week from eight to two. We agree ahead of time on nights off. We allow public and private lap dancing, you pay fifty per john for a private room, no touching of private parts allowed, panties on at all times. No drugs on the premises. The drinks that the johns buy you are watered way down for your own protection. You may not solicit sex on the premises. Capische?"

"I understand, Mister..." Melany said, questioningly.

"Call me Jake," The owner said. "You can start tomorrow night."

"I'll be here," Melany said with a seductive smile. "Eight sharp."

"That's eight sharp, ready to dance."

"I understand."

As Brad and Melany walked out of the Pussy Cat Club, Jake looked over at the bartender and said, "I'd have paid her to work here. Did you see her? The stupid shit with her insisted on haggling. Why is it the beauties always take up with simple fucks like that?"

2

"Carrie, she is absolutely beautiful," John said as he bent down to kiss his adopted daughter's perspiring, tired, smiling face. "I just came from the nursery. They are cleaning her and getting her ready for you. I can't wait until they bring her in."

"She is adorable," JT agreed. "All of her bones and appendages appear to be in their proper places as well," he smiled. "Again, this woman hits another home run."

The large, private hospital room was filled with smiling and chatting family members; all pleased with the day's outcome and excited that both Carrie and her new baby were doing extremely well. JT, the proud father, had a painted-on smile he couldn't seem to lose. He sat next to the bed, holding Carrie's hand and gently rubbing her arm. John and Joe stood back as the women gathered around the bed fussing, trying to make Carrie as comfortable as possible.

"Okay, JT and Carrie, what is the wee one's name?" John called out from the back of the room.

Everyone looked at JT and Carrie with anticipation.

"We haven't cast this in stone yet, but we were thinking about Priscilla Anne," Carrie said. "We wanted to honor your adopted mother, John."

"That would mean a lot to her and to me, but what about your mother, JT?" John asked.

"John, we plan to do this again. We haven't produced a JT yet, and at the rate this woman produces beautiful little girls, we should have no shortage of opportunities to honor everyone." Everyone in the room had a chuckle as Carrie rolled her eyes back in mock repulsion.

"Well this calls for some champagne," John said, opening several bottles and filling glasses on the side table. He handed out the glasses with his brother Joe's help. John held up his glass and said, "To Carrie and JT for providing this miracle today, and without expectation I vow to love Priscilla Anne Wingate with the same love I have for her mother and her other little charmer, Jennifer."

Carrie smiled up at John as her eyes began to glisten with the memory of the first, unfortunate daughter she lost to cancer. She remembered how much little Jennifer loved John and how John doted on her. She remembered the trip to South Carolina where Jennifer had the time of her life caring for and riding the Thoroughbred *Jennifer Too*, and how happy she was in the final days before her submission to cancer. She thought about little Jennifer often, and it was always with deep love, a little sadness, and a longing to have that type of relationship again. With her change in lifestyle, she knew that she wouldn't be spending the amount of personal, one on one, time with Priscilla Anne that she had done with Jennifer. Now there was JT, John, and the family as well as Double O to deal with, and JT's promise to the gathering that this would not be the last of the Wingate line. She smiled at the thought of having two or three more little Wingates running around the house. She and JT had talked about it and they both wanted the same thing, and they wanted to have them close in age. As soon as she was ready, they would try again.

"Here we are, ladies and gentlemen," the nurse announced as she paraded the cart into the room of guests and began to make the reports of record, administer the birth tests, and calculating the second APGAR score. They measured her head and her body length and took her weight, a healthy 8 pounds, 10 ounces. They gave her Vitamin K, a Hepatitis B shot and eye ointment. They wrist-banded the baby and Carrie to avoid mix-ups. They finished the cleaning, swaddled her, and placed a pink wool cap on her head to keep her warm and handed the tiny bundle to Carrie.

"A nine APGAR Score," the nurse said. "You have a very healthy, vital little girl, with two of the longest legs I've ever seen. I think you may have a ballerina in the family."

Carrie smiled and reached for the baby, grinning broadly as she kissed her on each of her plump little cheeks. One by one, starting with JT, the newborn was handed gently around the room. Her eyes were open wide in curiosity and she had an unmistakable smile for everyone. John was one of the last to hold the miniature package. He looked deeply into Priscilla Anne's little eyes with a beaming smile on his face. She blinked, kicked her little legs and smiled back, and John was hooked.

"That's it," John said. "I'm yours forever. Your wish is my command. I'll babysit for free, I'll take the three o'clock feeding, what university do you want to attend?" Everyone laughed as John listed his grandparental promises. "I know you have a stake in this too, brother Joe, I'm not trying to hog all the spotlight here, but I am declaring right now that I am this one's Papa, and I hereby demand all of the rights and privileges that title holds."

Joe put his arm around John's shoulder and looked down at the beautiful little girl. "I accede to most of your demands Papa, but you had best remember that the title of Grandpa holds a lot of sway in these parts, so don't be surprised if you run up against a little competition." Joe hugged his younger brother and they both smiled broadly at everyone in the room, still competitive boys at heart.

Joe, being the eldest, loved his brother in a retiring way. They had lost their mother at a very early age and their father, JT III, had talked Priscilla Anne Harcourt, his then personal assistant, lover, and eventual wife, into taking on the position of mother to the boys. They grew up loving her dearly, especially John, who adored her still at age 73. He still cared for her and went to see or talk to her daily. He couldn't wait to tell her the news of the family's new addition and the name that was chosen out of love and respect.

"Carrie, how long is your stay in the hospital?" John asked.

"I'm out tomorrow, assuming all is well, which it appears to be," Carrie replied.

"Wonderful. When are you coming back to work?" John went on.

"Gee, slave driver, give me a break," she smiled.

"I was thinking about handing over my Chairmanship to you and applying for the nanny job," John smiled.

"Hey John, how about giving someone else a chance holding the kid? You may have monopolized the shipping industry, but you can't monopolize that little one," someone called. The family was in rare form and having fun with each other. The joy that JT and Carrie brought was felt by everyone. Priscilla Anne was the first new blood in nearly a decade, and the entire family couldn't wait to watch her grow and flourish in the genuine love and care they all had for her.

"Okay, okay, who's next?" John queried reluctantly, as his wife Jennifer held out her arms, eager for the chance. "Enjoy, but don't get any ideas madam," John winked.

"My God, she's gorgeous," Jennifer said to Carrie in her round British accent. "Kind of looks like her mother, and I bet she'll have those signature Wingate blue eyes."

The gathering went on for another hour or so, and John noticed that Carrie looked tired and in need of rest. "Okay everyone, let's give this young lady and her mother a rest."

"I'm fine John," Carrie stirred.

"I'm sure you are sweetheart, but we have all had our first looks, we like what we see, and now it's time for you to be alone with JT and get some shut-eye," John insisted.

Everyone filed past the bed for one last look and a kiss for Carrie as they began to leave the room.

"One more thing everyone," John interrupted. "Big family get-together at Henri's this coming Sunday. We are going to give this little wonder a proper welcome party, everyone's invited. 5 PM sharp."

On the way home, John called his mother from the car. "She is absolutely gorgeous, Mom, and they have named her Priscilla Anne in your honor," John reported.

"Oh my, how splendid!" the Matriarch exclaimed. "I can't wait to see her, when is she going home?"

"Tomorrow, if all goes well, and if you like I will come get you and take you to see her."

"That's wonderful darling. What time do you think you will come by?" she asked.

"I'm not sure Mom, but I'll try to be there around four o'clock. That way I'm sure they will be home and settled by then."

"That will be fine dear, I'll be waiting," she said and rang off.

Priscilla Anne Harcourt – Wingate was now 73, and she had become frail after a very serious bout with the flu two years ago. She lived alone with a part-time caretaker since JT III had passed. John wanted her to move in with him and Jennifer, but she wouldn't think of it. *"You young folks have your lives to lead and you don't need an old hen like me hanging around,"* Priscilla had told him.

Priscilla Anne Harcourt was born in London, England in 1929 at the onset of the Great Depression. Northern England was breaking under the effects of the Great Depression while London in the south was quite a different matter. Housing construction and light industry were on the rise and James Harcourt, Priscilla's Victorian father, held a mid-level management position at an appliance manufacturing company. To give the twins the best life they could, Janis Harcourt, Priscilla's charming mother, went to work in James' factory when Priscilla and her twin sister Patricia completed primary school.

The family was close-knit and loving. The girls were inseparable, they did everything together. Priscilla embraced her early school years and participated with joy and commitment. She had to work for her grades, but she always had time for sports activities and playing, and she especially enjoyed her participation in the Girl Guides program.

As a Rainbow and Brownie Guide, she worked diligently to 'lend a hand' and took very seriously the 'Promises' to do her best, to love her God, to serve her King and her country, to help other people, and to keep the Brownie Guide Law.

WWII was beginning to escalate in Europe, and all of England was bracing for war. Most of England's finest men had signed up for the venture, and the women were working at men's jobs to support the homestead. In late 1939, the Harcourts decided to send their girls to the country to avoid the German Blitz. The decision was the most emotionally difficult one the two ever had to make. Janis began the process early by telling the girls what was to happen, explaining they would live with another family, most likely on a farm, that they would continue school and other activities and would communicate by mail until it was safe for them to come home again. The soon-to-be twelve year olds were well prepared when, in February of 1940, they were placed in the Pied Piper Program.

They were sent to Crewe, a railroad town in Cheshire. When they got off the train, it was cold, damp and dreary. They found a bench and sat huddled, scared and lonely with their ID tags displayed prominently on their coat lapels. Priscilla looked at Patricia, who was softly sobbing beside her. She put her arm around her and reassured her that everything would be alright. For an hour they waited, and Priscilla began to be concerned. She was cold and had to use the toilet, but she was afraid to leave the platform for fear she would miss the arrival of the host family. A man and a woman approached them and asked to see their ID tags. The woman looked at the man and then back at the girls and smiled.

"Welcome to Crewe," she said. "I'm Ester Thompson and this is my brother, Robert Avery."

Priscilla gave the woman a bright smile, saying, "I'm Priscilla Harcourt, and this is my twin sister Patricia." Patricia looked up with teary blue eyes, and tried to force a smile.

The sisters settled in quickly. They had house and farm chores, went to makeshift schools provided by Pied Piper, and Priscilla immediately joined the Crewe Girl Guiding group. She had become a full-fledged Guide just before leaving London and was anxious to continue helping others.

Over the first year Ester, grew to love the twins. Their goodness and willingness to please drew the girls closer and closer to her.

The girls also had regular visits from their parents, who brought them new clothes, books, candy and more love. Mrs. Thompson and the Harcourts were drawn to each other despite their different accents and lifestyles. James loved the country and its relative safety, Ester loved the stories and nice gifts that always accompanied the generous Harcourts.

In May of 1941, Mrs. Thompson was called to the Crewe office of Pied Piper. She was told that a German Luftwaffe bomb had made a direct hit on the Harcourt home and both of the Harcourt parents were deceased. Ester Thompson knew it would be up to her to deal with the children, now thirteen years old. She returned home to find the twins laughing and playing with the chickens. She called to the girls to come in; she had news for them.

"I don't know any other way to tell you, but we won't be seeing your mother and father anymore. They were viciously taken from us yesterday evening by a German bomb," she told them mournfully.

The twins broke down in deep sobs and hugged each other. Ester tried everything she could to bring them out of their sorrow, to no avail. The girls went to their bedroom, and were heard sobbing well into the night. They emerged from their room the next morning and walked up to Ester, faces swollen with grief and eyes that were now dry but puffy and red from the grueling night. Brave, clear voiced, and head high, Priscilla asked what was to become of her and her sister. Ester asked if there were any aunts, uncles or grandparents that the girls knew of.

"We are alone," Priscilla said, smiling bravely and shaking her head no.

"Then there is only one thing that we can do," Ester went on. "You will have to become my girls because I love you too much to let you go anywhere else," she declared, holding her arms out, wide apart.

Both Priscilla and Patricia fell into Ester's arms. The warmth of her breast, the doughy smell of her apron, the softness of her sweater enveloped them, and they felt safe. They had been so worried what would become of them.

"I will begin the process of adoption tomorrow," Ester promised.

The girls lived with the Ester for the next five years when Priscilla, now eighteen years old and fully blossomed, announced that she wanted to move to London to continue her schooling and strike out on her own. Mrs. Thompson tried hard to dissuade her, but Priscilla was too headstrong. Patricia was saddened, but she had no desire to leave Ester's care just yet; she had a beau in Crewe and she was reluctant to leave.

For the next three years, Priscilla continued on with higher education classes, working, and traveling back and forth to Crewe to visit her family. On her twenty-first birthday, she announced that she was emigrating to the United States. She had completed all of the necessary paperwork and preparation, received her work visa, and had set aside enough money for the trip and enough to live on for three months if she was very frugal. Patricia broke down and cried, and Ester held out her arms to her brave, young adopted daughter.

"I feel that I want to hug you forever, my sweet girl," Ester whispered into Priscilla's ear.

"I know it is a surprise, but I couldn't tell you anything until I was completely ready to make the move," Priscilla said, with tears beginning to blur her vision.

"Priscilla, I will miss you so much, but I know that you have to go and spread your wings. This isn't much of a birthday for me," Patricia lamented.

Priscilla had a week before she sailed, and she spent every moment with her sister and second family. She spent the week cooking with Ester, laughing and crying with Patricia, and playing card games in the evening by the fire with them both. She wanted to immerse herself in her family; she knew it would be a long time before she could feel their warmth again.

She arrived in New York on May 5, 1949, and immediately found a Women's Only Apartment in the West Village area of Manhattan. Her next task was to find a job, and she scoured the *New York Times* daily. A listing for a clerk/secretary caught her eye, as it was fairly close to her apartment. The ad read,

> Clerk/Typist required. Must have good math and typing skills.
>
> Must be prompt, orderly and of neat and pleasant appearance.
>
> Must be over 21 years of age. Starting pay is $180 per month.
>
> Progressive Medical and Dental Health Plans and Retirement Benefits provided.
>
> Contact Occident-Orient Shipping Company.

Priscilla put on her new calf-length skirt with a matching cropped, waist-fitting three-quarter sleeve jacket top that accentuated her slender figure, gloves, a modest hat, and two-inch heels. With CV in hand, she entered the nicely-appointed Double O office with all the self-confidence she could muster.

There was no one at the front desk, so Priscilla stood, hands clasped, in the foyer and waited. The great doors to the inner offices opened and out stepped Joseph Thomas "JT" Wingate III.

"I'm sorry, have you been here long?" JT III asked her, as she turned to meet him.

"No, I've just arrived to interview for your advertised position," Priscilla returned in her obvious round British accent.

"Please come into my office," JT gestured. "My assistant is out at the moment, so I will have to do. Do you mind?"

After introducing each other, JT scanned her CV and she let her eyes wander to take in the beautifully appointed office. They conversed for almost an hour. JT was mesmerized by her intellect, accent, and beauty. She delightfully charmed him, and without any further uncertainty he blurted out, "When can you start?"

Priscilla smiled broadly and said, "Now, if you like."

"Now it is, then. Take a seat in the lobby, Mona should be back shortly and she will get you started. Show you the ropes, as we say."

"We say that, too. It's an old British Navy saying, actually," Priscilla smiled back.

"Here is some information on the company you can read while you wait."

From that moment on, she began to fall in love with the twenty-seven year old executive.

Now the matriarch of the family, Priscilla Anne Wingate rode up in the elevator with her son John to meet and welcome her namesake.

3

THE GROWING MIRACLE

John sat watching little Priscilla Anne on her back in the crib, grabbing at the small teddy bears whirling around her head on the wind-up mobile. She smiled, kicked, and cooed like the happy and healthy child she was. At ten months, she was growing wispy blond hair, her eyes had turned azure, and she was beginning to hoist herself up on anything that would support her in her attempts to take her first steps.

As he watched, he couldn't help but remember little Jennifer, Carrie's first daughter. He remembered the feelings that she brought out in him. How he wanted everything for Jennifer, he wanted to hold her, protect her, give her happiness. She was a brilliant little girl with everything to live for but carried with her a fatal cancer. *Is it possible that I can somehow bring Jennifer back in this lovely little creature?* he asked himself. *Is it fair to little Priscilla Anne that I even have that thought?* He convinced himself that it was best that he see Priscilla as fresh and new, and reserve his old thoughts for little Jennifer only, keeping her separately alive in his remembrances. One day he would tell little Priscilla about his love for her sister.

"Up you get, little one," John smiled, as he gently picked up Priscilla to hold her. The nanny walked in with a nursing bottle and gave it to John, along with a burping cloth. "Okay my sweet, here it comes," he noted as he kissed her on the cheek and flew the bottle, like a fighter jet, to her waiting mouth, making a buzzing sound to her utter joy. She smiled broadly as John put the nipple in her mouth. She sucked quietly, all the time looking up into John's face. Her curious, smiling eyes seemed to study his handsome features; his gray hair, his sharp aquiline nose, his blue eyes, his signature dimples.

She let out a small gasp as the nipple popped out of her mouth and immediately smiled up at John. She was finished and ready to be burped at his shoulder. As he patted her tiny backside he hugged her as well, and she made small cooing sounds with each pat, and then a sudden belch. He wiped her mouth and placed her on her back on his thighs. He bounced her gently up and down and she giggled with joy. *Definitely a happy little thing,* he said to himself. He reached over and took a sip of his single malt Scotch and gazed down at her. He knew all of the young babysitters in the building were upset with him for usurping so many of Priscilla's babysitting hours.

"Come now Papa, it's not fair you have all of the fun," his wife Jennifer said, walking into the nursery they had set up in their apartment strictly for babysitting Priscilla. "Give me a chance, too." John moved to the love seat where he laid little Priscilla on her back between them. Priscilla smiled broadly up at them. They were forming a very solid bond.

"When do we get her again?" Jennifer asked.

"Carrie and JT have a big business trip planned, and its coming up soon. They will be gone for two weeks. Joe and Peg will take the first week and we'll take the second," John answered.

"Oh marvelous, if you can give me the dates, I'll arrange to take the week off," Jennifer offered.

"Perfect," said John. "We'll fly out to Tiburon and make a week of it. The baby will love it there. We'll get some sun and fresh air, and you and I can have the nights to ourselves. Should I ask my mother to go with us?"

"If you like, sweetheart. I'd prefer we were alone for a change, but suit yourself. I'm good either way," Jennifer said.

Jennifer and John were relishing their grandparenthood. Both of them had traded marriage and children for career, and it left a very large hole in both their lives indeed. They were starting to get the hang of things and felt extremely comfortable with little Priscilla.

"I'm going to find someone out there to turn one of the bedrooms into a nursery and baby-proof the place. I'll get on that today," John said.

"Great idea, darling. You think of everything."

"John, can you believe she is four years old already? Where does the time go?" Jennifer lamented, shaking her head.

Little Priscilla ran into the room, joyfully pirouetting and fouetté-ing as she came. Her lean body was developing well since she had begun dance lessons. The large nursery had been re-outfitted with full length mirrors, a fixed barre, and hardwood floors. A bed and desk adorned one wall to make sure she had familiar surroundings when she visited John and Jennifer, which was often.

"She is becoming quite the little ballerina, don't you think, John?" Jennifer asked.

"She's a natural," John replied. "Those long legs give her grace, even at this early age."

For Priscilla's first birthday, John and Jennifer gave her an old-world, well-made, hand-carved wood etui with a beautiful mechanical ballerina mounted atop. The child was mesmerized. She stared at it for hours, and always wanted it near her when she was awake. It played several classical ballet songs as the figure danced a fouette in time to the music. Swan Lake, Nutcracker Suite, and Rosamunde were heard over and over until, at three years old, little Priscilla could hum all three of the songs perfectly.

She especially liked Swan Lake. It started with dark passages and then became light and airy. At two, she would sit and sway back and forth to the music, and now she was doing pirouettes, pliés and fouettes.

Priscilla's teacher, a very attractive young girl who was fresh out of Juilliard, made ends meet by giving private dance lessons. She would teach Priscilla in whoever's home Priscilla was at the time. Priscilla adored the young girl, and the adoration was returned. They would sit opposite each other, cross-legged on the floor during rest periods, laughing and practicing arm movements and hand and finger placements.

"Melany, why do ballerinas place their fingers like this?" Priscilla asked.

"It makes the hand look very graceful and elegant, don't you think?" the teacher answered.

"Oh yes, yours very much so."

"Your fingers will get longer with time sweetie, don't worry. Then you must keep the nails clean and polished, and always well-manicured," Melany said.

Priscilla stared at her hands and fingers, and then at Melany's. She had a look of disbelief, but internally believed what she was being told. She vowed to stop biting her nails and sucking her thumb at that instant.

"Okay pumpkin, up you get and let's do some work at the barre," Melany instructed, and Priscilla jumped to her feet in obedience.

At five years old, Melany mysteriously didn't show up for lessons any longer. Carrie tried her number, even went to her apartment, and Melany was nowhere to be found. She tried Juilliard, but Melany hadn't been associated with the school for some time. Carrie asked the school if there was another young graduate or near graduate that might be interested in teaching little Priscilla. The next day a new girl called and asked if she could interview for the job. Melany was never heard from again.

Priscilla was sad to lose Melany, but the new girl, Sasha, soon took her place. Sasha was a Russian-born ballerina, whose mother had danced at the Mariinsky Ballet Theater in St. Petersburg. Sasha spoke perfect English with a slight Russian accent, which Priscilla found challenging and very interesting. Sasha's methods were very different from Melany's, and she worked Priscilla very hard.

"I'm only five years old, you know, and I'm not used to working this hard. I'd like to have some fun, too," Priscilla point-blanked Sasha one day.

"Oh you would, would you?" Sasha answered sternly. "When I was your age, I was dancing five hours a day. My mother had no mercy on me. Why should I be easy with you?"

"Because I am a little girl," Priscilla argued.

"That's why you need to work harder, because you are young and need more training," she said firmly. "Now, again."

At first Priscilla resented the girl for her hard work regimen, but soon began to see the change in her dancing abilities, and she saw the wisdom in Sasha's methods. Three days a week she had a two hour lesson and then would practice for three hours more. On the off days, she would practice for five hours and then rest on the week-ends at her mother's insistence.

She was becoming very strong, and very good.

At seven years old, Priscilla joined a small ballet troupe and began dancing in children's ballets. The very first was Swan Lake, her favorite. She was able to keep up with girls several years her senior, and she soon became the darling of the company. She was not yet the best dancer in the ensemble, but definitely the prettiest and the most supple. The boys liked working with her because she was light and easy to lift.

Now eight, she showed signs of real accomplishment.

"Well Papa, what did you think of that?" Priscilla asked as she finished her dance routine.

"You are a vision sweetheart. You are a sight to behold," John said, still clapping his hands. "Come here and let me hug you."

Priscilla gracefully tip toed into John's waiting arms to get the hug she so richly prized. John's praise was an inspiration to her, as was Jennifer's. At her young age she had an understanding of success, and she somehow knew and understood the difference between accomplishment and true success. She knew that John and Jennifer were truly successful people.

"My Lord, child, it is as if you are dancing on a cloud. Soundless, effortless gliding around the room as if defying gravity," Jennifer said with open arms. "I want to hug you as well."

JT and Carrie sat in the back of the room, their eyes and mouths wide with happiness and smiles. "Brava, Brava, Brava my little princess," JT applauded as Carrie just sat and smiled with love for her little ballerina.

Jennifer stood and walked to the door to pick up a large box. She carried it over to Priscilla and helped her place it on the side table. Jennifer stood back as Priscilla pulled gently on the black silk bow surrounding the three-foot diameter by one-foot tall round box. Priscilla's eyes were sparkling. She had an inkling of what was inside the ornate container. As she pulled off the lid, she jumped up and down with excitement.

"The Black Swan!" she screamed. "And the tiara, too." She dared not touch it and looked to Jennifer for help removing the professional tutu from its container. First Jennifer removed the tiara and placed it on Priscilla's head. The two then gently lifted the tutu and Jennifer held it out for Priscilla to step into. Jennifer carefully held the attached bodice so Priscilla could slither into the costume. Its form-fitting fabrication fit perfectly as Jennifer pulled and smoothed it into place.

"For your next performance, my sweet," Jennifer said.

"Oh my, Grammy, it is magnificent," Priscilla beamed.

"Give us a preview," Carrie called, and started the music.

Priscilla, tall for her age and incredibly graceful with her arms held out to the side, tip-toed to the center of the room to await the musical announcement of her entrance. When she heard the notes she danced around the room, leaping, turning, and smiling confidently at the family gathering. For over ten minutes she danced the Black Swan pas de deux without a partner and without missing a step. She had been working on it for weeks, and the premier performance was still three months off.

John sat wondering if it wasn't time for Priscilla to have a higher level of training, and he whispered his question to Jennifer as the dance went on. Jennifer was thinking the same thing, and before he could complete his sentence she was nodding her head yes. John made a mental note to talk with Carrie about it later.

There was not a single dry eye in the group, with the exception of Sasha, who stood head high, smiling, coaxing, and admiring her accomplished student. Priscilla's movements were those of students in their late teens and early twenties. Quick, sharp raises to her toes, pointed toe leaps, and centered spins were all done flawlessly and with no sign of the effort she was expending. As the dance completed, the family got to their feet and applauded excitedly. Priscilla bowed and curtsied several times as she tip-toed to the side of the room while the applause continued. She tip-toed back to the center of the room and took several more bows and curtsies. They brought her back for a third time and then they all rushed to hug her and kiss her. She pressed down the front of her tutu to keep the huggers from crushing her new costume. John didn't know why, but he was surprised to see how much Priscilla was perspiring. The young girl was not afraid to work.

"I would like to say something," John announced to the family. "With Carrie and JT's permission, of course, Jennifer and I would like to take Priscilla Anne and her namesake to St. Petersburg to attend a Kirov performance of Swan Lake at the Mariinsky Ballet Theater. There is a special performance scheduled for next month, and we understand Priscilla is on spring break at the time."

"What do you think, Priscilla?" Carrie asked excitedly.

"Oh yes mother, please, may I go, please?" Priscilla pleaded.

"Well, John, you have your answer," Carrie smiled.

"Fantastic!" John said. "We have the Tsar's Box booked, and all the flights and hotels have been arranged."

"As usual, sure of yourself, aren't you?" JT smiled. "How long will you be gone?"

"A total of four days. One day over, one day and evening at the ballet, one day seeing the sights in St. Petersburg and one day back. Priscilla has an interview and a short recital with Svetlana Zakharova, who is doing the special performance."

"What?!" Priscilla asked. "A short recital!"

"She would like to see your performance of the Black Swan pas de deux, and there will be a partner there for you," Jennifer said.

"Oh my God," Priscilla said, hyperventilating.

4

A PAS DE DEUX

"I'm so excited," Priscilla announced. The day had come for them to travel to St. Petersburg.

A short article in the previous Sunday's New York Times Society page told the story that young protégé Priscilla Anne Wingate was traveling with her grandfather Mr. John Wingate, Chairman of the Board of Occident – Orient Shipping Company, to St. Petersburg, Russia where it is rumored that Priscilla Anne would perform a recital of the Black Swan pas de deux for the famed Russian Prima Ballerina Sveltana Zakharova. There was an inset picture of Priscilla in her Black Swan tutu. There were a few more sentences about John and Double O and the article ended with a brava and good luck to Priscilla.

Priscilla was used to seeing John and Jennifer's names in the paper, but this was the first time she had seen hers, and she was thrilled. At first she was nervous about the recital, but in the last few weeks she felt that she had truly learned the dance and was confident she could pull off a respectable rendition. She wondered who her partner would be and what he would look like. Would he be a youngster, like she was used to dancing with, or a seasoned professional? She was dizzy with thought.

They boarded the direct First Class Flight to St. Petersburg. The 4,300 mile flight to Polkovo Airport was to take eight hours and twenty minutes. John made sure that Priscilla was able to get some rest and they all arrived in good spirits. Their stay was at the 4.5 star Corinthia Hotel, which was a short drive from the Mariinsky Ballet Theater and many of the other sights John wanted to take in. Their suite of rooms was palatial.

The day of the recital, Priscilla woke cheerful and confident. She ate a sparse breakfast as her meeting with Svetlana was at 11:00 AM. They packed her tutu in the hotel limo and arrived at the Mariinsky at 10:00 AM. Priscilla changed into her costume and came out to meet her partner. Serge Kabinov, a handsome young man in his early twenties, stood waiting for Priscilla. As she entered, he smiled and offered his hand gracefully. He was dressed in black tights, dance slippers, and a billowy white blouse. He appeared to Priscilla to be very strong, and it was the first time she had seen, let alone danced with, a man of his apparent prowess.

"Did you bring music?" Serge asked in halting English.

"I did," Priscilla said, handing him the CD.

As he walked to place the CD in the player, she couldn't help but notice his very firm, muscular backside and his rather large, protruding genitals. She told herself not to stare, but felt her young heart leap a little. They practiced together for thirty minutes until Priscilla felt comfortable. Serge knew the dance backward and forward, and quickly learned the little nuances Priscilla's choreographer had added. He was amazed at the little girl's competence, but said nothing.

"I think I am ready," Serge announced to Priscilla.

"I am ready as well," Priscilla said with a smile.

Ten minutes later, it was time for the recital. Priscilla had not yet seen the stage she would be dancing on and asked Serge to show it to her. They walked out on the large stage and she immediately noticed the old-world ornateness of the theater. The theater was filled with gold filigree, crystal chandeliers, red velvet seats, and luxurious curtains and backdrops. There was a very large box section at the very back of the theater.

"Who sits there, Serge?" Priscilla asked.

"The Tsar and Tsarina and their entourage used to sit there," he remarked. "But now it is used by diplomats, politicians, and others who can afford the price of admission."

"Should I be embarrassed to say that I think that's where I'm sitting for tonight's performance?" Priscilla asked.

"Absolutely not," Serge said. "Truthfully, I envy you."

"We should get into positions now. Svetlana will be here soon, and we must be ready."

They walked backstage and waited. Priscilla felt her heartbeat rise, but she knew it wasn't fear or anticipation, it was her normal body function to get ready to dance.

"She is here, seated and ready. The music will start momentarily," Serge said.

Priscilla smiled, smoothed her bodice, fluffed her tutu, and bounced up and down on her toes; as she performed her normal ritual before a dance. Suddenly the music started, and the two entered the stage. Priscilla could see no one, and immediately decided to focus on a central point in the orchestra section. She felt as if her feet had wings, and she danced like she was on air. She had never felt this way before, except a few times when she was alone in her studio. She didn't have to think about the steps, they came to her automatically. Serge lifted her like she was weightless, gracefully holding her, spinning her, and dipping her at all the right moments. Toward the end, as the pique and fouette turns got faster and faster, Priscilla performed with increasing precision and determination, always smiling, always calm.

When the music stopped, the theater was silent, and Priscilla, breathing rapidly, wondered if anyone was there. For fifteen seemingly endless seconds there was no sound. Suddenly a single clap began as Svetlana rose from her seat and shouted a single brava. Soon the theater hands, John, Jennifer, and Priscilla Anne senior clapped and cheered loudly.

Little Priscilla moved to the front center of the stage and the lighting was dimmed so that she could see her audience. Svetlana held her arms out to the side and moved them up and down asking for quiet. When everyone was settled and reseated, Svetlana, still standing, looked up at the stage.

"Serge, I hope you dance that well with me tonight," she said with a smile. "And Miss Priscilla, I hope I can dance as well as you tonight." She clapped several times again. "In fact," she went on, "I'm not so sure you shouldn't do the Black Swan pas de deux in my place."

Priscilla put her hands up to her face.

"I'm serious young lady, would you like to do that?" Svetlana asked.

"Oh, my God, yes," Priscilla blurted out. She knew she had done one of her best performances and felt very confident.

"You realize there will be sixteen hundred or so people here?" Svetlana warned.

"Oh, yes ma'am, I know everything about this theater, I have studied it in detail."

"Fine then, go change your clothes, you and your family are having lunch with me in my dressing suite," Svetlana said.

"Now young lady, who is your ballet teacher?" Svetlana asked over lunch.

"A young Russian girl named Sasha Kournikova," answered Priscilla. "Her mother actually danced here at the Mariinsky Theater."

"Are you referring to Marina Kournikova?" Svetlana asked.

"I believe so," Priscilla answered. "She mentioned the name to me once and I think that was it."

Svetlana told Priscilla that she knew Marina and that she was once one of the best of the troupe.

"Sasha works me very hard," Priscilla said. "But it is worth it. I know that I am a better dancer as a result of her slave driving."

"Dancing is very hard work, and you have luckily learned that at an early age. That is good. I don't call it work, however, I call it joy. Whenever I feel out of sorts, I dance until I no longer feel bad. It works every time. There is nothing like a thirty rotation fouette to chase away the blues." She smiled at Priscilla.

"Do you think it will upset your following if they don't see you dancing the Black Swan pas de deux tonight?" John asked the famous dancer.

"Not at all," she said. "The Russian people love to see newcomers, and your young lady is worth seeing. When she finishes her dance, I will come out on stage and speak to the audience. They will be overjoyed."

"Is it possible that I film the event?" John asked.

"All of our performances are professionally filmed. I will see to it that you get a copy of the entire ballet. It will be ready tomorrow afternoon," Svetlana answered.

"You are a most beautiful woman, but very quiet," Svetlana remarked to Jennifer.

"Thank you for the compliment, but I feel I am standing deep in the shadows of you two very lovely dancers," Jennifer answered.

"What do you do to stay so beautiful?" Svetlana asked.

"I am a model and a women's clothing designer, and I am under constant attack by the newcomers fighting for their place in the pecking order," Jennifer answered

"I know too well," Svetlana chided, pointing at Priscilla. "I haven't heard of the Jennifer Wingate line of clothing."

"It is under my maiden name, Jennifer Middleton," Jennifer responded.

"Ah, I know it well. I visit your shops often when I'm in Paris, London or New York," Svetlana said.

The group talked on for another half hour or so and Svetlana stood up from the table.

"I must go now and begin my preparations for tonight's performance. Young lady, I suggest that you do the same. You may leave your costume with me and join me here this evening at six sharp. We will dress and do our stretching together. Would you like that?"

"Oh yes, very much," Priscilla answered. "Thank you very much."

"As you know, your dance isn't until the third act, so you will have some time to wait, and you can watch from the wings back stage."

Priscilla was thrilled.

❧

John, Jennifer, and Priscilla senior arrived at the Mariinsky Theater at six PM to deliver young Priscilla. People were already beginning to arrive and mill around in the ornate lobby. Serge was there to meet Priscilla and escort her back to the dressing rooms.

John and his group were escorted to the Tsar's box. John was told that there would be others sharing the box. He had no idea who or how many. The box contained twenty seats.

Before they took their seats, they were offered champagne and caviar in the private vestibule. Jennifer and Priscilla senior sat in side chairs and John stood beside them as guests began entering.

"Hello, my name is Gordon Marinkov, I am the U.S. Consul General here in St. Petersburg," one of the guests said, walking up to John.

"Pleased to meet you sir, I'm John Wingate, this is my wife Jennifer, and my mother Priscilla."

"A pleasure to meet you all, and what brings you to St. Petersburg?" the man asked.

"We have brought our granddaughter to see Swan Lake," John answered.

"She will love it, we come to see it every chance we can and bring staff and resident Americans. Where is your granddaughter?"

"She is in Svetlana Zakharova's dressing room, getting ready for tonight's performance," John said proudly.

"We wondered why the front row was taken," the Consul said. "Now we know. That is marvelous. What part will she play?"

John related the story of how it was that Priscilla would dance to-night, and about the recital she had given Svetlana earlier today. The Consul General was genuinely interested and told John that it was a fairly common thing for Prima Ballerinas to introduce youngsters this way.

"How old is your granddaughter, Mr. Wingate?"

"Please, call me John. She is eight years old," John answered.

"My, so young. I will be looking forward to the third act. Again, a pleasure meeting you all."

The house lights dimmed, calling the guests to their seats. The performance would begin shortly.

The third act was nearing its end as Priscilla's music began. John and Jennifer sat up in their chairs as the two dancers entered the stage. The Consul General, sitting next to John, gave him a smile.

"You look like an expectant father," the Consul General quipped.

"Is it that obvious?' John asked.

Again, it was as if Priscilla was on auto pilot. She danced exquisitely and after each song she received a strong round of applause. Near the end, when she performed her thirty rotation fouette, she nearly brought down the house. Her spins were crisp, her head movements were sharp, and she never once lost balance. At the end of her dance, the entire audience rose to their feet in applause. Bravas could be heard from all areas of the house.

Svetlana came out on stage, as promised, and the audience quieted and sat back down.

"Ladies and gentlemen," she began in Russian. "I met this young ballerina this morning, and after watching her dance, I knew you would enjoy seeing her as much as I did. Her name is Priscilla Anne Wingate, she is eight years old, and she comes from America. She has been trained by the daughter of one of our own past Prima Ballerinas, Marina Kournikova."

There was a burst of applause from the audience.

"I know we will be hearing more from this young lady," she continued. Svetlana turned and looked at Priscilla, performed a ballerina's bow, stood erect, and shouted, "Brava, my child, Brava." The audience cheered again as Priscilla returned the bow. Someone came from the wings and gave Priscilla a bouquet of bright red roses. They were from John.

Both Svetlana and Priscilla ran hand in hand from the stage in pointe.

⚘

"You were marvelous," Jennifer said to Priscilla on the ride back to the hotel.

"Papa, I wasn't at all afraid. My heart was beating faster than normal, but I think that allowed me to do better. I knew every step, every arm movement, every spin. When I did my final fouette, I felt as though I was the ballerina on the etui you gave me, spinning almost automatically. That was the most perfect evening, Papa, thank you very much. I wish Mommy and Daddy could have seen it."

"We thank you sweetheart," John said. "Jennifer, your grandmother, and I are extremely proud of you."

The next morning, the front page of the Russian/English paper featured a picture of Priscilla doing her fouette. The article was titled *"Eight year old American ballerina wows the audience at the Mariinsky, last night."* Svetlana's speech was translated and reproduced for the article. The praise for Priscilla's performance clamored from the article.

"You made the front page, sweetie," John said, handing Priscilla the paper.

"Oh my God," Priscilla screamed. She knew she had danced well, but had no idea how well. The paper called her the future Svetlana Zakharova. Inside herself, Priscilla knew the difference between Svetlana's dancing and hers. She knew she still showed adolescence. She knew that her limbs lacked the muscular strength that it took to perform the crisp jetes, pirouettes and fouettes required. She also knew, however, that her abilities were far ahead of her years.

"Okay ladies, it is time to be tourists," John announced.

"Oh John, I'm not sure I'm up for it today," Priscilla senior said.

"Mom, I have a private limo that will take us to the front doors. If you don't want to make the walk, you can wait in the limo and do your tatting," John coaxed.

"John, your father took me on a four day tour of this beautiful city, and I remember it like it was yesterday. I'll just stay here in the suite and go down for lunch and high tea. When do you think you will return?" Priscilla senior asked.

"I have a dinner reservation for seven. I will have you picked up here at six thirty and you can join us."

"Wonderful," Priscilla senior said. "Now off with you all, and don't worry about me."

Little Priscilla was awestruck by the beauty of the amazing city, once besieged by the Germans in WWII. The Hermitage Museum and Winter Palace, overlooking the Neva, housed the unbelievable treasures of the Tsars. The list of sights seemed endless. St. Isaac's Cathedral, Peter and Paul Fortress, the Cruiser Aurora that fired the first shot of the 1917 Russian Revolution, Church of the Savior on Blood, Catherine Palace and Park, Palace Square and Nevsky Prospekt were all on the list of places to visit.

John, Jennifer, and Priscilla Anne were exhausted by dinnertime as they sat waiting for Priscilla Senior in the lounge at the Palkin. Priscilla Anne looked around the luxurious restaurant with its crystal chandeliers, gold filigree, rich draperies, and old-world inlaid wood flooring.

"My, my. We have a celebrity with us this evening," the maître d said, looking down at little Priscilla. "My name is Alexey, young lady, at your service." He made a sweeping bow.

Everyone smiled at the acknowledgement and nodded thanks.

"The cocktail waitress will be with you momentarily. Please enjoy your dinner."

"Alexey, we are waiting for a fourth member of our party. Please escort her to our table when she arrives," John requested.

"Certainly, Sir."

With Priscilla senior now in attendance, they were seated at their table. Perusing the menu was a mouthwatering experience in itself.

"May I take your orders?" the waiter asked.

"We would all like the lettuce salad. This lovely lady would like the Black Cod with beetroot risotto and scallops. The young lady would like the chateaubriand, and we both would like the Stroganoff Palkin," John ordered for the table. "We all will have Crepe Suzettes for dessert."

"Very good Sir, the Sommelier will be with you shortly," the waiter said.

The Sommelier arrived, and John explained what everyone had ordered and asked the wine expert to select the proper wines. The food and the wines proved to live up to the Palkin reputation.

"Papa, this has been the most wonderful two days of my life so far. Thank you very much, I love you with all my heart," Little Priscilla announced, eating the last of her crepes.

"You are very welcome, my little Prima Ballerina. I love you more," John answered. "We have a leisurely start in the morning, our plane is at eleven. Shall we go to the hotel?"

5

TOAST OF THE TOWN

JT handed his daughter Priscilla the morning paper the day after her return from St. Petersburg.

"Check out page B2," he said to his daughter.

"Local Girl Makes Good" was the title of the article. It went on to tell the story of Priscilla's trip to St. Petersburg and her successful performance at the Mariinsky Ballet Theater. *"Eight year old Priscilla Anne Wingate, dancing the Black Swan pas de deux, wowed the crowds. Prima Ballerina Svetlana Zakharova raved about the performance, bowing to the little star.* There were more lines about John and Jennifer and Priscilla senior. The article featured several archive pictures of the Mariinsky, Priscilla's third grade graduation picture, and the same picture that the Russian newspaper used of her in her Black Swan tutu.

"You are becoming quite the celebrity," JT said. "Don't let it go to your head." JT smiled.

"My little ballerina, I am so proud of you," Carrie said, leaning down and kissing Priscilla on her cheek as she entered the kitchen for breakfast.

"Charles will be picking us up a little early this morning and we are making the drive with you to school. I'm afraid there might be some newspaper people there wanting to interview you, and I want to get the school people on board to make sure you are protected from that," JT told her. "If need be we will hire a temporary bodyguard."

"Do you really think that is necessary?" Carrie inquired.

"It's better to err on the side of caution, don't you think?" JT replied.

"You're right."

"How did the school thing go?" John asked JT and Carrie as they walked into the office.

"It went well, John, the press was there, and the school agreed to protect Priscilla. I told them to call me if they thought a bodyguard might be required," JT said.

John was concerned, but he wasn't paranoid. He was used to being harassed by the press and made up his mind to always speak with them when they asked, always tell the truth, and always firmly cut them off if they went beyond their boundaries. He recalled the frenzy when he and Jennifer were married. Paparazzi followed them mercilessly for weeks. They stopped and posed once or twice, but then cut them off. He had given them what they wanted, and they weren't entitled to anything more than that. He had earned their respect and they stopped.

"Charles is going to pick her up today," Carrie said.

"Good, I'll go with him," John offered.

"That would be great," Carrie said. "Thanks Dad."

John smiled. He had not yet become completely used to Carrie calling him Dad. He loved it, thrived on it, and cherished it, but it was still alien to him.

"Brad, we need to make a big score. The dancing is okay, and we are doing well, but we need to find a pay day that will take us out of this stinking dump," Melany said. "I'm sick of it."

"Any ideas?" Brad shot back.

"As a matter of fact, I do have an idea," she said. "I was reading the society page the other day and found this," she said, handing the article to Brad.

"Isn't this the little rich bitch you taught ballet?" he asked.

"Yes it is, and her grandfather is one of the richest men in New York. He's the Chairman of the Board of some shipping company. I know my way around his home, his brother's home and the kids' parent's home," Melany boasted.

"What are you suggesting? Robbery? What?" Brad asked.

She told Brad her rough plans. They would kidnap the child and one of the adult family members and hold them for ransom. She thought that they should sweat the family for a week or two before calling them for the ransom.

"If we wait for a period of time, they will become desperate and agree to anything. I think that kidnappers are too fast to ask for ransom," Melany said.

"I've got to admit that we have an edge here in that you know the homes and the kid, but it is still a big risk. It will take a lot of planning and study," Brad replied.

She was impressed that he was being cautious, but still interested.

"I need to think this over, I mean really think this through," Brad said.

"Let's get high," came Melany's response.

He wasn't saying yes and he wasn't saying no, he was saying maybe. He was usually so lazy that any new thought she brought to the table was immediately poo-pooed. She was happy to see him rise to the idea.

"There she is Charles, over there," John said as Charles got out to meet the little girl.

"Hi Charles," Priscilla said with a smile as she got into the open door with Papa.

She hugged John and asked him why he was with Charles today. He told her that he missed her and wanted to spend some time with her.

"Papa, we were together just yesterday," Priscilla giggled. "You can't have missed me so soon."

"I miss you as soon as you leave my side," John said. "Give me another hug."

She slid across the seat and hugged her Papa.

"Charles, drop us off at the park, and wait at the end of the jogging path please. This one and I are going to have an ice cream and a nice walk."

John and Priscilla got out of the car and walked to Morg's Gelato Stand at 5th Avenue and E 72nd Street. John got a double decker Pistachio and Vanilla and Priscilla opted for Chocolate and Vanilla. They walked along holding hands, talking, licking and enjoying the afternoon. John felt wonderful spending time with his granddaughter, but for some reason he felt edgy. He stopped for a moment and looked around.

"Are you looking for someone, Papa?" Priscilla asked.

"No sweetie, I felt funny for a second and wanted to see what it might be. Looks like nothing," he soothed.

They kept walking and he couldn't shake the feeling. When they got to the limo, Priscilla got in as John swept his eyes in a 360 degree circle, to no avail. *Hmmm,* he thought to himself as he climbed into the limo.

"Thank you for the ice cream, Papa," Priscilla said sweetly, looking over at John. "I like it when you pick me up from school."

"Anything interesting happen at school today, sweetie?" John asked matter-of-factly.

"Not really," she said. "There were some people from the newspaper, but the principal told them to leave."

That's probably what it was, John thought to himself. He surmised that the press or the paparazzi were lurking in the trees and following them, probably taking telephoto snapshots of them. *Must be a slow news day,* he thought, and put his feelings aside.

"Well, we had best get back, Sasha will be waiting for you, and you know how she hates waiting," John said.

Priscilla couldn't wait to see Sasha and tell her all about her trip to Russia. She related the story of how she met Svetlana Zakharova and how Sveltana had remembered Sasha's mother Marina. Sasha beamed as the story unfolded.

"You told Svetlana that I was your teacher?" Sasha asked.

"Well you are, aren't you?" Priscilla said.

Sasha asked how it happened the she got the recital time from Svetlana, and Priscilla couldn't answer.

"I don't know," she said. "It probably had something to do with Papa though, he knows everyone and can do anything."

"All right, enough of this chatter," Sasha said. "Let's go to work."

Priscilla worked hard at her lesson, and then practiced for an hour before she showered and started doing her homework. She actually enjoyed school, studied hard, and brought home the report cards to prove it. Tonight she had a great deal of homework and the next day she had an exam in math and in social studies. She only took out one half hour to eat dinner. She ate in her bedroom as JT and Carrie hadn't gotten home yet. It was seven o'clock.

She wore headphones when she ate alone, which wasn't often, and listened to her ballet scores. She would imagine herself doing the steps demanded by the music and saw herself gliding, spinning, and leaping about the stage. She told Sasha once that it really helped to envision herself performing, and Sasha encouraged her.

At nine she was done with her homework and went downstairs to talk with Brenda, her nanny.

"Mom and Dad will be home in a few minutes, sweetie, why don't you have a glass of milk and some cookies?" Brenda asked.

"Good idea," Priscilla smiled. "I have had a lot of sweets today, so I think I'll not have the cookies, but the milk sounds good."

JT and Carrie walked in at nine twenty, and found Priscilla still up and waiting for them. JT fixed them a gin and tonic and the three sat in the living room and talked about their day. Priscilla told them about walking in the park eating ice cream, and how John thought the paparazzi were following them. JT and Carrie looked at each other, but didn't appear to be overly concerned.

"Okay young lady, it's past your bedtime. Get up to bed and I'll come up and tuck you in," Carrie said.

"Give me a hug and a kiss," JT said. "Goodnight my princess, sweet dreams."

Ten minutes later, Carrie walked up to Priscilla's bedroom to tuck her in. Dutifully, she was in bed, smiling, waiting for her mother's love. She felt warm and safe around her mother and father. She knew, without doubt, that they loved her. She wished that they didn't have to work so hard and could spend more time with her, but she knew their work was important and that she was loved and she was content with that.

"Goodnight, Mommy," Priscilla said, hugging Carrie very tightly.

"Goodnight my love," Carrie said returning the squeeze. "Think happy thoughts, and do well on your tests tomorrow. Are you prepared?"

"Yes, Mommy."

"Good girl, now go to sleep," Carrie turned out the lights and closed the door.

For a few minutes, Priscilla laid there in her bed thinking. *How did she know I have tests tomorrow?* Priscilla asked herself. She didn't remember telling her that she had tests. She thought that maybe it was in the way she acted. *Do I act differently when I have a test coming up? I'm not worried, I know I'm prepared.* As she started to drift off she made a mental note to ask her mother in the morning.

6

I DON'T FEEL WELL

The night was New York summer, hot and humid. There were a lot of drinking customers tonight, and the place was smokier than usual. Melany had finished three watered down drinks so far and she could feel them. As she walked up on stage, she stumbled slightly, caught herself gracefully, and continued on up the steps to the waist-high stage. Her music started, and there was a noticeable quieting of the customers, which gave her confidence. She knew she was an attraction, and she would give them something to look at.

She twirled effortlessly around the stage, discarding clothing as she went. She was down to her heels, mid-thigh stockings, bra and panties when she got to the pole, half way through the song. Her bra came first as she deftly removed it and threw it to the back of the stage, baring beautiful pert breasts. She pranced by the ogling eyes of the first row customers and saw the looks of desire on their faces. Her music came to an end and she still hadn't removed her panties, a requirement by the house. She did pirouettes back to the center of the stage, to the whistles and claps of the crowd. With one quick movement she dropped her panties, stepped out of them, and threw them to the back of the stage. She then walked to the far side of the stage, and then did a series of traveling pique turns slowly across the front of the stage, giving everyone in the room a full view of her beautifully toned, glistening body.

The men and women in the room cheered, whistled, and clapped wildly as she crossed the stage. At the end she stopped, ballet bowed, and tip-toe pranced to the back of the stage to retrieve her clothing.

"More!" "Encore!" and "Keep it going, baby!" Were the shouts from the lust-filled men in the room. They lined up for lap dances and all of them wanted private sessions. She completed four private lap dances before it was time to go back up on stage. She felt exhausted, but she was exhilarated by the crowd and climbed back up on stage.

She performed the same striptease, except at the end she did a series of jeté leaps across the front of the stage, and the men roared with pleasure. Again they lined up for private lap dances. She did three more private lap dances and again it was time to get back up on stage.

She felt woozy from the free drinks, exhausted from the dancing and lap dances, but kept going on sheer elation. At the end of her striptease, Melany walked naked to the front of the stage and from third position began a series of fouette spins. With each spin, the crowd cheered. She counted *six, seven, eight, nine,* as she spun in place. Her head began to feel light, and her stomach twitched. *Thirteen, fourteen, fifteen,* she counted and suddenly she fainted to the floor. The raucous room quieted immediately as two other dancers ran out from behind curtain to see what had happened. Jake ran on to the stage and covered Melany's genitals with his sport jacket.

"Are you okay, baby?" Jake asked, and there was no response. He called for two of his men to help him take Melany back to the dressing room.

"No, take her to my office instead and put her on the couch. Find something to cover her up," he ordered brusquely.

"Okay girls and boys, the show isn't over yet, girls get out there and do your thing. I'll see that Melany is taken good care of."

Jake went back to his office and looked at Melany, still out cold on the couch. The club's First Aid kit had smelling salts, and he cracked one under her nose. She shook her head once or twice and raised her head up in surprise. She looked around, wondering what had happened, one minute counting crisp fouettes, the next looking up at Jake in his office.

"What happened?" she asked.

"I was going to ask you the same question," Jake said. "You were dancing around the floor like Pavlova and the next thing we know you were flat on that beautiful ass of yours."

She scrunched her face in thought and remembered the seconds before she fell.

"I felt tiredness overtaking me, light headedness, and that's all."

"Baby, are you on any drugs?" Jake asked. "Is that asshole you live with keeping you in tow with drugs?"

"No," Melany lied, and Jake knew it. He had seen this happen too many times before. Young girls in the prime of their lives succumbing to weakness from overuse of meth and similar drugs.

"You're lying to me, baby," Jake said. "You really put yourself out there tonight, and at your age you should be able to do that stuff in your sleep. Something, or someone, or both has got their hooks in you, and you need to get some help."

"Honestly Jake, I smoke a joint every now and then, and that's it," she lied again.

"Don't bullshit a bullshitter baby," Jake snapped harshly.

Jake reached down and pulled her mouth open. With his other hand, he bared her teeth. He could see the telltale signs of meth smoking on her once pearly-white teeth. The meth was beginning to take its toll. She was on a pathway to oblivion.

"Baby, you knocked 'em dead tonight. How much did you make in the lap rooms tonight? Had to be a couple thousand at least. You got it all baby. Why are you trying to kill yourself?" Jake asked, somewhat sadly.

Melany looked away. She knew that he knew she was a meth-head. Early on, she had tried to quit, but now she was deep in the clutches of the horrendous drug. Oddly, tonight she felt a similar high, just from the dancing, an exhilaration she had had years before at Juilliard.

"Baby, I want to help you get your shit together, what do you say to that?" Jake said.

"I'd have to talk with Brad first," she answered.

"Why do you need to talk to that stupid fuck, what has he ever done for you, except leech off of that beautiful body of yours?" he fired back.

Melany started to tear and looked away again. She got up shakily and put her clothes on. She couldn't look Jake in the eyes, she was too embarrassed. The euphoria of the night was gone.

"Get some help Melany, before it's too late," Jake said, walking behind his desk, disappointed and shaking his head as she walked out of his office. "I'd hate to lose you."

Brad had decided to take the night off and had dropped Melany off, telling her to call him when she wanted to come home. She called Brad and told him she was ready to come home.

"It's early, what do you want to come home for?" Brad said. He was naked in his bed with an attractive Latina at his side. Both bodies were perspiring in the oppressive humidity.

"I had an accident on stage, and I need to come home, now," she said.

An hour and a half later, Brad rolled up to the club. He told the bouncer that he would only be there a few minutes, while he picked up Melany.

"What took you so long, you bastard?" Melany shouted.

"I was taking a shower," he said.

"It takes you an hour and a half to shower and drive ten blocks to pick me up?" she fumed. "I could have walked home four times. I'll bet you had some slut with you, didn't you?"

"Don't be foolish Melany, get in the car," he said.

They drove home in silence. They had to park two blocks away, and they walked in silence. When they got to the apartment she walked straight to the bathroom and slammed the door. She removed her clothing and stepped into the shower. The cool water felt good as she washed away the evening. She had earned twenty three hundred dollars in lap dances and nearly five hundred in tips, nearly three thousand dollars, and she didn't even finish the night. Where the ballet dancing idea came from, she didn't know. She had no idea the reception it would have. She felt magnificent while she was dancing, but now was concerned over her lack of stamina and control. When she was finished, she reached for a towel and held it to her face. She immediately threw it down on the floor. The towel was still damp, and the perfume on it wasn't hers. *That no-good prick did have another woman here tonight,* she thought to herself. As she dried with a new towel she decided not to confront the issue. She decided to let it slide, but would cut him off for a week or two to teach him a lesson.

She dressed in her pajamas and went out into the living room. She took a hit off of the meth pipe and went to bed.

7

RUN FOR IT

"**M**om, my PE teacher wants me to go out for the track team," Priscilla said to her mother. "He says my long legs will give me an advantage."

"I'm not sure if that is a good idea," Carrie said. "Runners use different muscles than dancers, it could interfere with your ballet. By the way, where will you find the time, what with school and ballet taking most of your time?"

"I'll ask Sasha today if she thinks it will hurt my ballet," she answered. "It's only one hour after school, and attending six meets a year. I can put off ballet for one hour."

Carrie was concerned that Priscilla might be getting tired of ballet, but decided not to ask the question for fear of the answer. Five hours per week didn't seem like much, but on top of twenty hours of ballet and thirty hours of school it was a lot, not to mention homework. She was skeptical, but allowed Priscilla her head.

"Sasha, if I were to make the school track team and start running, will it hurt my ballet? I don't really want to do anything to interfere with my ballet, but my PE teacher asked me specifically," Priscilla asked at her afternoon practice.

"Running is a high impact sport, like ballet is a high impact dance. Ballet is actually higher impact than running. Although running builds stamina, which helps the ballerina, the high impact can shorten your dancing life. Running uses muscles that ballerinas don't normally use and a lot of running can bulk up your thigh muscles, which is not attractive for ballerinas. I had the same desire as you when I was your age, and decided not to do it," Sasha answered. She knew this question would come up eventually, and she had prepared.

"Okay girls and boys, I want you to do two laps around the track today," Mr. Findley, the PE teacher, demanded.

All of the students took off running. For some reason, Priscilla felt frisky, and kicked up her speed. She ran as fast as she could. Not only did she complete the assigned laps first, she lapped two thirds of the class. She stopped at the finish line and doubled over to catch her breath.

"Priscilla, please tell me you have decided to join the track team," Mr. Findley said hopefully.

"I'm very flattered, Mr. Findley, that you have asked me to try out for the track team. I like running fast, but I have learned that too much running could have an adverse effect on my ballet, and that is my real passion. I hope that by declining I haven't let you down," Priscilla said.

"Not at all, my dear, it's just that you are a natural, and with the proper training you could be a force in the sport. I fully understand your passion for ballet, and respect your loyalty to it. It is an art, but it is one of the arts that exceeds sport in strength, stamina, agility and grace. Please carry on," Mr. Findley concluded.

Priscilla smiled up at the man, and ran off again down the track. She finished a third lap along with the two-lap stragglers. She wasn't showing off, she wanted to prove to herself that she was a runner and that now she could get on with her ballet without wondering if she was making a mistake.

When Priscilla got home, she told her mother of her decision, and Carrie seemed noticeably relieved.

"What drove your decision?" Carrie asked

"Sasha told me the good and the bad about it, and I knew in my heart that I would never do anything that might adversely affect my dancing," she replied.

"What did your PE teacher say?"

"He basically said that I should follow my heart, and be confident that ballet requires more stamina, strength, agility, and grace than any of the sports. That is what really impressed me," Priscilla said.

Priscilla was bright and athletic. She had it all. She was developing stamina by putting in the long hours at ballet. Strength was increasing with age. She knew her limits, but always kept her abilities honed to her development stage.

Agility is a given, grace, she thought, was learned. She wasn't sure about that, but that is what she believed. Sasha and Melany had told her that she needed to learn to be graceful. She must hold her hands just so, and arms just so, and always walk on her tip toes, and keep her shoulders back and down, chin and head high. At first she was dazzled by all the requirements, but now it was second nature. How far she had come in five years.

8

A BIG MISTAKE

Melany sat at her dressing table and looked in the mirror. She looked at her teeth and noticed the tell-tale signs of the meth. Some brown spots were appearing at her gum line, and she thought it looked horrible. She could see age lines developing around her eyes that shouldn't be there for at least another ten years. She knew that if she wanted to maintain her looks and her body that she had to stop. Jake was right. She knew she was in the fast lane to disaster.

She thought back about the other night when she introduced ballet into her strip routine, and how positively the crowd responded to it. She knew it was more her nakedness and the lust of the johns than it was an appreciation of ballet, but she didn't care. It worked, the crowd liked it, her boss liked it, and she was raking in the money.

"Jake, when you said the other day that you could help me, what did you mean?" she asked.

"Are you ready to admit you are a meth user?" he retorted.

"Yes, I am a meth user," she said, hanging her head.

"I was once a meth user, and I got help. Now I live day to day without it. You don't have to hang your head in shame," he confessed.

"I want help," she said, with tears coming to her eyes.

"What about that simple fuck you live with? What is his reaction?" he asked.

"I haven't spoken to him about it. I caught him screwing another woman in our apartment and have decided to cut him off for a couple of weeks," she told Jake.

Jake told her that if she maintained her dependency on Brad, she would never shake the habit. He was the enabler and she was weak at this moment in her life. In order for her to shed the meth habit, she had to shed Brad. He was using the meth to keep her. He told her that without the meth, she wouldn't look twice at the prick.

She mulled his words, and knew he was right.

"What do I do next?" she pleaded.

Jake couldn't understand how a woman this intelligent and this attractive could be so dependent and naive. She was now trying to lean on him, and he knew he couldn't let that happen.

"I can only tell you what I would do, I can't make up your mind for you," Jake said. "I'm not your keeper, I'm your boss and your friend, that's all."

She shrunk back in defeat. She actually thought she could go from one protector to another.

"I don't know what to do," she said as her eyes began to fill with tears.

"No, you don't go pulling that crying shit with me, Goddamn it. You have to stand on your own two feet. Find some inner strength. Get your shit together," Jake shouted at her, one sentence after another. He knew he had to put her through this in order for her to begin the healing process.

She put her hands over her ears to calm the shouting and began to sob. Jake momentarily wondered if she wasn't a lost cause.

"How much stuff, that you actually need, do you have at your apartment that belongs to you and that you can use going forward?" Jake asked.

"I don't understand," she said, wiping her eyes and nose with a tissue.

Jake explained to her that she had to leave the asshole, and that she should take only what she needed with her. Taking a lot of familiar things with her was not good. They would only remind her of her addiction, and trigger old desires.

"I don't have a lot of street wearable clothing," she said.

"What do you mean?" he asked.

She explained the two years that Brad had prostituted her to high paying johns. She told him the clothing was sort of kinky, like the school girl, the nurse, or the dominatrix outfits she had worn to stimulate the johns. She said that she could probably fit everything else she had into a small suitcase.

"The fucker pimped you out?" he asked, incredulous. "Why in hell are you still with him? Don't answer, I know. The meth."

She hung her head again in shame.

"Look, sweetie," he said calming down and raising her face to his and looking her straight in the eyes. "You are better than this."

"I know," she said, smiling up at him.

He told her that he knew of a group that would help her with the initial withdrawals. He also told her he would stand by her, since she had no one to support her. He told her that she could use one of the apartments he owned until she got on her feet. It was located right next to the club.

"I'm not going to be your crutch, mind you, but I will support you and be there if and when you need someone," he said consolingly. "But that's it. You have to do this on your own."

"Brad, I told you I am through with this crazy life we live. I want to try and get well and rid myself of this dependency on meth," Melany argued. "I'm leaving until I can get myself together, and then we can see where we go from there."

"Over my dead body, bitch. What am I supposed to do in the meantime?" Brad countered.

"You'll just have to find a job," she said shakily.

"Bullshit," he bellowed as he swung at her and hit her squarely on the cheek.

She went down and lay there motionless for several minutes while he got a beer from the kitchen. She stirred, and he kicked her in the ribs. She cried out and begged him to stop as he kicked her again.

"You're not going anywhere, bitch," he yelled.

He straddled her waist while she was lying on her back. He hit her with closed fists again and again, left then right, until she finally passed out. He got up and looked down at her. *She'll be out for some time now, I'm going to track down the prick that put her up to this*, he thought to himself, and walked out the door.

Ten minutes later she stirred. She blinked her eyes open and suddenly felt the pain. She could barely raise herself, but managed to get to her feet and staggered into the bathroom. Her face was a bloody mess. Blood ran from her nose, her mouth, and from a cut near her left eye. *He nearly killed me*, she thought. Melany knew that she had to get out of there as fast as she could. She stumbled to the bedroom and packed a small roller suitcase. She put on sunglasses and a ball cap and hoodie and left the apartment. She had no idea how long she was out cold, and she had no idea where Brad was; she only knew that she had to get to the Pussy Cat Club as best she could.

The neighborhood was rough, but people tended to leave the homeless and destitute alone. She decided to go the long way, avoiding the regular route she and Brad normally took. It added two city blocks to the walk, but she thought it was best. Her ribs ached and her head pounded with pain. It had been too long since she'd had a hit of meth, and the pain was now becoming excruciating. Finally one block to go as she rounded the last corner.

She stopped suddenly when she saw Brad being bodily thrown out of the Pussy Cat Club. She ducked quickly back behind the building. She watched him pick himself up, flip off the bouncers, and childishly scream obscenities at them. He staggered to his car and drove off. Quickly she hobbled her way to the entrance and went in to the club. Jake immediately intercepted her.

"My God, what happened to you?" he asked, genuinely concerned.

"Please help me Jake, the bastard nearly killed me," she cried. "I think I need to go to the hospital. I think my jaw is broken, it hurts badly when I move it."

"Phil, take Melany to St. John's Emergency, and stay with her until I come. I'll try and get there as soon as I can. Don't let anything happen to her. If that prick shows up there, you know what to do," Jake ordered.

Phil and Jake's driver took precaution to take her out unseen and drove a circuitous route to detect if they were being followed. By the time they got to the hospital, they were sure no one had followed them.

"How did this happen, young lady?" the male triage nurse asked.

"I fell down a flight of stairs," she lied.

"Where does it hurt?" he continued.

She explained that she thought that her jaw had been broken, that maybe her nose had been broken, and that she had a terrible, terrible headache. She showed him the ribs that she thought might be fractured. The nurse thought that she was not being truthful about what had happened, and was sure she had been abused. None the less, he quickly completed the triage and wheeled her back to the emergency room, Phil following close behind.

"First, we are going to get some x-rays to determine the extent of your injuries, and then we will have the doctor have a closer look at you."

"Can I get something for the pain?" Melany asked.

"Not until the doctor has seen you, I'm afraid," the nurse apologized, knowing that she must be in very serious pain.

"Please hurry," she begged.

The x-rays showed that she indeed had a broken jaw, a broken nose, and two fractured ribs. The doctor also asked how it happened, and Melany lied to him as well.

"We are going to send you to the OR immediately to get tended to," the doctor said. "I wish you would reconsider your story as to how this all happened, however. Who is the man outside your room?"

"That's Phil, a good friend of mine. He found me and brought me here," she answered with difficulty.

Four hours later, she was out of the operating room: jaw wired, taped and braced. Her nose was reset and taped, both eyes were blackened, and the cut at her left eye socket looked carefully stitched.

"She looks a lot worse than she is," the doctor said to Jake. "She's fortunate that everything will heal properly and she will maintain her looks. I want her here for observation for two days, then you can take her home."

"Her friend, Phil, the big guy over there, will stay with her day and night," Jake said.

"That's fine. Can you tell me how this happened?" the doctor asked.

Jake leveled with the doctor, telling him that he thought it was a jealous boyfriend who did it. He also told the doctor about Melany's drug habit.

"It's a good thing you told me that, I'll prescribe a methadone regimen for her until she gets over the healing hump," the doctor said.

Jake asked the doctor a flurry of questions. How does she eat? When does she come home? How do we deal with the bandages? The doctor answered all of his questions, Jake thanked him, and went to give Phil instructions and see if Melany was awake yet.

"Where the fuck are you bitch, I know you are here somewhere!" Brad yelled as he stomped through the apartment.

He looked everywhere, including the fire escape, to no avail. Brad suddenly stopped, sat down, and tried to think things out. He knew she didn't have a car, so she would have had to walk, which means she couldn't have gone far. He knew that in her condition, she would be in a lot of pain and would have to go slow. The logical place for her to go would be to the Pussy Cat Club. He decided to stake out the club, and see what he could learn.

He drove to the club and parked across and down the street. It was a perfect spot. He could see the entrance, there were no working street lights near him, and it was the last available space near the busy strip joint except for the space in front where Jake usually parked his big black SUV. He noted that there was only one bouncer at the front door.

Brad thought that Jake had probably had Melany taken to the hospital in his vehicle. He sat there for another hour when he saw Jake's vehicle drive up and park. Jake got out, and his driver stayed in the SUV. Jake said something to the bouncer, looked around, up and down the street, and walked into club. A few minutes later, a big bruiser, one of Jake's inside men, came out of the club and walked down the other side of the street, away from the club. He had a flash-light and was shining it into the parked cars. He walked a full block away, crossed the street and was coming back in Brad's direction on Brad's side of the street. Brad decided that it was probably a good idea to leave. He started his vehicle and began to slowly pull away from the curb. He noticed that the bouncer started to run toward him from half a block away. His flashlight was aimed at Brad's car. He accelerated rapidly and turned left at the next corner, and then right into an alley. He waited for ten minutes to see if he was being followed, and then drove home.

He decided to wait until tomorrow to continue his search, so he grabbed a beer from the refrigerator, sat down on the couch, put his feet up on the coffee table and lit a cigarette, something he never would have done if Melany was there.

Suddenly the door burst open, and Jake and his bouncer entered the room. Brad struggled to his feet, but the bouncer was on him before he could get his balance. The first stinging blow to his left eye stunned him. The second and third blows brought him to his knees. Jake walked up to him with what looked like a fungo bat.

"I'm going to beat the living shit out of you, you low-life scum," Jake said. "What kind of a man does to a woman what you did to her?"

The blows rained down on Brad's upper body, arms and legs; breaking bones and fracturing ribs. Six blows in all, avoiding the head area, and Brad was still conscious.

"If I ever see you anywhere near her again, I'll kill you. Do you understand me?" Jake threatened.

Brad didn't move. Jake viciously hit him again.

"Answer me, asshole!" Jake yelled.

"Yes," was Brad's only meek reply, as Jake and his man turned and left the apartment.

9

INVITATION FROM JUILLIARD

"Priscilla, there's a letter for you," Carrie called.

Priscilla dutifully bounced out of her bedroom and gleefully skipped up to her mother in the kitchen. She did not receive many letters, and was excited to see what it was. She opened the large manila envelope and took out its contents. She read the letter aloud.

> Dear Miss Wingate,
>
> We have received a letter from Ms. Svetlana Zakharova, telling us of your dance at the Mariinsky Ballet Theater. Ms. Zakharova raved about your dancing and suggested we bring you in for a recital. Our board has agreed, and we would like you to fill out the attached document, giving us an outline of your training and experience, the number you would like to dance to, and several dates and times that would be acceptable to you.
>
> We look forward to your favorable reply.
>
> Sincerely,
> Maria Zukova,
> Director, Ballet School

"Priscilla, that's wonderful!" Carrie raved. "Juilliard is one of the most prestigious dance schools in the country. You must write a letter to Svetlana and thank her for her thoughtfulness."

"Will you help me with the questionnaire, mommy?" Priscilla asked.

"Certainly, sweetheart," Carrie answered. "But first you must get ready for school. Papa is going to take you this morning, he has something he wants to talk with you about."

"Papa, you will never guess what happened," Priscilla said breathlessly as she ran to John's limo. "Good morning Charles," she politely added.

She got into the car and told John about Svetlana's letter. Her excitement was electric and John was very pleased with her reaction.

"That's wonderful sweetie, when will the recital be held?" John asked.

"Mom is going to talk with everyone to make sure that the dates we pick will be suitable to all."

"Well I don't know about everyone, but Jennifer and I will clear our calendar to be there, no matter what," John said, smiling at her. "Wouldn't miss it for anything."

Priscilla hugged her Papa. He was such a positive influence in her life. The love that she had for him was special. It was like they were very best friends. She felt she could tell him anything, talk with him about anything, and felt completely safe when she was with him. She trusted him completely.

"Well that news makes what I have to say sort of inconsequential," John said, faking a pout.

"What Papa, tell me," she said.

"Well Jennifer is going out of town next week and I have to attend a Board dinner. I wondered if you would be my date," John said. "I have checked with your mother, and she says you have the evening clear."

"Oh, Papa," Priscilla said with delight. "I would love to be your date."

John explained to her that it was a formal affair, and after school today he would pick her up and take her to Jennifer's shop to get fitted for a formal gown. The Board dinner had gotten some play in the *Times*. John would be speaking and giving out awards to executives from various Double-O offices around the world. John thought it would be fun for Priscilla to meet some of the attendees, and he also wanted to show her off. He was sure there would be press coverage.

"Sounds like a lot of fun, Papa, I can't wait," she said.

The night of the Board dinner arrived, and Charles and John picked up Priscilla precisely at six thirty. Priscilla looked very grown up in her new formal gown. Most of the attendees were already there when John arrived. He proudly stepped out of the limo and then helped Priscilla out. They walked into Henri's, and all heads turned to greet John.

The crowd applauded as John and Priscilla were seated at the head table.

"To copy a famous speech, hi, my name is John Wingate, I'm the fellow who has accompanied Priscilla Wingate here tonight," he stated with a smile, looking down at Priscilla smiling up at him. There was more applause from the crowd.

"It is wonderful to see you all here tonight, and I look forward to chatting with each of you. First, let's get to business," John continued.

John talked at some length about the successful year. Tonnage was up fifteen percent over the previous year, and forecasts indicated that it was still climbing. He praised the domestic agents for their very prosperous year. There were no graphs and charts or overhead projectors. John had the numbers memorized, he knew every detail backwards and forwards. When he was finished, there was polite applause.

"Okay," John continued. "Under your charger plates, you should find an envelope. Make sure your name is on it before you open it. JT and I, the Board, and all of the home office executives and staff want to thank all of you for your efforts this year making Double-O the most successful shipping company in America," John said as the applause increased. "Now, let's get on with the festivities. Henri, please begin the service." The room came alive with conversation as waiters and waitresses took orders. John and Priscilla walked around the tables greeting the guests.

Priscilla was the hit of the party and had her picture taken standing alongside John with most of the invitees. The following day, many of the pictures were published in the business section of the *Times*.

"This fucking snooty little bitch is everywhere," Brad said out loud.

The head of America's biggest shipping company must be worth a bundle, he thought to himself, reading the morning paper. Brad wondered how a broad like Melany could have gotten wrapped up with people like that.

Brad had been laid up in the hospital for three weeks from the beating that Jake gave him. He now had a permanent limp, and he vowed that no matter how long it took he would get back at Jake and Melany for what they had done. Somehow he would even the score. He was getting out of the hospital today and he would go home and have a long think about his next steps. He was seriously low on cash, and needed to find some income soon. Tomorrow, he would call around and see what he could scare up.

"How are you getting along, Melany?" Jake asked as he picked her up at the doctor's office.

"Nearly mended," she said. "The ribs are still sore, but the doctor says they are healing well and I should be good as new in a couple of weeks."

"How about the jaw? I see your nose has completely healed."

"The doctor said I can start eating firmer foods, but that I shouldn't eat hard foods for at least another two to three weeks," she said.

"When do you want to get back to work?" Jake asked. "The customers have been asking for you."

The rib pain was holding her back, and she told Jake she would like to get past that before she started dancing again. Besides, she had to practice and get back into shape. She had started her meth-heads anonymous meetings and was completely off of the methadone. Everything in her life was looking up, and Jake was bending over backwards to help her. If his reasons were selfish, she didn't care. He was the first bad boy who had ever treated her properly, and he wasn't always taking advantage of her. In fact, it was the opposite.

"Jake, you have been such a great help to me, and I don't know if I can ever repay you," Melany said, putting her arms around him.

"All I want is for you to get well, all around, and get back out there and make us some money," he answered honestly.

"So all I am to you is a piece of dancing meat, ready to be devoured by the johns?" she fired back sassily, and then mock pouted.

"You are the best piece of dancing meat I've seen in a long time," he smiled, with a hint of playfulness. He was not a playful person generally, and that gave Melany a little confidence.

Jake took Melany next door to the Pussy Cat Club to her new apartment. Jake had the apartment furnished except for one bedroom he had left empty for her to exercise and practice in. He had installed mirrors on one wall with a barre on the other.

"Jake, how thoughtful of you," Melany smiled and kissed his cheek.

"Nothing but the best for my star attraction," he said.

"If you feel up to it, come down to the club this evening, and I'll buy you a drink," Jake said as he headed for the door.

"No drinks, I'm afraid, chairperson's orders, if you remember," she said.

"Sorry, I wasn't thinking, a soda it is then," he smiled and walked out of the apartment.

At the club, everyone hovered around Melany, all with the same questions. When would she dance again, will she still do the ballet routines, will she lap dance again? She smiled at their persistence but she answered them all. She knew they were her bread and butter. She kissed them all on the cheek, did a pirouette, flaring out her miniskirt, showing her panties, and walked sexily to Jake's office.

"That was quite a performance you just did out there, I watched you through the one way glass," Jake smiled.

"Ya gotta keep 'em coming back for more," she said happily.

"Look Melany, I want to change our working relationship," Jake announced.

"Really? Why?" she asked.

"I know what we make every night without you. We will tally the differences when you get back to work, and I'll give you half of the total net," he offered.

"I was making upwards of twenty five hundred to three thousand a night previously," she said.

Jake told her that he knew exactly what she was making and that the new arrangement would easily net her the same and more.

"Let's give it a try," he said. "If you don't like it, you can go back to your old arrangement. I'm trying to get you a few more bucks, and give you some incentive as well."

"Thanks Jake, I trust you completely," she said, sipping on her soda straw. "I'm a little bushed, Jake. If you don't mind, I think I'll get to bed early."

"There's a stairway behind my office that will keep you from having to run the gamut out there," Jake said. "See you tomorrow."

10

CAT AND MOUSE

John was in the park at his usual time and Carrie joined him. He gave her a hug and a kiss and the two took off down the jogging trail.

"Dad, we've gotten the Juilliard dates agreed. The recital is the eighteenth of next month, a little over a month away," Carrie said.

"Jennifer and I are very excited, aren't you?" John asked.

"Very much so, as is Priscilla. She and Sasha are working very hard on her new routine."

"I know. When we babysat her the other day, we could barely get any time with her she was working so hard," John said.

The two jogged on and John suddenly got that feeling in the back of his head that they were being watched.

"Carrie, let's stop at that bench up there for a moment," John said.

They stopped, John put one foot up on the bench pretending to tie his shoe as he scanned the area behind them. He could see nothing out of place, but the feeling remained. He put his foot back down and they started down the trail again.

"What was that all about, Dad?" Carrie asked.

John explained to her that he had the feeling they were being watched, and that he had the same feeling when he was with Priscilla just a short while ago. He didn't want to alarm her, so he made light of it.

"I'm getting old I guess, and maybe a little paranoid," he told her as they jogged on.

Back at his office, John picked up his phone and called Trent McSpadden.

"John, how are you?" Trent began. "We haven't spoken in a while."

"I'm fine Trent, and yes, it has been too long."

They caught up with families and activities and then John got down to business.

"Trent, when I'm out and about lately, I've gotten a feeling that I am being watched. It happened recently with my granddaughter, and this morning with my daughter as we were jogging in Central Park," John related. "It is a very strong feeling, and no I don't think I am getting old and paranoid."

"John, aware people who have this feeling usually have it for a reason. I have many clients who have had the same experience. Believe me, it's real," Trent told John.

They talked for several more minutes, and John asked Trent to come up with a plan to try and get to the bottom of the issue. John wanted to do it quickly and asked Trent to get right on it, and Trent agreed.

Two days later, John was out on the trail at his regular hour. This time he was alone. About fifteen minutes into his run, the feeling came to him again. He tapped the speed dial number Trent had given him on his cell.

"Yeah, got the feeling again," John said, a little breathlessly.

"Great," Trent answered. "Do what I told you to do, we'll do the rest."

John kept on jogging for another fifteen minutes, and slowed to a brisk walk to catch his breath like he often did. Fifteen minutes later, he picked up his pace and jogged to the end of the trail where Charles was waiting with the limo.

"Good run, Sir?" Charles asked, as he always did.

"Yes it was, Charles. If you would, take me to the office, and I'll clean up there."

"Very well, Sir."

As John was finishing his shower, the phone rang. It was Trent.

"John, I'm sorry, but we got nothing. There was no one suspicious on the trail within a hundred yards of you in any direction," Trent said. "What that usually means is that whoever it is has a stationary position and watches you from there. Are you jogging again tomorrow?"

John told Trent that he would be at the same place at the same time, and would call again if the feeling came back.

"John, vary the time a little each day you run," Trent said. "We can learn a lot from that, and it confuses whoever may be watching, keeps him off balance. He may make a mistake during his confusion."

"John, I had four men scouring the windows of the buildings, the heavily wooded areas, the other side of the pond you run around, nothing," Trent said, frustrated.

John shook his head in disbelief. The feeling this morning was as strong as it had ever been. It had started on the trail, and ended when he got to his limo.

"Trent, remember Eric Erickson, one of the Seal team leaders we had for JT and Carrie's extraction?" John asked.

"I do, John."

"Get hold of him please, and let's set up a bodyguard operation where he observes me at all times. I want to get this thing figured out. Please have him call me," John said and hung up.

Eric called John later that afternoon. They discussed the issue, and Eric told John he would be at John's office at nine the next morning.

"Eric, John has had feelings of being watched, and it is not always at the same place or same time," Trent started the meeting. JT, Carrie, and Joe were also in attendance.

John explained that the family had been involved in some very high profile events lately, and that usually brings the creeps out of the woodwork.

"We get threats, hate mail, graffiti, everything you can think of, but it is also the periods when I most get the feelings of being watched." John told the men that the family was well aware of the situation, they all took precautions, and all the family drivers had been trained in diversion and evasion tactics.

"Are all of the drivers trusted?" Eric asked.

"Yes," John answered. "Most have been with us for generations."

"You vary your travel patterns and times?" Eric asked again.

"Yes."

"What are the events you have coming up?" Trent asked.

John had Patricia run off a copy of his next two months' schedule. He had JT, Carrie, and Joe do the same. Several of the events were mutually attended by all family members, but the majority of events were separately attended. The family, especially John, was involved in many charity events.

"Do any of the others of you have feelings of being watched?" Eric asked.

They all shook their heads. John told Eric that during the most recent incident, he was jogging with Carrie, and she didn't seem bothered. It had happened to John many times in the past, and some panned out, but in the majority of cases nothing had happened.

"It would take an army of men to follow all of you everywhere, so we should probably set ourselves on an on-call basis. The moment anyone has the feeling they are being watched, tailed, harassed, or stalked, they should call Eric and he will deal with it," Trent said.

"If you are attending an event that you feel is high-risk and high-profile, it would be best if you call me before leaving your homes. Also, if you are not going to attend an event shown on your schedules, we should get a phone call as well. We will try this for a couple of weeks and see how it goes," Eric explained.

"John and Carrie, are you two running this week?" Eric asked. "If so, I would ask that you run together for two reasons. One, it will make my job a lot easier, and two, it will be much safer for you both. What I would like to do is run along behind you at a discreet distance and look for anomalies. If anyone is out there stalking you, he or she will show themselves sooner or later as they get more and more confident of your seeming lack of awareness. Act as natural as you can, even if the feeling comes to you."

The week went by without a sighting. John and Jennifer attended two charity galas, JT and Carrie had four out-of-office meetings, and Joe pretty much stuck to the office. The group got together and discussed the week. No one, including John, had had any premonitions. Everything seemed normal and uneventful.

"Eric, JT, and I are out of town all next week, which means my daughter will be staying with John and Jennifer," Carrie said. "It is your turn, correct?"

"That it is," John said with a smile. "Can't wait."

"Well, carry on as normal," Eric said. "How far out of town?"

"London."

"I don't think a crank stalker is going to follow you there," Eric smiled.

The following week, John rode to school with Priscilla every other day, and Jennifer took the other two days. They explained to her what was going on and watched her closely from car to school and school to car. They told Priscilla never to allow herself to be alone, and certainly not to talk with strangers alone.

On Wednesday, John picked up Priscilla on time. Priscilla ran to John's limo the minute she saw it drive up.

"How was your day, sweetie?" John asked, hugging and kissing Priscilla on the cheek.

"Very exciting, Papa."

"What was so exciting?" he asked.

She explained that one of the teachers noticed a man sitting in his car across the street from the school, watching the kids. The teacher told the principal and he called the police. Before the police arrived, the man drove off. He was described as a man in his mid-thirties, dark haired with sunglasses, and he was driving an older model car.

"Why was it so exciting?" John asked.

"The principal got the whole school together in the auditorium with the policemen and told us to be watchful of that sort of thing. They gave a presentation on the stalking and molesting of children. It actually scared me a little bit, Papa."

"I'm sure it did, sweetie, I'm sure it did."

The next day John called Eric and told him Priscilla's story.

"I completely forgot all about little Priscilla, and she was with me on one of the occasions when I thought I was being watched," John said. "This puts a whole new spin on things. Eric, can you full-time guard Priscilla?"

"I can," Eric answered.

"We start that as of today. I don't think it is necessary for you to be at hand if Priscilla is with one of us, but if she is alone anywhere, I want her guarded," John said. "That includes school, ballet lessons, anywhere, any time."

"John, if you would, I'd like you to call a meeting of the immediate family, so we can have a discussion about this," Eric said.

"Is tonight, here at the office good?"

"Perfect John, thank you."

It was necessary now that Priscilla be added to the schedule requirements. Eric was to know the movements of every family member and any situation when any family member might be left alone or caught alone. Eric explained that if someone took someone else to a function and then returned home alone, or was left home alone, he wanted to know it. He insisted that everyone have his number on speed dial.

"You might think I'm paranoid, but something as innocent as one of you saying to the other that you are going out for a newspaper, or a jog, or a stroll, anything; that constitutes a situation where both of you are now alone. It puts each of you at higher risk," Eric explained.

It was very easy for a family of this stature, wealth, and exposure to make a mistake and end up alone somewhere. Eric told the family story after story about how abductions happen at the most innocent of times when the guard is dropped and the perpetrator pounces on their victim.

"You are assuming that someone is trying to abduct one of us," John said.

"It is adding up to that," Eric said. "First it was your premonition with you and Priscilla, then you and Carrie jogging, and now we have the school incident. That tells me that more than one of you is being studied. He or she might be looking for the easiest target, and when to do the deed. That's what it looks like to me."

They all looked around the room at each other in silence, and then rapidly began asking each other questions. John asked the group if anyone else had feelings of being watched, and all the heads shook. JT asked if it could be a disgruntled employee, but no one could think of anyone, at least not off the top of their heads. Carrie wondered if it could be her first husband, and she threw the thought out for the group to consider.

"Why would you say that?" Eric asked.

Carrie told him that he was a loser who got her pregnant and walked away from the marriage at age seventeen. She mentioned that she hadn't heard anything from him since then, but he might have heard about her adoption and was plotting to abduct her for ransom.

"Is Priscilla his daughter?" Eric asked.

"No, her name was Jennifer, and she died of cancer at age eight," Carrie answered.

"The fact that it was you who was with John when he had his hunch on the jogging trail makes it a possibility," Eric surmised. "But Priscilla is an unknown to him, unless he has done some research. We'll keep him on the list and see what happens."

11

MELANY AND JAKE

Melany was completely healed and back to work at the Pussy Cat Club. The johns were happy, she was happy, and Jake was making lots of money. Each night she would vary her routines to close with a ballet move. In her complete nakedness, she felt free and airy, and as long as she was appreciated she felt good about herself.

She finished her last dance for the night and Jake asked her to come to his office.

"You've made two thousand, eight hundred dollars tonight so far," Jake said. "What do you think of that? And there's still two hours left to go."

Melany smiled. She was on the right track and she knew it. Everything was falling into place. The only emptiness was her lack of male companionship.

"That's wonderful," she said as she walked up to him behind his desk. She sat on the wide surface and crossed her legs, facing him. Her miniskirt barely covered her, and she knew she looked desirable.

"Whoa, what's this?" he said, rolling back several feet in his desk chair.

She explained to him that she was extremely grateful for all he had done for her and wanted to show him her appreciation. She leaned back on her elbows and her top rose up, revealing her flat stomach.

"I want you," she said, uncrossing her legs.

Jake stood, stepped up to her, pulled her legs apart gently, and bent to her waiting mouth.

"I want you, too," he said, kissing her gently and pulling her up to him.

Jake was concerned about mixing business with pleasure, but he was caught off guard and decided to rise to the occasion. He reached for the desk phone and buzzed his bartender.

"I'm leaving the office. Lock up, I'll see you tomorrow morning," Jake said firmly and hung up, not waiting for any further conversation.

She was as light as a feather, and he picked her up and carried her up to her apartment. She reached behind her and undid her top, shrugging it to the floor. She removed her miniskirt and panties and walked up to him to put her arms around his neck. She kissed him long and hard, let go, turned, and walked like a ballerina to her bedroom.

Jake hesitated a second before following her to bed. She was aggressive and yet submissive, soft and yet firm, wet and probing and without doubt skilled at pleasing a man. He fondled every inch of her body, he breathed in, kissed, and tasted every curve and orifice. Her love-making made him feel manly and strong, but he found himself being gentle and controlled with her, taking his time, not wanting it to end in a frenzied flurry.

When he finally climaxed, she released a split second before him, making it the best experience he had ever had with a woman. He rolled her over on her side, positioned himself behind her, and enveloped her in his strong arms. She fit dreamily into the curve of his body, her buttocks seemed to embrace his still erect penis as they both raised their knees to a fetal-like position. He buried his face in her hair.

"God, that was marvelous," he whispered in her ear.

She wiggled closer to him. She was smiling and he could feel it.

"Everything up to this point has been fucking," he said to her. "That was love-making."

"Are you telling me you love me?" she asked.

"I'm telling you that felt like love-making," he said. "Don't get any ideas."

Jake got out of bed and went to the doorway, giving her a playful pat on the fanny. He put on his Jockeys and went to the hall for a smoke.

"I'll be right back, I'm getting a smoke," he told her.

"Are you alright?"

"I couldn't be better, baby."

The following night, Melany danced with a new commitment. There was a sign-up sheet for lap dances. She was averaging three lap dances per performance, and she performed five times a night. Doing the math, she was bringing in over three thousand a night. When she stopped in to Jake's office for her pay, he smiled at her and told her how pleased he was with her contribution to the club.

"It's like it's a whole new place here. The clients seem to be of a higher caliber, they are spending more money, and we are coining money both in the lap rooms and at the bar. I'm starting a pub food menu, to see if that won't get 'em in here earlier and keep 'em here, what do you think?" Jake asked her.

"You want my opinion?" she asked in amazement.

"Certainly, partner," he said kissing her on the shoulder.

She told him that she loved the idea, and asked how that would be financed. He told her that the guy who was going to do it was footing the costs and splitting the costs of the waitresses with Jake.

"He keeps all of his profit, and except for the waitresses, we keep everything separate," he said.

"What is he doing for kitchen space?" she asked.

"He prepares everything off site, and brings it in daily. He has a refrigerator and a bank of microwaves in the back. He paid for the installation, we split the electric bill and clean-up costs. All the food is served in specially designed hard paper containers, with napkins and plastic utensils. I personally have tried several of his dishes, and they are very tasty, just what these bozos want," Jake said.

"I think you are on the right track Jake, sounds great," she said.

The food idea was a great success. Within two months, the average guy was spending five hundred a night on dances, food and alcohol. That worked out to twenty five thousand every weeknight and fifty thousand or more on Friday and Saturday nights.

Jake was sleeping with Melany two to three nights a week. The lap dancing would often get her worked up, and she needed the release. She was also beginning to have feelings for Jake.

"Jake, I haven't paid you any rent yet," she told him one night.

"I'm there half of the time, so I'm letting the club pick up the cost," he told her. "That way, we share the cost fifty-fifty".

They were sitting on the new sofa that had mysteriously arrived that day. She straddled him as if doing a lap dance.

"You've never asked me for a dance," she said, mock pouting.

"Down there it's all business baby, up here I think of you—of us—differently," he confessed.

She cocked her head, looked at him, smiled, and kissed him on the mouth. He gently pulled her to him and eased her down on the couch.

"Let's see how this thing feels?" he crooned.

"Umm, yummy," she said, laying on top of him.

They necked and petted like high school kids for an hour before going to bed. Melany was ecstatic with his tenderness. Jake had never felt this way before. He liked the way he felt.

"Baby, Sunday I want to take you for an all day trip to the country. We can have a picnic and be in the fresh air and sunshine all day. Then we can come back and make love all night. What do you say?"

Melany rolled over and kissed him. He wanted to spend his free time with her as well. This was a change, and she wanted to keep it going.

"That would be lovely Jake, I can't wait," she murmured, and nestled her head into his chest.

Jake decided to take Melany to Cheesequake State Park in New Jersey, a little over an hour away in good traffic. He had gone there many times as a boy, and it held good memories for him. The lake, beaches, and walking trails were all part of his recollections, and he felt like sharing them with her. She was dressed in a sweatshirt, jeans, a T-shirt, and tennis shoes, and she was ready for the outing. Jake had his new food man pack them a lunch and he carried it along the walking trail until he found a good place to stop.

Jake found a camping spot he had used as a boy, not too far from the trail but far enough to be reasonably quiet and semi-private, and the view of the lake was calming. He spread the blanket Melany was carrying and they both took off their shoes and laid down. The sky was a radiant azure, the temperature was eighty-two degrees, there was a slight easterly breeze, the birds were chirping loudly; overall, it was a perfect day. Melany shrugged off her sweatshirt, rolled it into a ball for a pillow, and laid back with a contented smile on her face that was so appealing, Jake couldn't take his eyes from her. He lay on his side next to her, his head propped up in his hand.

"Like the place?" he asked.

"It's beautiful Jake, I feel peaceful and happy here," she answered.

He told her the stories of his boyhood, how he and his buddies would often come here and camp. They snuck cigarettes and beer in, and at sixteen they thought they were men. They laughed, told ghost stories, roasted marshmallows, and never got into any real trouble.

There was the time they came upon a couple skinny dipping in a remote part of the lake and they swiped their clothes and dropped them about two hundred yards down the trail. They waited in the bushes and got an eye full as the young pair came looking for their clothes.

"You meanie," Melany mocked.

"Aw, it was all in good fun, they were laughing as they walked away," he said.

She enjoyed his stories. Each tale gave her an insight to who he was and what he stood for. She was getting to know him. She rolled over and gave him a short kiss to let him know she was enjoying herself.

Jake sat up and looked around. He saw a man across the lake with what appeared to be binoculars, and the man turned away when Jake fixed his gaze. The man walked away with a limp into the crowd and never looked back. *That was strange,* Jake thought. He shrugged his shoulders, reached into the cooler for a beer for himself and an orange juice for Melany, and again fixed his attention on her. The day passed much too quickly.

"Ready to go, babe?" Jake asked.

"Oh, must we?"

"I'm taking you to a little local trattoria back in the city for dinner, and then I'm taking you home," he said.

The word *home* rang like chimes in Melany's ears.

12

THE RETURN OF BRAD

When he thought he was completely out of sight, Brad changed his jogging pace to a brisk walk as he approached the Park's parking lot. He went straight to his car, but decided to sit there and wait for Melany to leave. He knew Jake's big black SUV and had his eyes on it in the lot. He waited four hours before he saw the pair come to the vehicle. He quickly slid down in the seat, peeking through the gap formed by the wheel and the dashboard.

As Jake opened the passenger side door for Melany, she stood on her tip toes and playfully kissed him on the mouth. She hopped into the vehicle as Jake patted her on the fanny.

All lovey dovey, Brad thought. He watched them until they drove out of the lot. He decided not to follow them. Jake was smart, and he would recognize a tail. He decided to wait another half hour before he left. As he drove home, he passed the Pussy Cat Club and noticed that Jake's SUV was missing from its usual parking space.

He drove home, grabbed a beer from the refrigerator, and went to sit on the seedy living room couch. He noticed the blood stains from the beating he had sustained at Jake's hands and seethed. He lit a cigarette and leaned back against the cushion.

Brad started thinking about his lot. He had sold the car he and Melany had purchased. He got six thousand dollars and bought an old clunker to get around with. He had four thousand of that money remaining, and very few prospects for more. He was selling meth as a side job, and busted drifters for extra change. He was barely getting by, and he knew he had to come up with a plan quickly.

The first thing he had to do was get Melany back. Then he had to get her hooked on meth again before he could proceed with his grand plan.

⚬

"Hi honey, this is Brad, how are you?" Brad said into the phone.

"I'm fine Brad, what do you want?" Melany said coldly.

"I want to see you honey, I miss you and want to make sure you are okay."

Melany looked into the phone, rolled her eyes back in her head and thought a few seconds.

"I don't want to see you Brad, I'm fine, and I want to leave it at that," Melany said, but stayed on the line.

"Aw come on Melany, I'm really sorry for being such an asshole with you, and I want you to know that I've changed and am trying to clean up my act," he said, pleading. "Maybe we could have a cup of coffee sometime?"

"I'm not ready for that yet Brad, please understand," she said and hung up.

He sounds so sad and remorseful, she said to herself. She knew she no longer had any interest in him, but she did hear a little of the old Brad in his voice. *Maybe he has changed,* she thought.

"No, I'm not going down that road again, and that's final," she said to herself aloud.

She walked down the back stairs to the club and noticed Jake sitting on a bar stool talking to the bartender. There were only one or two customers, it was early. She walked over to Jake and sat down beside him.

"Hi," he said. "Ready for the evening crowd?"

"You bet," she answered, smiling brightly.

The bartender asked her if she wanted her usual orange juice and soda, and she nodded.

"Brad just called," she offered.

"Oh yeah, what did the asshole want?" he asked.

She explained the reason for the call and that she told Brad that she definitely was not interested. Jake smiled at her.

"Good decision, that guy is a creep. I've heard that he is dealing meth and rolling bums for change. What a loser," Jake said.

Melany finished her juice and got up to go on for her first number. Jake watched her closely. Old habits are hard to break, and he wanted to be sure she wasn't going to get back with the loser. Her dance was well received by the growing crowd, which for a Tuesday night was beginning to look pretty good. She came down off the stage and two men approached her for a lap dance. With her sexiest smile, she led them to the lap rooms. She came out about a half hour later and went to the dressing room. Jake walked in a minute or two after she got there.

"What's up?" Jake asked.

"One of the guys who asked me for a dance gave me a message and that from Brad," she said, looking down at the small box on the seat next to her. She explained that it was a silver necklace with a small heart on it. "I suppose he is trying to get back in my good graces."

"Want me to take care of it?" Jake said threateningly.

"No, I'll send it back to him," she said. "I asked the guy to come back later. I want to write a note back to him."

Jake watched her very closely for any sign of weakness in her approach to the situation. He knew that she had a fragile, needy, and enabling side, and he wanted to make sure that she didn't lapse and take backward steps.

"You are doing so great baby, promise me you won't let that worm get to you," Jake entreated.

"I won't, it's just that he is so contrite in his note and says he can't get along without me."

"He wants his meal ticket back, that's all. Don't do it, he used you and abused you in the past, don't ever forget it," Jake said with finality and left the dressing room.

"I won't," she said as her eyes welled slightly.

At the end of the evening, Jake called her into the office. He said that they had an okay night for a Tuesday. He asked her how she was doing and if she needed anything.

"No, I'm fine," she said.

"I'm having an alarm hooked up in your apartment. You can use it to alert me, my bodyguard, or the bartender if you have any intrusions. You know what I'm talking about. I wouldn't put it past that bastard to break in on you."

"I don't think that's necessary, I'm sure he won't try anything," she said.

"I'd rather be safe than sorry where he is concerned."

Two nights later, after her last dance, she went to her apartment to shower for bed. There was a knock at the door, and she thought it was Jake. She went to the door in her towel and smiled broadly as she opened the door.

"Can I come in?" Brad said, sliding his foot in to jam the door open.

"That's not a good idea," she said, voice shaking. The beating he had given her flashed back into her mind.

She stepped back into the room and stood next to the newly installed alarm.

"I want you to leave, and now," she said.

He looked at her with a smile that soon changed to an evil sneer.

"You don't understand Melany, you and I are a team. You need to come back right now, I insist," Brad demanded.

"You have two minutes to get out of here in one piece. I just pressed this alarm button and either Jake, his bodyguard, or both are on their way here."

Brad hadn't done anything and decided to test her. Two minutes later, both Jake and his bodyguard barged in.

"What the fuck are you doing here?" Jake roared.

"I just wanted to talk to her, I haven't done anything," Brad answered.

"Is that right?" Jake said to Melany.

She nodded and he noticed that she was shaking.

"Look asshole, I'm going to let you walk out of here this time, but be assured that this is the last time. If I catch you here, or anywhere near here again, they will have to carry you out in a bag. I'm not putting up with your bullshit. Do you understand me?" Jake yelled.

Brad nodded his head and eased around Jake's bodyguard and out the door. As he walked away, Jake noticed his limp, and he flashed back to the man at the lake. Brad quickly walked down to his car and drove off. He was going to have to come up with a different plan, but he was satisfied with the night's effort, having learned the lay of the land at Melany's apartment.

"Look baby, we can't trust that asshole," Jake said. "At the beach the other day, I saw a man with binoculars watching us from across the lake. When he turned and walked away, I noticed he had a limp. Something is going on, and until we get to the bottom of it, I'm going to stay as close to you as I can."

"Jake, we were together nearly three years, it's hard to just throw him away," she said.

"All you were to him was a meal ticket. He was sucking off of you. He pimped you out, for Christ's sake."

"I know, I know," she said, putting her arms around him. "You're right."

Jake smelled her freshly washed hair and the lotion on her taut dancer's body and it aroused him.

"I'd like to stay with you tonight," Jake said.

"I'm a little shaken up, do you mind if I ask to be alone?"

"Not at all baby, but I would like to sleep on the couch at least. I don't trust that bastard."

"Suit yourself," she said. "I'll see you in the morning, and thanks."

Jake lay on the couch thinking. He knew Brad would persist until Jake did something permanent about it. He knew the only way to stop him was to kill him. *I'm not going to risk jail over that piece of shit.* He decided to look into other ways of getting rid of him. Maybe he could set up a drug issue with the people he sold drugs for, maybe he could make sure one of the bums that Brad rolled for change died and see to it that Brad got blamed for it. Neither one would be difficult to do. He fell asleep.

Ten blocks away Brad laid on his rumpled bed. He too was thinking. He knew that Jake would now throw up a shield around Melany to protect her. He knew that he wouldn't get anywhere near her at her apartment or the Pussy Cat Club. He somehow had to get her out of there and into the open.

He also knew that if he was successful in abducting Melany, he would have to take her to a different place, because his apartment would be the first place Jake would look. For his complete plan to work, he needed a two bedroom apartment near a grocery store or convenience store. He needed to keep the tank of his car full at all times and he needed a hand gun. With this many people to handle, his hunting knife wouldn't be enough.

13

FORTRESS PUSSY CAT

As Brad suspected, Jake threw up a virtual fortress around Melany. He hired a body guard to be with her at all times. The only time he was allowed to leave her side was when she was safely in the club between the hours of six PM and midnight or one AM on the nights Jake didn't stay with her, and six PM to nine AM if he did. During that period he could sleep or do whatever he needed to do personally.

"Max, this is a picture of the creep we are concerned about. He is pretty burley, somewhat fearless, and he walks with a limp, left leg. He drives an old rusty Ford Ranger pick-up, blue," Jake told the new member of his crew.

"Do I need to carry?" Max asked.

"Do you have a permit?" Jake asked.

Max explained that he has been a bodyguard for the last thirteen years. He had guarded celebrities, the wealthiest of whom insisted that he carry a weapon. He was a sharpshooter in the military, keeps himself current, and shoots every two weeks. He also told Jake that he has never had to use his weapon, but was ready for the first time should it be necessary.

Jake liked the quiet, sharp-featured, six-foot-three, wiry man. He looked as though he could handle himself, and so far he felt very comfortable with Max on the team.

"Max, the next time you go to the range, I'd like to go with you. Please let me know a day in advance," Jake asked.

"I'm going this Friday, if that will work for you," Max said.

"It will, and we're taking Melany with us. I want her to be more gun savvy. What gun do you use?" Jake asked.

"I carry the Smith and Wesson, model 649, .357 Magnum," Max said.

"A heavy piece," Jake said. "I'm impressed."

"It gets the job done."

Max and Jake's driver sat in the front seat of Jake's SUV, he and Melany sat in back. They drove out to the Metropolitan Rod and Gun Club where Max knew the range coach. After the introductions were made, they all went to the range. Melany was jittery, never having fired a pistol. She remembered watching her father skeet shoot when she was a very little girl. She hated the noise, and resolved to stay away from firearms.

The first up was Max. He fired five rounds from each of three positions and three distances, a total of forty five rounds. He hollowed out the head and the heart. There were no stray shots. Jake was next. He fired ten rounds of his 40 Caliber Glock 27 at three different distances. His patterns were not as precise as Max's, but he was deadly.

Melany dreaded her turn, but she knew that Jake was serious about wanting her to be ready for any situation. Range Coach Dale showed her the workings of her new Smith and Wesson .357 Magnum, Titanium Air Lite.

"You'll be firing 38 caliber rounds today miss, a lot easier on the hands," Dale said.

He showed her the proper stance, grip, and squeezing techniques.

"Okay, point down range, take a breath, let it out, and squeeze," Dale instructed.

Melany closed her eyes and fired. She missed the target completely. Dale stood behind her, put his arms around her and helped her fire her second round. This time she hit the lower stomach area of the target. Dale explained that she would do better to keep her eyes open and always pull straight back on the trigger using only the pad of her trigger finger. She fired eight more rounds, one of which hit the head and three hit the torso. She was improving.

"Hey Dale, there's some guy sitting in his pick-up outside the gate. He's got binoculars," one of the range members said.

Dale went to the closed circuit TV system and took a look.

"You folks know anyone with an old Ford Ranger pick-up?" Dale asked.

"Unfortunately we do, he's the reason we're all here," Jake said.

As if he had heard the conversation, Brad started the Ford and drove off.

"I don't like guns," Melany said on the way home, "I know that I should learn, especially since we saw him there today, but I want to make it clear that I don't like it."

"That's okay, baby," Jake said. "Max is going to take you shooting every day this week and then twice a month."

"How did you get to be such a good shot?" Melany asked Max the following day at the range.

"Practice, practice, practice," Max said. "I assume you understand that, given that you are such a good dancer."

Melany smiled at the offhanded compliment, and assumed her shooting stance. She fired three rounds and turned to face Max.

"Whoa," Max raised his voice slightly and quickly grabbed the gun to point it at the ground. "We don't want to kill anybody now, do we?"

"How stupid of me," she said. "I didn't even think."

"It's okay, everyone does it once. Leave it at that," he lightly admonished. "Every time you want to leave the range, you first place your weapon on the table and then turn around. Try to make that a habit."

Max wanted to use the outdoor range and show Melany a few things about what she was doing. He got her in position at the firing line. He told her to hold the gun down at her side.

"I'm going to stand behind you, and when I tap you on the shoulder, I want you to raise the gun, aim, and shoot at the close target as quickly as you can with accuracy," Max directed.

"What are you going to do?" She asked.

"I'm going to run in the other direction."

"Why, afraid I'm going to shoot you?"

"No, just do as I said, you'll see."

Max tapped her shoulder and took off running. Before she could shoot, he had traveled over twenty five feet.

"That's how far a target can run toward you in the time it takes you to shoot him. You can see that if he was closer than I am to you now, he would have been on top of you before you could shoot."

Melany was amazed. She was beginning to see the importance of protecting herself. Max told her that if that situation ever arose, she should change her tactic and raise the gun to chest level and fire as many shots as she could until the target got to her. Hopefully, by that time, enough bullets would stop him or kill him.

By the end of the week, Melany felt comfortable with the gun. She still didn't like it, but she felt she knew how to use it. She was hitting the targets consistently with fewer and fewer misses. She liked the feeling of having the gun handy in her apartment.

"I think you have come a long way miss, you are shooting well for a novice," Dale said. "By the way, your friend in the Ford Ranger was out there again today. He left the minute I moved the camera."

"Well you're no Annie Oakley, but knowing what I know now, I'd be afraid of walking in on you uninvited," Max told her.

She smiled confidently as they drove back to the city. She wondered to herself if she would be able to pull the trigger when and if the time came, especially if it was Brad. The thought of the beating he gave her came back to mind.

The bitch just keeps digging her hole deeper and deeper, Brad said to himself as he drove away from the range. *I'm going to have to completely surprise her,* he thought.

"Max tells me you're becoming a decent shooter," Jake told Melany as she came down to work that evening.

"I'm not as afraid of it as I was, and the noise doesn't bother me as much now," she said. She told him that she still didn't like it, but knew that it was the best thing for her to do.

Her music began and she walked up on the stage. Max had just finished the meal Jake had the caterer prepare for him and he started to walk out of the club. She waved at him, he waved back, and he was off until nine AM.

As he walked out the door, he noticed the blue Ford Ranger parked up the street. He pretended not to notice, got in his car and drove off in the opposite direction. He turned left at the next intersection, then a second left and a third left, and he was back on the street where the Pussy Cat Club was. He pulled up next to the Ford, rolled down his passenger side window and motioned Brad to do the same.

"What's your problem, asshole," Brad asked with attitude.

"You," Max answered.

"I'm not doing anything illegal," Brad smart-mouthed.

"As long as you keep it that way, you'll be okay," Max smiled. "The minute you do anything illegal, you'll be dead. Have a nice evening," Max said as he threw his last paper target into Brad's window and drove off.

He called Jake and told him that Brad was lurking outside his club. "He may have left by now, but he was there three minutes ago, and I had some serious words with him."

Jake sent his bodyguard outside to have a look, but Brad was gone. Jake thought about a restraining order, but opted against it. He knew that Brad would be able to get to Melany, with or without a restraining order, if he really wanted to get her. No, he had to keep the ring around her tight.

14

A NIGHT AT JUILLIARD

"Jennifer, you need to hurry up or we'll be late," John called from the living room.

At that moment, Jennifer stepped around the hallway corner and into the living room. She looked regal with her nearly white gray hair in an up do, a royal blue, floor-length gown, and pearls.

"Would you mind putting this on me, please?" she asked, handing John the Lapis bead bracelet he had gotten her years ago on one of his trips through India. It had a particularly difficult clasp that she never mastered.

"Thank you darling, I'm ready to go. Do we need our opera glasses?" she asked.

"No, I understand it is a rather small venue and we have excellent seats," John answered. "By the way, you look stunning."

Charles was waiting for them downstairs as they walked out of their apartment building and into the limo.

"Are we running late, Charles?" Jennifer asked.

"No ma'am, we are right on time," Charles reassured her.

John and Jennifer were excited about the evening. Seeing Priscilla dance at Juilliard was going to be a milestone, in both their and Priscilla's life. Priscilla had been working extremely hard on her number, The White Swan. Everyone in the family knew the piece backwards and forwards, having watched her practice it so often. Jennifer had a big smile of excitement on her face as she got out of the limo at 60 Lincoln Center Plaza. John had a momentary feeling of anxiety, but didn't know why. He shuddered, and the feeling was gone. He looked around to see if anyone was watching or acting suspiciously, and saw no one except the anxious crowd that included all the Wingates, as well as John's mother Priscilla senior.

The venue was one of the practice halls converted into a small theater with thirty seats and a dance platform three feet above the floor. The Wingates were afforded the first row of seats, then the other performers' families, then various Juilliard teachers and administrators. The lights dimmed, and Priscilla stepped out on the stage from behind a curtain. She walked to the center of the stage and stood in third position waiting for the music to begin, a faint glimmer of apprehension in her eyes. The familiar strains of Swan Lake mesmerized John as he watched his little flower dance gracefully and artfully around the stage.

At the beginning, she had a hesitant look on her face, and as she began to realize she was nailing the movements and dancing without thinking, her face became serene with a confident smile. The dance teachers were experiencing something they hadn't seen in a while; a student of obvious rare talent becoming one with her music, allowing it to move her around the floor in perfectly centered steps; never shaking, faltering, or wobbling. She danced with an eight-year-old's strength, and a twenty-year-old's grace.

As the music came to an end, after the White Swan pas de deux, the crowd roared with applause. John felt compelled to stand and clap adoringly. Jennifer handed him a bouquet to bring to Priscilla. John was in tears as he made the presentation. Next Carrie came forward and gave her a lei of orchids and plumeria. Lastly, eighty-year-old Priscilla senior, with John's help, rose from her seat and approached the stage with aged difficulty. She stood in front of the smiling ballerina, cocked her head, and began clapping her gloved hands.

"Brava, my dear, brava," she said quietly, handing Priscilla a single red rose.

Priscilla junior did a deep bow to her namesake with a sweeping arm gesture of profound love and respect. With a teary smile out to the gathering, she turned and, on tip toes, left the stage.

There were two more dancers participating in the recital, an eighteen-year-old girl in her first year at Juilliard and twenty-year-old male in his third year at dance. Both danced extremely well. The evening ended with a small reception. The Wingates gathered together and hovered around Priscilla junior, praising her, congratulating her, and adoring her. She was definitely the jewel in the family crown.

The Chair of the Dance Department, Sarah Martin, approached Priscilla, now changed into her evening clothes, and shook her hand.

"A very fine performance, my dear," Mrs. Martin said. She talked a little more about Priscilla's dance abilities and asked her questions.

"How many hours a week do you practice?" she asked.

"Three to four hours per weekday, and two hours of limbering exercise on the weekends," Priscilla said with a nonchalant seriousness that had even John marveling at her maturity.

"How did you come to meet Svetlana Zakharova?"

"I think my Papa was instrumental in arranging that meeting. It came as a surprise to me. I will remember that experience as long as I live," Priscilla said, smiling and looking lovingly up at John.

"I would like to give you this," Mrs. Martin said, handing Priscilla a manila envelope. "It is a letter of recommendation to the Juilliard school of dance, signed by all of the ballet school administrative and teaching staff, ten of us in all."

Priscilla's eyes widened in surprise as she looked gleefully at everyone around her. She had an idea of the value of such a letter, and was deeply thankful.

"How old are you, my dear?"

"I'm eight, I'll be nine in October," Priscilla said.

"That means in another ten years, you will have your high school diploma, at which time we would be very interested in you submitting an application to Juilliard. Svetlana Zakharova has also given us a recommendation letter, which will be kept on file here. You have a copy in your envelope. Please keep dancing my dear, we would love to see you in ten years."

Priscilla explained to the administrator that she currently had only seven years to obtain her diploma, as she had been advanced twice since starting school. She smiled shyly at the woman and looked down at the floor, not wanting to seem boastful.

"That's magnificent, we will be seeing you sooner than we thought. Goodnight my dear, and goodnight to you, Wingate family. You have a marvelous protégé on your hands," Mrs. Martin concluded.

Brad put down his program on the seat of his chair and moved to leave the ballet venue. *Not a bad little dancer,* he thought. *That ups the ante a little, I think.* He felt out of place and didn't want to get caught up in the pleasantries of the reception. He got to the door and let himself out.

John noticed the limping man without any recognition. He even smiled at the man before he returned his attention to his group. John noticed a purple-blue trace of a tattoo sticking out above the starched collar to the man's blue dress shirt. His brow furrowed momentarily, but again, thought nothing out of the ordinary.

"Jennifer, did you see that man?" John asked.

"What man?" she replied.

"The one that just limped out of the room and into the court-yard," he added.

"No, I didn't," she said. "There is no one else in the room except little Priscilla, as far as I am concerned."

"Charles, please take us to Henri's," John asked his driver. "We'll get a bite to eat before we go home."

"Very good, Sir," Charles said. "By the way, there was a man looking around the car this evening. A big man with a limp."

"Was he wearing a blue shirt and tie with a brown sports jacket?" John asked.

"Yes, how did you know?" Charles asked.

John looked at both Charles and Jennifer and furrowed his brow. He made a mental note to speak with Eric in the morning. He called JT and Carrie and related the story to them.

"I'm not trying to scare you, but I thought you should know and keep a sharp eye out," John told Priscilla's parents. "I'll have Eric beef up protection first thing in the morning."

15

PARANOIA?

"**Y**ou need to keep an eye out for a man about six foot, two inches tall, two hundred and twenty pounds, light brown hair and a tattoo on the nape of his neck," John told Eric over the phone.

"Anything else John?" Eric asked.

"Yes," John said. "He walks with a pronounced limp."

John told Eric about the previous evening at Juilliard. Eric was very concerned. If this was a stalker, he was showing very bold moves. He wasn't timid.

The two men decided to publicize a family event that would make the news. They thought it might attract the man so they could apprehend him when he showed up. They needed to have words with him.

"SHIPPING MAGNATE AND HIS FAMILY CELEBRATE THEIR JUILLIARD DANCER," read the Society Page headline. The article went on to say that the closed event would be held at Henri's restaurant, gave the date and time, and another two paragraphs extolling Priscilla's prowess on the ballet stage.

These people are so stupid, Brad thought as he put down the newspaper. *They advertise every move they make as if it was of worldwide importance.*

"Who gives a fuck?" he said to himself aloud.

Brad had a hard-on for the wealthy. As a young man growing up in New York, he would see them all the time around Central Park, in their limos and their fancy attire, at the theater, at the Met, and at the expensive seats at Giants Stadium, where he worked selling peanuts to the fans.

He never understood why there were rich people and then people like himself who had to scrape for every cent they had. Somehow it didn't seem fair to him. He thought about the snooty little Wingate brat who had everything handed to her. He developed a true hatred for the affluent and did stupid things like keying their limos, soaping their windshields, or placing dog feces in places where they were likely to step in it.

He was caught twice marring the limos and went to juvenile hall for thirty days for the second offense, and he was made to work to pay for the damage he had caused, which really sealed his loathing of the rich. It was at this time in his life that he got involved with the seamier boys his own age—and older—he had met at reform school.

He got involved in drug sales the day after his sixteenth birthday. He was walking the streets, feeling sorry for himself, when he was approached by a boy his same age selling cocaine. He engaged the other boy and they became friends. Before long, he was selling cocaine as well, which put some change in his pockets. He got busted at age eighteen and served two years for possession with intent to sell. Now he had a criminal record and a reputation with his peers of being fearless, but a brick short of a load. It seemed that everything he did turned bad. He served a second two year sentence and was now on the police radar, one of the so-called usual suspects. He would get rousted and harassed on a regular basis. He soon realized that the harassment came with the job, and he learned to live with it. He also learned that if the authorities didn't have any evidence against him, he knew how to wiggle out of their net. Deny, deny, deny.

Henri's was an intimate restaurant that held probably fifty to sixty guests at fifteen tables comfortably spaced around the open floor. The decor was definitely of French origin with chandeliers, velvet drapes, and French provincial-style furniture. There was ample room between tables to move around to serve the guests and allow guests to visit one another. John particularly liked Henri and his food.

Eric stood at the door checking invitations and looking for the man with the limp. A man boldly stepped up to him and started to move past him and into the restaurant.

"One moment sir, may I see your invitation?" he said to the casually dressed man.

"Left it at home pal," the man said unconcernedly and tried to continue on.

"Sir, please stop," Eric said firmly.

The man stopped and looked defiantly at Eric. He knew that if he was going to get in, he would have to keep up the bluff and hope the man caved. John noticed the commotion and walked over to the front entrance.

"Any problems, Eric?" John asked.

"This man says he has an invitation, but has left it at home," Eric offered.

"Are you sure you're in the right place?" John asked the man.

"I think so. This is the Anderson wedding party, isn't it?" the man asked.

"I'm sorry, you have the wrong function," Eric said.

The man said a few more words and turned to leave the restaurant. John immediately noticed the tattoo peeking out from under the man's collar and motioned to Eric by tapping the nape of his neck. Eric instantly noticed the tattoo, and walked up the sidewalk after the limping man.

"Hang on a minute there, I'd like to talk with you," Eric called.

"Fuck you pal, now I'm already late for my party," the man muttered and continued walking.

Eric grabbed the man by his shoulder and the man swung around with a big left hand headed for Eric's jaw. Eric ducked and easily subdued the man, and soon had him on his knees. Eric reached down, grabbed and pulled on the man's mustache, which came off with some pain. "Who are you, why are you in disguise, what is your name?" Eric asked, rapid-fire.

"The mustache is a joke man, just trying to have a little fun with the people at the party I'm supposed to be at. Now you've gone and fucked that up too."

"Why did you take a swing at me?" Eric asked.

"Why did you grab my shoulder?" the man returned. "I don't like being grabbed, and my name is none of your fucking business."

The man stood, brushed off his pants, and started to walk away. There was nothing that Eric could really do to get any more out of the calmly belligerent man. Eric decided to let the man walk away.

"Well, what happened?" John asked as Eric returned to the restaurant.

"The guy was definitely in disguise, but he gave me a reasonable explanation. I drew a little blood while we were scuffling, and got some of his on my coat jacket. We can have it analyzed, if you like. Maybe we can learn his name that way," Eric suggested.

"Good idea, get that done," John said and walked back to his guests.

The next day Eric contacted a friend of his who ran a private forensics lab and asked to have the DNA analysis work done.

"I need to know who left the blood on this jacket," Eric said.

"We are going to have to cut the blood out, it will ruin the jacket," his friend told him.

Eric shrugged, it had to be done. He needed the man's identity.

The lab offered overnight service and the next day they had their man, Brad Waterman, aka Waters, aka Watson. He had a long rap sheet, mostly drug related, nothing violent.

"What do you make of it, Eric?" John asked.

"I don't know, sir. Has he ever worked for you or a subsidiary in any capacity?" Eric returned.

"I'll have that checked immediately," John said, leaving the room. He went to his brother Joe's office and gave him Brad's name and information and asked to have someone check payrolls back fifteen years, as Brad looked to be in his early thirties. John knew this would take time, and asked Joe for a priority effort.

"Put as many as you think you can spare on it, Joe," John said as he turned to go back to his office.

Double O was a fast-growing shipping company that hired some un-savory people for their sailing fleets. Human Resources had developed a hiring system, complete with background checks, and for the most part they hired good hard-working mariners, but the occasional bad apple slipped through the net.

John was sure that there must be some disgruntled employees in the company's long history. He recalled an incident when they mistakenly hired a murderer that was trying to flee the country. The FBI caught up with him just as the ship was being towed away from the pier.

Sitting in his seedy living room, Brad drank a beer and relaxed. He was thinking hard about his plan and it was coming together rapidly. He felt that he had most of the t's crossed and i's dotted. The only loose end was how to get Melany away from her bodyguard long enough for him to grab her undetected.

He laid his head back against the sofa cushion and stared up at the cobwebbed ceiling fan. He closed his eyes and drifted into a momentary reverie. Suddenly he bolted straight up in his seat.

"That's it," he shouted to himself aloud. He stood, clapped his hands together, and walked into the kitchen for another Budweiser, tossing the dead soldier in the trash.

16

STEP ONE

Brad packed everything he owned into two medium suitcases, one plastic garbage bag, and an Igloo cooler. It was late at night, and he intended to leave his apartment, skipping his last month's rent. *Fuck that chink son of a bitch slum landlord,* he thought.

He loaded his car and drove to the other side of town, where he had earlier rented a two bedroom, one bath, walk-up flat. It was seedier and cheaper than the one he had just left, but it would work for his purposes. It hadn't been deep cleaned in ages, and it was filthier than even he felt he could live in. He got to work cleaning and scrubbing the rust-brown stained sinks and toilet. He worked hard on the dark gray tile grout, with negligible results. He thought it smelled a little better, at least something for his efforts.

The apartment had two twin beds, one in either bedroom. He moved them both into the master and purchased two cheap blow-up mattresses for the second bedroom. He bought two heavy-duty, plate-mounted, restraining U bolts and installed one on the floor near each blow-up mattress.

After everything was cleaned and liberally sprayed with Raid, he taped sheets of newspaper over all of the windows, blocking most of the light and all of the unwelcome eyes. He got a beer and took a stroll through the apartment, looking for failings, finding none. His three days of hard work and elbow grease was complete. He was ready.

The absence of an elevator was a problem, but he felt he could manage it. The stairs were narrow and poorly lit. In the week he had been living here, he had seen no one in the stairwell, at the front or rear entrance, not even on the steps. There were three apartments, and his was the middle. He decided to delay the beginning of his plans for one more week until he fully learned the comings and goings of his fellow apartment dwellers.

In the week that followed, Brad learned that the elderly woman upstairs lived alone and a visitor dropped by on Monday, Wednesday, and Friday at precisely six in the evening and left two hours later. He noticed that on the Wednesday visit, the old woman was taken for a short walk up and down the sidewalk in front of the flat. Her visitor was a fifty-year-old or so man who was very attentive and hugged the woman at the door when he left. *More than likely the woman's son,* he thought.

The apartment below him was also very quiet. The first three days he saw no one and wondered if the apartment was vacant. He decided to check things out and dressed like a handyman with a ball cap, aviator sunglasses, and his fake moustache and knocked on the door.

"Who is it?" a frail voice called from inside.

"I was sent here by the landlord to check all the fans and air conditioners in the building," Brad deftly lied.

The door opened slowly and an old man with a menacing-looking shillelagh-type cane slowly and cautiously opened the door.

"He didn't call me first. He usually calls me first to let me know someone is coming," the old man blurted out.

"Sorry sir, hope this isn't too much of an inconvenience," Brad said. "I won't be long."

Brad looked around, checked the wall switches on the fans, and turned on each window air conditioner.

"Don't go in there," the man said. "My wife is ill and sleeping."

"Had any troubles with the fans or AC in there, Sir?" Brad asked.

"Can't say as I have," he said.

"Well, it looks as though everything is okay in here, sorry to have troubled you," Brad offered as he began to leave the apartment.

"Oh, that's okay son, can't be too careful these days, though."

Brad smiled at the old man, turned, and closed the door behind him. *I think I've stumbled into the perfect spot*, he thought as he walked up to his apartment. *Elderly, quiet, hard of hearing, and probably of poor eyesight neighbors make for good neighbors*, he said to himself with a very pleased look on his face. The residents of the upper and lower apartments were dead to the world by ten PM.

The week ended with Brad feeling he knew the apartment routine well. He lived very quietly, not wanting to draw attention or upset his geriatric neighbors.

Brad purchased clothesline rope, extra towels, duct tape, four cheap blankets, four pillows, some bar soap, and a week's worth of food and water for two. He bought two cases of Budweiser at the neighborhood liquor store.

"Hi, Audrey, this is Brad, Brad Waterman," he said into the phone.

"Yes, Hi Brad, how are you, and how is Melany?" the woman asked.

They talked on for a few minutes and it became obvious to Brad that Audrey wasn't aware of his split with Melany. *Audrey was a bit of an airhead, not the sharpest tool in the shed*, he mentally recalled.

"Well Audrey, we had a bit of a spat, and I really feel bad about it, and want to make amends, but she won't see me," Brad told her.

"What can I do?" Audrey asked.

"I wonder if you could call her and have her come visit you and we could surprise her when she got to your place. I just want to talk to her. You can be with us the whole time she's there. You could tell her something like you lost your boyfriend, or your job or something like that. You know how she loves to help people, she is such a good soul," Brad said.

"I don't know Brad, if she doesn't want to see you, she probably has her reasons."

Brad started pouring on the charm, virtually begging Audrey to help him, sounding almost in tears. He told her that he loved Melany and wanted to start over with her. He asked her please to try, and gave her his cell number to call him back with a time and date to meet Melany.

Two days later, Audrey called back. She told him that Melany was coming over to her apartment tomorrow night. She said she would be there at seven o'clock.

Brad decided to case Audrey's apartment house, and get a feel for the layout. He had been there several times with Melany when they were together and remembered the interior, but wanted to check the entrances and the exits and make his plans accordingly.

The next day he showed up at Audrey's apartment an hour early. He brought with him a bottle of wine and a bouquet of roses.

"You're early," Audrey said as she opened the door.

"You said six o'clock, right?" Brad feigned surprise.

"I said seven, but it's okay, come on in. I'm just finishing my make-up, I'll be with you in fifteen minutes. Have a seat in the living room," Audrey offered. "There's beer in the fridge."

Brad put the wine and the roses on the kitchen counter and got a beer. He wandered around the apartment, familiarizing himself again with the floor plan, fidgeting with the packet of white rohypnol powder in his pocket. Audrey had changed the furniture around a little bit, but it was still mostly as he had remembered it.

Audrey returned to the living room wearing white, low-rise, skin-tight jeans and a short-sleeve white crop top baring a flat, tanned midriff. She had finished her make-up, and she looked very desirable to Brad. Brad asked her if she was seeing anyone, and she said she was still dating the same man Brad had met several times with Melany when they had double dated. They were still getting along very well, and were thinking about moving in together.

There was a knock. As Audrey got up to open the door, Brad went to the bathroom. He heard Melany come in, the sharing of hellos and hugs. He waited a few minutes and joined them. Melany was visibly shaken when she saw Brad.

"Melany, I hope you aren't upset, but Brad asked me to get you here so he could apologize to you and try to win you back," Audrey stammered.

"I told you that I didn't want to see you again, Brad, and I meant it," Melany said. "I'd like you to leave immediately. Besides, there is someone waiting for me out front."

She had just told Brad what he needed to know.

"Oh babe, come on and relax, I just want to talk with you and make sure you're okay."

"I'm fine Brad, you need not concern yourself," she answered.

Brad got up to get a glass of wine for Audrey, and something for Melany.

"There's some Perrier in the refrigerator," Brad called. "Melany, would you like a glass?"

"That would be fine," she answered, her voice agitated.

Brad came back with the drinks and placed them in front of the girls who were sitting together on the sofa. Brad took a seat across from them and drank a second beer. The two girls started talking and sipping their drinks. The girls talked several minutes as Brad sat quietly and patiently smiling at them. He didn't want to get Melany upset by confronting her so he just chimed in with the small talk.

Five minutes later, Melany stood to go to the bathroom, and reeled backward onto the couch. Audrey moved to catch her, and fell over onto the floor. Brad sat and watched with a smile on his face. Melany raised her head to look at him, but fell back without making eye contact. She tried reaching into her pocket for the alarm buzzer Jake had given her, but couldn't coordinate her movements.

Pleased with himself, Brad stood and stealthily approached the apartment front window, looking down at the cars below. He saw Jake's black SUV with Phil and Jake's driver in the front seat. He needed to act fast now, and get Melany out of the apartment.

He wiped down the glasses and everything he had touched. He pulled out his straight-blade hunting knife and walked over to where Audrey was laying. He stabbed her three times in the heart, and then slit her throat for good measure. Audrey moaned once with the first blow, and then not a sound. Brad went to the kitchen and cleaned his knife and put it back in its sheath behind his back. He put on the fake moustache, dark glasses, and a ball cap pulled down as low as he could and still navigate.

He picked up Melany, put one of her arms around his shoulder, and grabbed her waist in support. Her head dangled down, and she looked like a drunk being hauled off to bed with her feet dangling inches above the floor. Brad left the apartment and closed the door behind him. He was immediately confronted by one of the apartment dwellers opening the door to 3C.

"A little too much of a good thing," he said and smiled, walking off toward the elevator, which was still at the floor, having just brought the 3C occupant. He pressed the *level 1* button and calmly rode down with his burden dangling at his side. He turned in the direction of the rear alley exit and pushed open the door. He had parked his Ford Ranger less than fifty yards away behind a dumpster.

He gently placed Melany into the front seat, fixed her seat belt, and tilted the seat back so her head would rest against the headrest. He drove without headlights to the end of the alley and turned away from the front of the apartment, turning on his headlights as he entered the dark and empty street.

17

AW SHIT!!!

"Phil, she said she was only going to be an hour, and it's nearly been an hour and a half. Think you should check on her?" the driver said.

"Yeah, I guess so," Phil said, easing his six-foot-four frame out of the SUV.

Phil walked up the front steps and into the apartment building. He walked up to the third floor to apartment 3B and knocked on the door. He waited a full minute and knocked again. There was no answer and he knocked a third time, this time trying the door knob. To his surprise, the door opened and he walked in, closing it behind him. He immediately noticed two feet in high heels sticking out beyond the end of the living room sofa, toes pointed up.

He approached the sofa and saw the attractive young girl with blood coming from three wounds to her bare midriff and pooled on the floor around her chest. He also noticed that her throat had been cut. *A little bit of over-kill,* he thought to himself as he touched her throat for any signs of life.

He looked around the rest of the rooms and found nothing. There was no sign of Melany. Only the wine glass, water glass, and Budweiser beer can gave any testimony that someone else had been there. With his handkerchief, he lifted the water glass and sniffed it. Nothing. There was a lipstick stain that looked like Melany's color. The lip gloss stain on the wine glass was that of the dead woman.

He called Jake using his cell phone.

"What the fuck do you mean she's not there? You took her there, didn't you?" Jake growled into the phone.

"What I meant boss, was when I went to check on her in the apartment, she wasn't there, only a dead girl."

Jake calmed his voice. Phil was his best man, and Jake didn't want to piss him off.

"Are there any indications of a struggle, or what else went on there?" Jake asked calmly.

"Nothing. Only that there was a wine glass, a water glass, and a beer can on the coffee table, indicating to me, at least, that there were probably three people in there," Phil replied.

"Don't touch anything, Phil, and get back here as soon as you can."

Jake's driver pulled up in front of the Pussy Cat Club twenty minutes later, and Jake met them at the curb. He got into the back seat and told his driver to go to Brad's apartment. Phil and Jake stormed into the apartment, breaking the jamb.

"Where are you, you useless fuck?" Jake screamed.

A very scared, nerdy-looking man in horn rimmed glasses and two piece pajamas stepped out of the bedroom and looked at the two men.

"What are you doing in here?" the man stammered.

"Where is Brad?" Jake shouted.

The man winced and answered, "There isn't anyone here by that name. I'm the only one here, you can look around if you don't believe me," the man said, voice still noticeably shaky.

"I will," Jake said, pushing past the man and walking into the bedroom. He trusted no one.

Phil looked around the kitchen and bathroom and found no one.

"He's alone here, Boss."

Jake asked a few more questions like how long had he lived here and did he know the man that had lived here before him, and did that man leave a forwarding address. It was obvious to Jake that the man was telling the truth, and he and Phil left the building.

The two men went back to the club, directly to Jake's office. They called everyone who knew Brad, talked to the other dancers, and then decided to go back to the apartment where Melany had gone to visit her friend. As they got closer to the apartment, it was obvious they weren't going to get a chance to get close to the place. There were police everywhere. They parked a block away and watched the first responders at work. Jake decided to walk into the building alone and see if he could find anything out.

"You can't go in there, pal," a uniformed police officer said.

"My girlfriend came here earlier this evening to see a friend of hers, and she hasn't come home yet. She said she would only be an hour or so. It's been over three hours now," Jake told the cop.

"Who was she here to see?" the officer asked.

"Whoever lives in 3B, I don't know her name," Jake answered. "That's where my driver said he dropped her off." Jake was trying to protect Phil by stretching the truth slightly.

The officer motioned to one of the detectives standing at the entrance, who walked over to where Jake was standing.

"What's up, Officer?" the detective asked.

"This man says his girlfriend was in 3B earlier this evening."

"Really, sir? What's your name?" the detective asked.

"Jake O'Malley," he said.

"Can I see some ID?" the detective asked.

Jake showed him his driver's license. The detective wrote the name and number in his pocket note pad.

"What happened here?" Jake asked.

"Your girlfriend's friend's throat was cut, and there's blood everywhere," the detective said, leaving out some of the facts for later questioning.

"I can tell you right now that my girlfriend didn't do it. She is a gentle soul and wouldn't harm anyone. She's not your perp," Jake offered.

"Thank you Sir, now if you'll let us do our jobs we will keep you informed of our progress," the detective lied.

"Wait a minute, what about my missing girlfriend? When does that get some attention? I'm really afraid she may have been abducted, I have had her under a bodyguard's care for the last several weeks," Jake said assertively.

"I understand your concern Sir, but we have work to do and lots of it, and we will include the abduction angle in our investigation. Officer, take this man's information. Get what you can on the missing girl, possible abductor, pictures, IDs, the works." With that, the detective turned and went back into the apartment house.

"Can I go in and see if she left any of her stuff behind?" Jake asked the detective as he disappeared into the building.

Jake gave the officer everything he had on Melany. He even had his driver go back to the club and retrieve a publicity picture of her.

"She's a real looker," the officer said, as he folded the poster-size photo in fourths.

"Officer, can you go and see if my girlfriend left anything behind, like a purse or something?" Jake tried again.

"I'll see what I can do," the officer replied.

"Persistent fucker," the detective told the officer. "Tell him we didn't find anything out of the ordinary. And Officer, don't say anything else to him. If he starts to ask questions, just tell him you aren't allowed to discuss an ongoing investigation."

The officer returned to Jake, shaking his head.

"What does it look like in there?" Jake asked.

"Not at liberty to say, Sir. Now if you don't mind, I have work to do. Go home, you can check with the precinct tomorrow."

"I told you I'm concerned she may have been abducted, and tomorrow may be too late to help her," Jake pleaded. "Has the detective interviewed the tenants yet? Did they see anything?"

"As I said, Sir, the investigation is ongoing. Please check with the precinct tomorrow."

Jake tried, but wasn't able to penetrate the Blue Line. He walked back to his SUV and told his driver to go back to the club.

"I know that prick Brad has something to do with this, and I'm going to rat him out to the police tomorrow," Jake said to Phil.

"That may not be a good idea, Boss. Brad will just tell them all about our beating up on him and trashing his apartment," Phil wisely offered.

"You're right," Jake said. "We'll mount our own search for that bastard tomorrow. Someone was bound to have seen something. You guys go home and get some rest, we'll get an early start in the morning."

"Boss, were still good, right?" Phil asked Jake.

"Were good, Phil. Short of chaining yourself to her, there was nothing you could do. Get some rest."

Jake, Phil, Jake's driver, and two other bouncers gathered at the diner down the street from the Pussy Cat at seven the next morning. They had all had a good night's sleep and were ready to go.

"Phil, I want you and one of the others to check through the neighborhoods to see if Brad is still rousting bums. See if they know where he might be living now," Jake began.

"Sure, Boss," Phil said.

"Johnny, you take the other guy and see what you can find out at the precinct house."

"Will do, Jake," Jake's driver said.

"I'm going back to that apartment house and see if I can't talk to the other tenants. We'll all get back to the club by tonight's opening time," Jake ended.

They finished their breakfasts, Jake winked at the proprietor, and they all walked out.

❦

Jake noticed that all of the yellow tape was gone from the front of the apartment, but apartment 3B still had the tape across the jamb. He walked over and knocked on 3A's door. No one answered and he knocked again, a little louder.

"Hold your horses, I'm coming," said a female voice from inside the apartment.

The door opened and a sixty-year-old woman in her robe and pajamas appeared.

"Yes?" she asked.

"I'm with the insurance company, and I need to ask you some questions about the incident here last night," Jake said, producing a fake ID.

"I've already told the police everything I know," she said

Jake talked with her a little longer, and found out that she wasn't here last night during the incident, and couldn't get back into the building until late last night when the police completed their investigation.

"I'm sorry, but that's all I know."

"Did the murdered woman have a boyfriend that you know of?" Jake asked.

"Oh yes," she said. "A handsome young fellow. The police asked me that, too."

"Can you describe him? Do you know his name?" Jake persisted.

"He is about six to six-foot-two tall, trim, brown hair, and blue eyes. I heard Audrey call him Andy once, never got the last name," she answered.

"Anything else you can remember, other boyfriends, girlfriends, cars, anything?" Jake finally said.

"I did notice that Andy's hands always had that dirty/clean look, like a mechanic," she said.

"Thank you, ma'am, you have been very helpful," Jake said, and moved toward apartment 3C.

After several knocks a man answered.

"Hello Sir, I'm with the insurance company and I'd like to have a few words with you if you don't mind," Jake said, showing his ID.

"Yes, would you like to come in?" the man asked.

"No, I won't intrude," Jake said. "I just have a few questions. Did you see anything last night?"

"I told the police that I saw a man come out of the apartment holding up what looked to me like a very drunk young woman and walking to the elevator," the man said.

Jake reached into his jacket and took out two pictures.

"Is this the woman you saw?" Jake asked.

"Yes it is, very pretty girl."

"Is this the man you saw?" Jake asked.

"It could be, but the man last night had a moustache. He wore dark aviator glasses and a ball cap pulled down low on his forehead. He was friendly enough. Said something like *she's had too much*, and smiled."

"Can you describe the guy?" Jake asked.

"Yeah he was tall, with a good build. I think his hair was brown, but I'm not sure," the man said.

"Anything else?"

"Yeah, I noticed that he walked with a pronounced limp."

Bingo, Jake thought.

"Did you see anything else, Sir," Jake continued to probe.

The man said that about a half hour after he had seen the man with the girl, he heard someone go into the apartment. He said that he went to his door and looked through the peephole. He described the man that came out and it was Phil's description to a T. He made a mental note to tell Phil to lay low.

"Thank you very much Sir, you have been very helpful," Jake said as he turned and walked toward apartment 3D.

There was no one home at apartment 3D, and Jake thought better of using his tools to pick the lock. He was satisfied with the information he had received and decided to go to the precinct house. There were still four hours left before shift started.

"Jake O'Malley, here to see Detective Johnson," Jake announced to the precinct officer on duty.

Jake stood looking around at the Gallery of Uniformed Officers Killed in the Line of Duty. There was a picture, a name plate, and a badge on each plaque. Jake was surprised to see the extent of the precinct's losses. There must have been seventy or eighty men in the line-up. He noted the first picture was of a man killed in the year 1933 and the last was this year, 2009. Jake did the math and estimated that the precinct averaged over one death per year. On the other side of the hallway were pictures of detectives and others killed in the line of duty. Not as many, but still a shocking number.

"Mr. O'Malley, how may I help you today?" the detective asked with a somber look.

"Have you made any progress with the investigation into my missing girlfriend?" Jake asked politely.

"We have some information, but very little to go on," the detective said.

"I'm going to tell you something and I know it is going to incriminate me, but her ex-boyfriend is a jerk. A while back he beat her up so badly that she had to spend time in the hospital and over six weeks in recovery. It really pissed me off, so I beat the crap out of him, causing him to have a permanent limp," Jake confessed.

"Does he have a moustache?" the detective asked.

"Not normally, but that doesn't rule out disguises," Jake offered.

"Do you know his name and where he lives?"

"It's either Brad Waterman, or Waters or Watson, and he no longer lives at the address I knew. I was there yesterday hoping to find him, I know he has something to with this. You said the other woman had her throat cut, and I know that the guy carries a straight-blade hunting knife."

"Mr. O'Malley, you've been very helpful here, and I wouldn't worry about any retaliation from Mr. Waterman if he is the man who did this," the detective said.

"I just want to get my girlfriend back. She is also my business partner and we need her back."

"I will keep you informed Mr. O'Malley, I have your contact information."

Jake shook the man's hand and started to walk out.

"By the way, I have some of my own men on this checking out Brad's old haunts. He used to roust bums for pocket change and we are checking to see if he is still doing that. I'll keep you informed as well."

"A word of caution, Mr. O'Malley. Don't get too deep into police business, please. We appreciate your inside information, but you don't want to cross the line."

"I understand, Detective," Jake said and left the precinct house.

18

HOOKED

Brad pulled up to the front of his apartment house at nine PM. There was no sign of life in the top apartment and only one light coming from between closed curtains in the bottom apartment, it had the blue hue of a television screen. There were several people, mostly bums, walking the street. He waited with Melany, out cold beside him. Looking down at her, slumped in the seat, he was still attracted to her, but his vengeance clouded his feelings. He wanted to get back at this woman and the asshole she was shacking up with.

The street finally cleared. He got out and walked around to the passenger's side, lifting Melany out of the car. He handled the one hundred and twenty pound burden easily. Again he put one of her arms over his shoulder and held her up at her waist. Head bobbing, he walked into the building.

He quietly entered his apartment and switched on a light. He carried Melany to the bedroom and flopped her down on one of the twin beds. He tore off a six inch strip of duct tape and placed it across her mouth. He then stripped her down to her panties and spread-eagled her arms and legs before he hog tied her to the bed with clothesline. After ogling her for several minutes, he threw a blanket over her and went to the kitchen to get a beer.

The seedy apartment was essentially a box. The front door opened into the living room. The kitchen was behind the living room on the left, the bathroom was behind and to the right, both accessible from the living room. The two bedrooms were to the right of the living room. Brad left the bedroom door open so he could see Melany from where he sat. He sipped at his beer and then nodded off. He didn't know how long he was out, but when he woke up he saw that Melany was struggling with her restraints. She was stretched out so she could only pull at the ropes holding her, which made them tighter.

"Well, look who's back in the land of the living," Brad said, looking down at her with a sneering smile.

She looked up at him and glared. She tried to mumble something and couldn't get it out. Frustrated, she stopped tugging and squirming and in frustration, stared directly up at the ceiling.

"We're going to have a little fun tonight, sweetheart, but first I want to get you into the mood," Brad said.

Brad pulled the cover from her and she raised her head to look down at her nearly naked body. He sat down on the other bed, reached into the nightstand drawer and pulled out a box of paraphernalia. He dissolved the meth in warm water and then sucked it up in a needleless syringe. He untied her legs and flipped her over on her stomach, then he pulled down her panties. She began to squirm violently and tried to turn over. He re-tied her legs when she was face down again and the squirming stopped.

He rubbed her buttocks softly and then slapped her hard. She moaned a muffled scream. Out of the corner of her eye, she saw the syringe in his right hand and she blanched with horror. *No, he can't be doing this to me,* she cried to herself. *Oh God, please don't let him do this to me.*

He slapped her buttocks again and again as tears came to her eyes. He transferred the syringe to his left hand, spread her cheeks, and injected the fluid directly into her rectum.

"Welcome home, Melany," he said snidely.

He pulled up her panties, rolled her over on her back and re-tied her legs. He put the blanket back on her and left the bedroom turning out the lights.

"Sweet dreams."

She lay sobbing, defeated and beaten for thirty seconds before the dopamine began to flow and the room and the world slipped away from her. She swooned.

The next morning she woke with a screaming headache. He wasn't in the room with her and she pulled at her ropes with no affect. She lay quietly, trying to figure out what to do next. She looked around the room and noticed the newspapers on the windows, the cracked ceiling, the smudge marks on the walls. *He really has come up in the world,* she thought with a scowl.

At around noon he came back into the room with a half a sandwich and a glass of water.

"If I take the tape off, will you promise to be quiet?"

She nodded her head up and down.

"If you make any noise I'll tape you up again and you won't get any food or water. Do you understand?"

He pulled the tape from her mouth with one quick swipe and she winced and moaned. The headache throbbed, her butt cheeks still stung, and now her mouth hurt. All this and the comedown was almost more than she could handle. He sat on the bed next to her and he fed her the peanut butter and jelly sandwich. He held up her head so she could sip her water. When she was finished, he taped her mouth again, left the room, and closed the door.

Later that evening, Brad turned on the TV to see if the six o'clock news had any reports of the murder. He was instantly shocked to see his image on the screen.

"Brad Waterman is a person of interest in the case," the newscaster said. "Anyone seeing or knowing anything about this man is asked to call the police. Do not approach this man, he is armed and dangerous"

The phone number flashed on the screen. There was a scene of the police milling around Audrey's apartment and then the news shifted to the weather.

Brad momentarily wondered how the police got his name so quickly, and he realized that Jake had ratted him out. *He'll pay for that, too,* Brad said to himself.

He looked at his watch and realized it was time to give Melany some more food and water, and get her high again. Four or five days of this and she'd be begging him to slap her ass.

"Time for dinner," Brad announced as he walked into the room. "Same rules apply if I remove the tape. Got it?"

She nodded her head. Her eyes were closed waiting for the pain of the tape being pulled from her lips. When she finished eating, he rolled her over on her stomach and tied her in that position. Again he slapped her and administered the drug.

"Is it necessary for you to slap me so hard?" she asked.

"Brings the blood to the surface, gives you a quicker high somebody told me. If you'd rather I didn't do that I won't, it's your high not mine. I do like rubbing your sweet ass, though," he told her. Again, he re-tied her and replaced the tape.

After the fifth day, Melany was begging for the meth, and Brad started giving it to her twice a day. Soon it would be three times a day and he wouldn't have to restrain her any longer.

"How are you feeling?" Brad asked her on the sixth morning.

"Please give me a hit," she begged, rolling over and pulling her panties down.

Brad did what he had to do and she was off again in a stupor. She was completely hooked, and she was his again to do with that he pleased.

He went food shopping and when he returned, she was still on the bed, out cold. He looked at her with disgust. He had no desire to have sex with her, he'd have to look elsewhere for that.

He checked the news again. There were no new leads in Audrey's murder case and the story had slipped to page four of the paper. He was feeling pretty safe in his new surroundings. It was time for the next stage of his plan to be set in motion.

Brad went to the kitchen window that he had covered with newspaper. The previous Sunday's *New York Times* Society page was taped up in the middle of the window. Circled in black felt pen was an article about John Wingate and his granddaughter.

"Three more days," he said aloud.

19

GETTING READY

John Wingate rose from a sound sleep and dressed for his run in the park. The last week had been a quiet one, and John was thankful for that. His foundation's fundraiser event was in three days, and he was looking forward to it. The goal this year was eight million dollars, and six million plus had already been pledged.

He was upset that Jennifer couldn't attend with him, and unless he could get little Priscilla to go with him, he was on his own. It had happened many times in the past, and he was prepared, but he preferred to have someone from the family with him. JT and Carrie were out of town.

"Good morning, Charles, great morning for a run," John said with a smile as he got into the limo.

"Yes it is, Sir," Charles answered.

"Drop me off at Museum of Modern Art and pick me up at the East 97th Street entrance. I feel good today and that's an invigorating run."

John stepped out of the limo into the brisk morning air. He walked to the Central Park entrance just north of the museum at East 84th Street. He leaned on the four-foot high black chain link fencing and did his normal stretching routine. He took off toward West Drive and turned north, and jogging all the way to the north end of the park and North Woods. He then turned onto East Drive and south toward

East Meadow and Jacqueline Kennedy Onassis Reservoir. He opted out just before the reservoir onto East 97th Street, where Charles was patiently waiting for him.

"I'll clean up at the office this morning, Charles," John instructed.

"Very good, Sir. Good run?" Charles routinely asked.

"Yes it was, Charles. You know, I've never asked you if you were a jogger," John said.

"Oh no, Sir, I prefer the low impact exercises. I do yoga, race on a recumbent bike, and do light weight lifting," he told John.

"You look very fit, and I have always wondered what you did to stay that way."

"Thank you, Sir, I try to take care of myself," the chauffeur replied.

John Wingate had one of very few slow days at the office. JT and Carrie were away on a trip, Joe Jr. was on vacation, and all serious business had been rescheduled for their return. John decided to use his time to prepare his speech for the foundation's fundraiser. The most important need was funding for cancer research in young children. The loss of his daughter's first child to cancer at age eight had always perplexed him. He couldn't, or didn't want to, understand how a child of four could be diagnosed with stage four cancer.

His foundation was funding research that would detect cancer in embryos and possibly earlier stages, such as the likelihood of parental genes coming together and forming cancer. He didn't understand the technical aspects, but he did understand the need.

An integral part of his foundation was dedicated to providing last wish grants to children under the age of eighteen. His foundation worked with other similar foundations, but his foundation was mainly for children like his deceased adopted granddaughter who had a love for horses. He had talked his old girlfriend Sammy into establishing a wing at her property that would house up to five or six children at a time, and be run and operated by professional staff and volunteers. The current cost is roughly two million dollars a year, and was in need of one million, three hundred thousand dollars for the next year's operation.

John already had pledges totaling six million dollars for cancer research, so his speech needed to stress his "Make a Wish" division. He decided that his speech would center on his adopted daughter and her deceased daughter.

John could not hold back the tears that came as he wrote about little Jennifer and Carrie. He recalled the period in his life when he himself struggled with cancer, watching a precious young girl wither and die, watching a young single mother lose everything, nearly kill herself and then spring back to life to become a force in the shipping industry.

John asked his secretary Patricia to listen to and critique his speech. She sat quietly, listened carefully, and took some notes. When it was over, she had tears in her eyes and was dabbing them with a tissue.

"How much do you want? Where do I donate?" Patricia said, smiling.

"You liked it?" John asked.

"John, if that doesn't get them digging into their pockets, nothing will," she said.

"Do you have any comments or advice?"

"You use the term *"Make a Wish"* several times. Won't that be confusing?" she commented. "I would use something like "Wingate Wish Organization" or "Jennifer's Wishing Well," so as not to confuse. I know we work with the Make A Wish organization, but we don't want to compete with them for funding."

"Good point, Pat," John said. "I like "Jennifer's Wishing Well," by the way. We'll formally change the Wish Division's name."

"Mom, Papa wants me to go to the Wingate Foundation fundraiser with him, but I have exams this week," Priscilla said to her mother on a long-distance phone call.

"This particular fundraiser is very important to him because he is trying to raise money for the Wish Division, which involves your deceased half-sister," Carrie told her. "Are you sure you can't see your way clear to attend with him? Take your exam book with you, and study as much as you can that evening. What exam are you taking anyway?"

"History."

"I don't think you have to worry sweetie, you aced the last test, and by your own admission, 'you get it,'" Carrie said reassuringly. "Please tell him you'll go, it will mean the world to him."

"You're right as always, Mommy," Priscilla said. "I'll call him right now."

"Thanks sweetie. We miss you. Goodnight and I love you. Daddy says he loves you, too."

"Hi Papa, it's me," Priscilla said into the phone.

"Hi my prima ballerina. How is the love of my life?" John said with obvious excitement in his voice.

"I'm fine Papa, and I'd really like to go to the fundraiser with you. Mommy said it was okay if I did."

John was nearly beside himself with joy. Having Priscilla with him was his forever joy, and her presence at the event would really drive home the impact of his speech. Yes, in a way he was using her, but for good, not selfish evil.

"That's fantastic, sweetie. Number one we are going to have a grand time of it, and number two you are going to make the foundation a bundle of money," John told her.

"How am I going to make a 'bundle of money?'" she asked.

"I'm going to ask you a very big favor. Would you please do a very short dance for the audience, say five minutes?" John pleaded. "Pretty please?"

Priscilla chuckled and told him that she would. She asked if it was to be in full dress, or could she do it in leotards. He asked her to do the closing minutes of the Black Swan pas de deux in her tutu. She agreed and realized she would have to rehearse. She only had two more days before the event.

John met with Eric "Hulk" Hendersen the next morning for a briefing on the surveillance operations. Eric told him that things had been very quiet for the last week to ten days.

"Maybe he has given up his plans," John opined.

"Possibly, Sir, but I wouldn't let my guard down just yet. You have your fundraiser to deal with Friday evening, and your daughter and son-in-law come back on Saturday," Eric cautioned.

"I know, Eric, I guess it was wishful thinking on my part. What do you have planned for Friday?" John asked.

"I'm going to ride in front with Charles. This is a pretty well advertised event, and it is one of the few events you have planned with Priscilla for a while."

"That sounds great Eric. Charles is a good man, but with an event this big, I'm sure he'll welcome the help."

"Sir, much of the event is wide open. Can we have you and Priscilla use back entrances and such?" Eric asked.

"This is a very important event, and it's going to showcase my granddaughter. We are honoring her deceased sister and Priscilla will be doing a short recital dance number for the people," John said. "We're going to have to keep a high profile, I'm afraid."

"Very well, Sir, we will plan accordingly," Eric said and ended the briefing.

"Have you looked at the venue?" John asked Eric.

"I haven't, but I'm planning to spend some time there this evening so I can see it in the same light. I'd like to have Charles drive me through the sequence of how he plans to drop you off and pick you up. We'll look for issues," Eric said.

John thought that was a good idea. Get the lay of the land. No surprises. John liked Eric, the detailed way he planned, his dedication and loyalty, his thoroughness. Navy Seals are trained to avoid surprise and they are trained to handle surprise on a split second basis. It was comforting to know he would be nearby.

"Charles, how long have you been working for John Wingate?" Eric asked as they drove toward the fundraiser venue.

"My father was his father's family driver, so I guess you could say two generations," Charles proudly replied.

Eric knew that Charles was loyal, protective, and would do whatever it took to protect the family, he was not questioning that. He wanted to hear the emotion in Charles' voice when he spoke of his employer. He got what he wanted.

"This is where we will let John and Priscilla off," Charles said, stopping at the curb.

Charles explained that there would be an attendant opening doors and letting the people out of the limos.

"Normally I would do that, but the event producers don't want to waste time and want to keep the limos moving through as fast as possible," Charles said.

"Ok, what's next?" Eric asked.

"We will go around the corner and find a place to park and wait. It will be three to four hours. Mr. Wingate will call on his cell phone when he is ready to leave the building. He may have to wait in a line, but being the boss, he probably won't have to wait long," Charles said.

"What is it like where we will be waiting?" Eric asked.

"I'll show you," Charles said as he pulled away from the curb.

There was a parking lot next to the venue where the limos parked in such a way that they could leave at any time without being blocked in by other limos.

Eric thanked Charles for walking him through the situation. He now understood what to expect, where the weak points were, and what his role would be.

20

A FRIDAY NIGHT TO REMEMBER

"You look lovely, my dear," John said to Priscilla as she came out of her room.

"I gave Charles my tutu. He's going to have Eric carry it up to the auditorium with us, and give it to the attendant who will help me dress for my number," Priscilla smiled.

"Seems like you have everything under control," John said with a smile. "Are you ready to go, do you have everything you need?"

"I was going to take some books and study, but I really don't think I need to," she said.

"Very good then, let's be off," John said, grabbing her hand and opening the door.

"Charles, Eric, how are you two this evening?" John asked.

"Fine, Sir," Charles answered.

"Very well, Sir," said Eric. "And how are you, little lady?"

"I'm fine, Eric, and it's nice to see you again," Priscilla said.

"I have a small gift for you, Priscilla, and I'd like you to wear it this evening at all times if you would," Eric said. "It's a GPS finder that is difficult to detect. Don't forget to transfer it to your tutu and then back to your dress, Okay?"

"I won't forget," Priscilla said with a troubled look on her face.

John thought it was a good idea that Eric had, but he didn't want to scare Priscilla.

"It's just a precaution dear, think nothing of it," John told her.

She pinned the small broach on her shoulder strap. It looked nice, she thought. The limo pulled up in front of the venue, and the attendant came and opened the rear door for Priscilla and John. Eric got out of the front seat and went to the trunk to retrieve the tutu. The three walked up the two flights of entrance steps and into the large entrance hall to the auditorium. Charles pulled the limo ahead thirty feet to allow others to pass as he waited for Eric to return.

There were so many people there that John knew personally, and he smiled and waved as he and Priscilla were led to their table.

Eric dropped off the tutu and took one more glance at John and Priscilla to make sure they were seated and safe. He checked the GPS, and it blipped Priscilla's position accurately. He was satisfied. He quickly returned to the limo and he and Charles moved to the limo parking area. A parking attendant directed them to their spot where they stopped and turned off the engine. They were the last in the row, it was on the dark side, and Eric decided to get out and look around. He walked up and down the long parking area and counted over fifty limos, and they were still coming in. When he returned, he got back into the limo with Charles and they began the long wait.

"Ladies and gentlemen, please take your seats," the emcee said into the dais microphone.

The crowd began to settle, waiting for John to address them. John sat smiling, his arm around the back of Priscilla's chair. Priscilla beamed at everyone who caught her eye. She was getting used to the gathering and calming herself before her performance.

"I think it's time for you to change into your tutu sweetie, break a leg," he said with a big smile.

She rose quietly and walked to the side of the room where her attendant met her and brought her to the dressing room.

"Ladies and gentlemen, this is the annual Wingate Foundation fundraiser and I know all of you are waiting to hear from the man himself. So without further delay, John, they are all yours," the emcee said, beginning the applause.

John rose from his seat and walked to the podium, shaking hands, smiling, and schmoozing as he went, followed by a spotlight in the dimmed room. He knew he had a job on his hands, the last one and a half million was always the hardest to squeeze out of his followers, but squeeze out it always did. He respected this crowd of generous donors, most of whom had some sort of experience with the horror of cancer.

"Thank you, thank you, thank you," John said as he steadied himself at the dais.

The group settled again and John waited a full minute in silence before he began his speech.

"I once knew a beautiful little eight-year-old girl named Jennifer. I met her at a cancer clinic where I was beginning my cancer treatment, and she was finishing hers, unsuccessfully. We sat next to each other in the treatment room, where she grabbed my hand and told me not to worry, that 'we were going to beat this disease together,'" John's eyes began to glisten and his voice momentarily faltered. He looked down, choked back his sadness, and went on.

"I literally fell in love with that little waif, with her Aunt Jemima head scarf balanced jauntily on her bald head, and we developed a lasting, binding relationship. She was an accomplished artist and drew lifelike pictures of horses, running, standing, rearing and lying down. She loved horses, but never had the chance to really be with them and experience them." John turned to the second page of his speech. As John spoke, pictures that Jennifer had drawn were being flashed on a large screen behind him, and the audience gasped as each picture came up.

"Well, I couldn't have that, now could I. I just so happened to have a very good friend who owned a racehorse breeding farm in South Carolina. One phone call was all it took and little Jennifer was off on the wish of a lifetime. She spent the last five months of her life grooming, walking, petting and riding her horse she named Jennifer Too. She had a painted on smile for the entire five months."

Pictures of Jennifer with Jennifer Too projected up on the screen. There were oohs and aahs from the crowd. John was setting the hook.

"The saddest day of my life, bar none, was the day that little girl died. There was a happy ending, though, when little Jennifer's mother allowed me to adopt her as my daughter, and she married my brother's son."

John looked out at the gathering with a big smile on his face, eyes shining as he turned to page three.

"What happened next was sheer fate. My adopter daughter and nephew created the amazing child who I want to introduce to you tonight. You may have noticed her sitting next to me during dinner. She is beautiful, smart, and an accomplished ballerina. She has danced at the Mariinsky Ballet Theater in St. Petersburg, Russia, at Juilliard School of Dance, and tonight she is here to dance for you, and of course, your substantial donations. She will perform the last movements of the Black Swan Pas de Deux, alone of course. As you know, in the final scene, the Black Swan does thirty fouette spins. My granddaughter, little Jennifer's step-sister, has agreed to attempt the rigorous task, but wants fifty thousand dollars for each spin. I am purchasing spin number one," John said, producing a check from his inside suit pocket, to the applause of the generous gathering.

The lights dimmed further and the spotlight moved to the rear of the podium stage where Priscilla appeared, standing in third position, waiting for her music to begin. The onlookers clapped loudly for her and she smiled broadly. The music began and she flew like a bird around the stage, and near the end positioned herself, again at center stage. The familiar music sounding like a French Can-Can piece heralded the next scene, and she began her spins. The crowd began to count the spins aloud and by spin six they were clapping loudly to the time of the music. Twenty-seven, twenty-eight, twenty-nine, thirty, they shouted in unison as she completed the last few movements of the piece. When she finally stopped, the donors went wild. She bowed and curtsied to all three sides of the stage as the wives began elbowing their husbands, prodding them to write their checks.

Priscilla walked to the front of the stage and did one last deep sweeping bow, then stood erect facing the now silent crowd.

"My Papa asked me to do this for you tonight, and I hope you enjoyed it as much as I did. I told him I would do it only if he changed the name of the foundation to *Jennifer's Wishing Well Foundation*, and he agreed. Please give generously so that we don't have to lose more young people like my very talented sister. Thank you," she turned and tip-toed to the back of the stage.

That was an added surprise, John said to himself as he walked back to the dais.

"I'll stay here all night if need be, to make sure we reach our goals," John said to the applauding gathering.

The evening was a resounding success, raising nearly one and three quarter million dollars. John was pleased. Priscilla, still in her Black Swan costume, shook hands, smiled, and chatted with the donors, thanking them for their generosity.

"Why don't you get changed sweetie, and I'll meet you in the foyer in a few minutes," John said to his young ballerina.

21

THE CURTAIN FALLS

"**S**houldn't be too much longer now," Eric said. "Should we get in line or something?"

"No, they let us go according to who is ready to be picked up," Charles said. "The boss can pull strings, however, so we have to be on our toes."

Just then there was a tap on the driver's side window with a gloved hand. A man in chauffeur's uniform was standing there, signing Charles to roll down his window.

"Can I help you?" Charles said as the window opened.

"No," the man said and shot Eric in the head. He held the gun to Charles' head and asked, "How do we know when to leave for the pick-up?"

Charles was hesitant but answered the man immediately. A second, silencer-muffled shot was fired as the man shot Charles in the head in a downward trajectory to limit the amount of blood to be cleaned up.

The man quickly yanked Charles from the driver's seat and opened the trunk. He effortlessly threw the body in the trunk and went around to the passenger's side to remove Eric's body. Eric's size and weight made this a little more difficult, but the man finally prevailed.

Next he had to clean up Eric's blood from the passenger's window, which would be an immediate red flag if anyone were to see it. He worked fast, knowing the event would soon be over. Many of the limos had already left to retrieve their patrons and employers. So far, not a hitch.

Charles's phone rang.

"Charles, we're ready to go," John said.

"Yes, Sir," Brad answered and hung up. He threw the phone out the window and started the engine. Slowly, he rolled out of the parking area and into the line of limos. He was five cars back from the front. He closed the window between the driver's seat and the rear of the limo. They inched steadily forward. He could see the little Wingate brat holding her grandfather's hand and smiling. *I'll wipe that smile off your ritzy little face,* he thought to himself and he pulled up in front of John and Priscilla.

The attendant stepped forward and opened the door for John and Priscilla, who entered first. John then slid in next to her and the attendant handed John Priscilla's Black Swan tutu container, which he placed on the floor in front of him. The two buckled their seatbelts as the window slowly came down between the two compartments as the limo rolled forward about thirty feet.

John was about ready to speak when the limo stopped and a strange man turned, pointed his gun at John, tossed him handcuffs and told him to cuff himself to the door handle.

"No," John said defiantly.

A shot squirted out of the pistol and lodged in the seat between Priscilla and himself.

"Do it, or the next one goes right between the brat's eyes," Brad shouted.

John immediately complied.

"You next, miss priss," Brad said, throwing her a set of handcuffs. She cuffed herself as tears began to well up in her eyes.

John looked over at her and wanted to hold her and tell her everything was going to be alright. Always the protector, he looked at her beseechingly in an attempt to calm her.

The vehicle began to move forward again. John began to concentrate on the route the driver was taking them. He watched for signs and landmarks that he could remember and stored them in his head. Soon he noticed the same landmarks began to appear, and realized that the man was taking them on a circuitous route that he wouldn't be able to recall or describe.

The limo finally stopped in an alley next to an an older model car Brad had swapped for his Ford Ranger. The driver got out and opened Priscilla's door, pulling her harshly out of the seat. She fell to the ground, her arm and hand stretched in pain. He picked her up roughly and dragged her to the other car where he cuffed her to the rear door. He noticed the pin on her shoulder strap and pulled it off, tearing her clothing. He threw it under the limo.

"You won't be needing that tool to pick the lock on your cuffs," he said snidely.

He walked over to John's side and opened the door, slowly, this time.

"One false move from you, and my partner in the other car shoots the brat," he said. "Got it?" John looked and thought he saw another head in the car, but wasn't sure in the darkness.

He complied straightaway and moved toward the other car. He knew that somewhere, sometime, somehow he would get an opening, an opportunity, and he would have to strike quickly. He looked around and realized this was not the time. He slid into the seat and cuffed himself to the door handle and noticed that Brad was alone. There was no accomplice.

Again, the man drove a convoluted route to their final destination. John was thoroughly confused and had no idea where they were.

He looked over at Priscilla, whose eyes were now dry and determined. He saw her resoluteness in the glow of the streetlights as they passed under them. Somehow she had gone through a transformation and realized that she needed to be on her toes at all times. She needed to be there for John and be able to react for him when she was needed. She looked over at him without turning her head. A small upward curve of her mouth appeared that told John she was no longer cowed, but ready for whatever was to come next.

The ride took nearly half an hour. John guessed that they were still in the city, but did not recognize the neighborhood or the street names. He searched for anything that might announce their whereabouts. He noticed a small neighborhood market near where they finally stopped. The market's sign was in a strange writing that he thought might be Thai or Lao, but he wasn't sure which. It was definitely a market, though, and he needed to use something as a landmark.

The car finally stopped and the driver went to Priscilla's side of the car. She was ready this time, and the man wasn't able to hurt her again getting out of the car. Her wrists ached from the first episode. *Once burned, twice learned,* she remembered her Papa telling her. The man unlocked the handcuffs and told John to relax.

"Any funny business while I'm gone and you know what happens next. Remember, I've got two of you and can afford to waste one and still go through with my plan," the man said with pure evil. "And I don't give a shit which one of you it is."

For the first time during the evening, John noticed that the man walked with a limp. A high collar and what appeared to be a wig hid the back of the man's neck.

John knew he had to be there for Priscilla and decided to be a model prisoner until he fully understood his circumstances and could assess properly his prospects for escape. He was confident that this man knew what he was doing, but also felt he was capable of making mistakes.

The man was gone for about fifteen minutes, but now returned to deal with John.

"I'll have this gun pointed at you the whole time, so I suggest that you cooperate," the man said.

"Don't worry, my whole purpose is to see that the little girl is safe, and is going to survive this ordeal," John assured him.

The man walked John up the flight of stairs and into his rat-trap apartment. As he walked toward the back bedroom, he noticed someone lying in the bed in the front bedroom. It was a quick glance but he definitely noticed an arm sticking out from under the covers, and it looked female.

"Welcome to your new home," the man said.

John looked around the small bedroom. He first noticed Priscilla sitting on a blow-up mattress, legs tucked under her, one hand chained to a restraining u-bolt attached to the hardwood floor. The handcuff looked humane in that it was cloth lined. He saw a second mattress with a similar u-bolt next to it, and he assumed was for him. John didn't see anything else in the room.

"Can I remove my suit coat before you put the handcuffs on me, Brad?" John asked.

The man stiffened and then smiled.

"You have done your homework, Mr. Wingate. Very good, and yes, you may remove your suit coat," Brad said.

After removing his coat and loosening his tie, John sat down on the air mattress and submitted to the cuffing process. The cuff was snug around his hand. If the u-bolt was strong enough, he was secure.

Brad said good night and left the room, dark, smelly, and foreboding. John thought the smell was insecticide. He laid back on the mattress which had a thickened end that acted as a pillow and he heard Priscilla do the same.

"Are you alright, sweetie?" John asked.

"I'm scared, Papa," she answered. "I don't like that man."

"I don't blame you, neither do I, but as long as we are here, we need to humor him and do as he says. Do you understand, sweetie?"

"Yes, Papa."

John talked to Priscilla for a few more minutes, trying to reassure her and help build her strength and resolve. John needed time to get the lay of the land, think, and plan.

"We'll come up with a plan tomorrow after we've had a look around, and get a feel for the routine here. I think I saw someone else in the other bedroom, looked like a female, but I can't be sure. It could have been a boy or a young man. Try to sleep now. It's very important that we stay as strong and as healthy as we can," John said.

"Good night, Papa, I love you," she said, with fear still in her voice.

"Good night sweetie, I love you more."

John heard Priscilla sniffling.

"Are you warm enough, Priscilla?" He asked.

"I think so, Papa."

"If you get cold, use my coat to keep you warm," John said, sliding the coat to her.

"Thank you, Papa."

"Please don't cry, honey, we are going to be fine."

John wanted to reach out to her but couldn't. He could only guess how frightened she must be.

22

A GRIZZLY SCENE

Two NYPD detectives stood at the side of John's limo. They had popped the trunk and found the two bodies. They found Priscilla's GPS broach under the limo, and they found her tutu in the box on the rear seat floor. There was a lot of blood on the front passenger's side door and seat, and the window appeared to be wiped clean.

"The registration reads Orient Occident Shipping Company," Detective Blake said to his partner Detective Johnson.

"What is the address?" Johnson asked.

"East Forty-Sixth Street."

"Let's get over there and see what we can dig up. I think we're done here. It will be a few days before we get any forensics," Johnson said.

The two detectives drove to the Forty-Sixth Street address and took the elevator to the Double O office level. They knocked on the locked office door several times. After the third attempt, Patricia, John's assistant, opened the massive double doors.

"Yes, may I help you? The offices are closed," Patricia said quizzically.

"Detective Johnson and Blake of the NYPD," the detective said, flashing his badge and identification. "May we come in?"

"Certainly," she said, backing away and opening the door wider. "Please have a seat there in the waiting area."

The two detectives sat down looking around at the lavishly appointed reception area. There were ship models, nicely framed photographs of the Double O shipping fleets, and several Double O brochures neatly placed on the coffee table. Detective Johnson took a copy of each and put them in his inside coat pocket.

"How can I help you?" Patricia inquired.

"Well Ma'am, we're bearing bad news. We found one of your company limos in an alleyway with two dead bodies in the trunk. One of the victims was a Charles Bannerman, and the other was an Eric Hendersen."

She recoiled in shock. For a moment she was speechless. She choked back her thoughts.

"Where and when did this happen?" she asked.

"We think it was sometime around ten to ten fifteen last night, Ma'am," Detective Blake said.

"How many limos does Occident Orient shipping company own here in New York?" Detective Johnson asked.

"The company owns five of them, but the one driven by Charles Bannerman is used mainly by the Chairman, John Wingate, and he was at his foundation's fundraiser last night with his granddaughter," Patricia offered.

"Is the granddaughter a ballet dancer?" Detective Blake asked.

"As a matter of fact she is, and a very good one. She performed at the gala last night."

The two men looked at each other with disappointed looks on their faces, and told Patricia that there were no other bodies in the limo, and no blood in the rear passenger compartment. They then asked her who was in charge of the company, could he or she be located now, and would it be possible for them to meet with the detectives now.

Patricia explained that the President and his wife were out of the country, but returning today and that the CFO was on vacation, not to return until Wednesday next week. She told them that there were several department managers that she thought she might be able to find and assemble on short notice.

"When are the President and his wife due to arrive?" Detective Johnson asked.

"They are arriving Terminal Four at JFK at three this afternoon from Amsterdam on KLM," she said efficiently.

"They fly First Class?"

"Yes," she said. "Oh my God, Charles was supposed to pick them up, I'll have to find another driver."

"And another limo. We will be impounding the one we found last night and will have it for some time. I don't mean to sound callous, but this investigation is shaping up right now to be a kidnapping and they usually take some time to resolve, especially when there is a murder involved," Detective Johnson said, apologetically.

"The granddaughter is the daughter of the President and his wife," Patricia volunteered.

"Thank you for that," Detective Blake said. "We'll be sensitive to that when we meet them at JFK this afternoon."

The detectives stood and turned toward the door. They thanked Patricia for her helpfulness, and asked her for a business card of John's, the President, and the CFO for their files. She gathered them from the reception desk and handed them to Detective Blake as they left.

Detectives Johnson and Blake stood to the side of the jet way, holding a placard with the name Wingate as passengers began to deplane the KLM arrival from Amsterdam. JT and Carrie appeared in the doorway and immediately noticed their name. JT walked up to the two men.

"I'm JT Wingate, and this is my wife, Carrie."

"I'm NYPD Detective Johnson and this is my partner, Detective Blake. Would you please follow us to the KLM office, they will deliver your luggage to you there."

JT looked puzzled, but followed Detective Johnson as Detective Blake took up the rear.

"Please take a seat Mr. and Mrs. Wingate, would you like some coffee or water?"

"No, thank you," JT said. "Why are we here?"

Detective Johnson began telling them the story, and was as tactful and gentle as he knew how to be. He knew that no matter what he said, the Wingates were going to be distraught.

"I hate to be the one to tell you this, but two bodies were found in the trunk, the driver Charles Bannerman and Eric Hendersen, your security advisor," Detective Johnson said.

"Was there any other indication of a struggle?" Carrie asked.

"No, Ma'am," said Detective Blake.

"We did find a tutu, which Mr. Wingate's assistant told us belonged to your daughter, however. The incident is shaping up to look like a kidnapping to us."

JT and Carrie looked at each other with tense, worried looks. They lamented to each other over the losses of Charles and Eric, but were deeply concerned about John and Priscilla.

"Mr. Wingate, has there been any indication that something like this was about to happen?" Detective Blake asked.

"Actually, there has been," JT said, and went on to explain what had been happening over the last several weeks and months. The detectives took notes and asked questions as JT revealed, in detail, the happenings of the last month.

"Do you know a Brad Waterman, or Waters?" Detective Johnson asked.

Both JT and Carrie looked at the two detectives and shook their heads. The detective offered an arrest photo and mentioned that the man walked with a limp.

"There have been recent discussions regarding a man with a limp and a tattoo on the nape of his neck, but we have no idea who he is," Carrie said.

Detective Johnson got up and walked to the door to talk with an airline representative who had peeked in the door. He nodded his head and returned to the Wingates.

"Mr. Wingate, your driver is here and your luggage has been taken care of. Thank you very much for your time, we understand that you have had a long day. We will be in contact with you tomorrow to discuss a plan to deal with this whole mess," Detective Johnson concluded.

JT and Carrie rushed to their limo and began the hour and a half ride to the office. On the way, JT called Trent McSpadden, told him the story, and asked him to join them at the office in the morning first thing. JT wanted McSpadden's advice before committing to any plans with the NYPD.

"The police are coming to see us this morning sometime and want to speak to us about where to go from here, and I want your input first," JT asked the security advisor.

"JT, let me say first, if we had any inkling that this would turn this violent this quickly, we would have handled things completely differently. I know that is 20-20 hindsight," Trent said.

Trent went on to say that he always welcomed police involvement, but always advised that the victim's families be completely involved in the decisions before anything happened. Trent knew that most police departments were cooperative with their victim's families, but he also knew there were those out to make a name for themselves, especially when a high profile person like John Wingate was involved.

"Has there been any contact with the perpetrator yet?" Trent asked.

"Not with us," JT answered.

Trent explained to JT that it took at least two or three days, and up to a week before perps showed their hands.

"They are nervous and scared like we are. They don't know what's going to happen and they know they are vulnerable as soon as they stick their heads out of hiding. If we don't hear from them for a while they are either getting their act together, or trying to make us worry," Trent continued. "Either way, they'll keep John and Priscilla alive as long as need be, to make the deal."

"If that's what's going on, they are doing a great job of it," Carrie said.

"It's just like when you and Carrie were in captivity in Hobyo. If they were going to make any money at the deal, they had to play by some sort of rules," Trent reminded JT.

"What does that mean in this case?" Carrie asked.

"Like Hobyo, we are going to ask for proof of life on a regular basis. It is going to be very difficult for you, JT and Carrie, to see Priscilla on a cell phone video, scared, crying, wanting her mom and dad."

"Where do we go from here?" JT asked.

Trent explained that it was important that they give the police their full cooperation. He suggested that a command post be set up either at home or at the office, preferably at home. Carrie dreaded the thought that strangers would be walking around the house and expressed the thought to Trent.

"We can keep a handle on that," Trent said. "We can limit where the police are allowed to go, and I would suggest that we turn the dining room into an 'ops room'. It has direct access to the kitchen, and we can make rules for that as well. We can set up two-way communications with them so they aren't walking into your private spaces to try to contact you. You have plenty of room."

"We'll leave it to you to set all that up. You will stay until they arrive, won't you?" JT asked.

"Certainly, when do you expect them?"

"They said around lunchtime."

"Great, that will give me time to get a plan together and discuss it with you before they come."

23

JENNIFER

J ennifer Middleton-Wingate met her new driver, Franklin, at JFK airport. He was waiting outside of the First Class skyway with a placard saying Mrs. Wingate.

"Mrs. Wingate, ma'am, I'm Franklin, your new driver. Please give me your ticket information and baggage claims, and I will have your bags retrieved," the man said as he motioned her to a nearby British Airways office.

"Thank you," Jennifer said with a slightly bewildered look.

"I'll be back in a few minutes, ma'am," he said and closed the office door behind him.

Jennifer immediately got on her cell phone and called the Double O office.

"Hello, this is Mrs. Jennifer Wingate, may I speak to JT please?" she asked.

"Yes Mrs. Wingate, I'll put you straight through, he is expecting your call," the receptionist said.

"Jennifer, welcome back. I'm sorry it has to be under these conditions, but suffice to say we are on top of things and are all very anxious to see you," JT said.

"JT did you send a new driver for me, and is his name Franklin?" Jennifer asked.

"I did," JT answered.

"Is he muscularly built, about five foot eleven inches, blond hair and about thirty-five years old?" Jennifer continued.

"That's correct Jennifer, why, is there something wrong?" JT asked.

"Does he say ma'am a lot?"

"Yes he does, he's is a retired Navy Seal, ordered by me through Trent," JT answered.

"Thank you, JT. I was confused to see a new face. I haven't quite got my head wrapped around everything yet," she said. "Is there any word from John?"

"We haven't heard anything yet, and the consensus is that whoever has them is trying to work on us psychologically," JT offered.

Jennifer asked a few more questions as Franklin returned. She held up her hand to signal Franklin to wait a moment and continued her conversation.

"Jennifer, please get to the office as soon as you can, and we'll brief you completely on where we are and where we think we're going. I know you're tired, but please hold out for a little while longer," JT said.

Jennifer reassured him and hung up the phone.

"Ma'am, I have your bags in the limo, are you ready to travel?" Franklin asked.

"Yes Franklin, off we go," she replied, gathering her coat, gloves and purse from the office table.

The entire family was gathered in JT's office when Jennifer arrived. As she came through the door, everyone rose to greet her and give her reassuring hugs. This was the thing she appreciated most about being married to John Wingate. Shortly after she met John, she lost everything, and even though she had a large group of friends and colleagues, her true support base was definitely this family. Carrie hugged her for a long time, and Jennifer thought it felt like a mother/daughter connection. She was moved by it, and savored the embrace.

"Jennifer, it is so good to see you," JT said. "Please sit here, would you like a drink?"

Jennifer waved off a drink as she sat in the chair opposite JT's desk. She looked around at the faces, trying to assess the mood of the room. She could definitely feel the empathy, but could also feel a strong underlying anxiety. She knew that like herself, these were people who have been through it all and their combined strength radiated through their distress, giving her a profound sense of understanding and safety.

JT conveyed all of the details of the past several days and told her that there was a team of police as his home, dealing with the issues.

"What about John's mother, how is she taking it?" Jennifer asked.

"We all decided to keep her in the dark until after it's all over," JT said. "We thought it might be too much for her."

They all looked at each other and then back to Jennifer.

"I suppose that is best. Hasn't she wondered why he hasn't contacted her?" Jennifer asked.

"We told her he was out of town on an extended stay and unable to contact her," JT answered. "Jennifer, we would like you to stay with us for the time being, it will put you closer to the action as well as afford you a higher degree of personal security. Our apartment is a fortress at the moment."

"Thank you, JT," she said. "That would be wonderful."

"Do you have any questions for us?" JT asked.

"Yes, what are we doing about Charles and Eric?"

"We've reached out to both families, and have assured them that they would be financially cared for, and that when they were ready, and if they were interested, there was employment here at Double O, the least we could offer. The funeral for both men takes place on Saturday, and we have handled all of the expenses."

"I would like to attend the funerals. Is that possible?" Jennifer asked.

JT assured her that it was, and that all of the family would attend, and make a show of it. They all agreed that love and solidarity was what was needed now. Jennifer was through with her questions and started to get up to leave.

"Jennifer, go directly to our apartment please. Make a list of the things you need and Franklin will gather them at your apartment with the help of your housekeeper," JT said. "We need to tighten everything up here, 'go to the mat', as the Mafioso's used to say," he added in an attempt to ease tensions.

Jennifer managed a tight smile as she hugged everyone again and left the office. When she arrived at JT's apartment, she introduced herself to the detectives and uniformed officer, shaking hands, and gave Vince Packard a hug.

"Mrs. Wingate, after you have unpacked and freshened up, we have a few questions for you, if you don't mind. All routine, mind you," Detective Johnson said.

"Certainly, Detective, I'll be right with you."

Twenty minutes later, Jennifer came back into the operations area of the apartment and took a seat at the large dining table. Detective Johnson asked her if she needed anything, coffee, water, and she said no.

"Mrs. Wingate, when did you leave on your business trip?" Detective Baker asked.

"It was the day before John and Priscilla went missing," she responded.

"How long did you intend to stay abroad?"

"It was my semi-annual visit to my franchised boutiques in London and Paris, which usually takes me about two weeks, depending on the events they have planned for me to attend," she said. "With a few exceptions, we don't have a rigid schedule."

"Do you always take your trips at the same time of year?"

"Usually, yes. They coincide with the spring and fall line debuts. We have a show here in New York first, then London, and then Paris. Then there are the private events put on by the shops for some of our oldest and best customers."

She sat with a thin smile, looking down at her hands while the detectives took notes and finished their line of questioning. She was very quiet and reserved.

"Mrs. Wingate, do you know why anyone would want to kidnap your husband and granddaughter?" Detective Johnson asked.

"Other than the obvious, no. He is a beloved man, a philanthropist, and a hardworking man of the highest integrity. I have never heard anyone speak badly of him, and vice versa," she said proudly.

"What do you mean by 'other than the obvious'?" Johnson asked.

"He is an extremely wealthy man," she said.

"I see, yes, certainly," Johnson said with a hint of embarrassment.

"Mrs. Wingate, you don't seem to be very upset about all of this?" Detective Baker said.

Jennifer straightened, looked over at the man, squared her shoulders to him, and smiled.

"Detective Baker, I can assure you that if I thought it would make things better that I sat here crying and whimpering, I would do so. Our family has been through this before in spades, and I can assure you that everyone, including myself, remained composed and unruffled. When this is over and we bring John and Priscilla safely home, which we will, I'm sure I will have my moments. Until then, I will keep myself in check," she said with firm resolve.

"Thank you, Mrs. Wingate, we don't have any further questions."

"I have a few questions, if you don't mind," Jennifer said.

"Certainly, Mrs. Wingate."

"Where do we stand today?" she asked, wanting to hear it from the detectives own mouths.

Detective Johnson told her that they think they know who the perpetrator is, and they have distributed his picture to all the precincts, to the newspapers, and to television news programs for the last week.

"We have visited the suspects last known address, spoken with his acquaintances, and everyone says he has disappeared. This is the main reason we suspect that this is a kidnapping for ransom. He has planned this for some time. We also know that he has kidnapped an old girlfriend of his, a Melany Barton, his one-time live-in."

"Melany Barton the ballet instructor? My God, she knows this apartment and the other family apartments inside and out. How do you propose to handle this situation?" she asked, showing the first sign of a reaction.

"The first move is always his, and you can see that we have set up Vince Packard who is acting as JT. You know Vince's capabilities, and we will all take our cues from him," Johnson said. "He will know what the next move needs to be. JT and Carrie have explained the Melany history to us. We are taking it all into consideration."

Jennifer looked over at Vince, who gave her a consoling smile.

"Vince, are you here day and night?" she asked the seasoned negotiator.

"No ma'am, there will be a night negotiator who begins at ten PM and goes until ten AM. I take the ten AM to ten PM shift," Vince said. "If the suspect wants to operate during the night shift, then we will switch. We have it set up to where the night shift negotiator acts as an operator, go-between only, and insists he cannot act on my behalf and will get me to the phone as soon as he can, or suggest that he can call in the morning after ten AM."

"Do you think that will work?" she asked.

"Always does the first time," Vince said. "Remember, he wants money, he is heavily committed to his task, and he isn't going to give up easily."

"He also knows that he can't sit on a live line for any length of time or he risks the chance of being located," Detective Johnson said. "He'll call again at the appointed time."

Jennifer was satisfied that things were being handled properly. She trusted Vince completely, but thought the police were a little clumsy. She fully understood that everyone was a suspect until ruled out, but their questions seemed so pointed that it wasn't hard to see through their façade. She wasn't sure that the police understood how wealthy John was and how big a target he really is.

24

THE ROUTINE

"Papa, I have to go to the bathroom," Priscilla said to John. "Hey, Brad," John yelled loudly. "My granddaughter has to use the bathroom."

Brad stumbled into the room in his boxers and a t-shirt. He had obviously been drinking. This was news for John, and he catalogued it along with the amount of time it took Brad to respond. He watched Brad closely as he walked over to free the eight-year-old.

"No funny stuff, brat, or you'll wish you hadn't," Brad said as he roughly lifted her and pushed her toward the bathroom.

"She's an eight-year-old, for God's sake. Do you have to be so rough with her?" John exclaimed.

"Shut up, old man," Brad retorted, walking out the door.

John waited anxiously for Priscilla to return. He was concerned how Brad would treat her in the bathroom. He counted the seconds and minutes that she was gone. She returned in six agonizingly long minutes, and John was relieved. Brad chained her back to the floor and left the room, leaving the door slightly ajar.

"Did he go into the bathroom with you, sweetie?" John asked.

"No, Papa, he stayed outside," Priscilla answered.

"Did he touch you in any way?"

"No, Papa."

"Did you see where the front door was?"

"Yes, Papa."

"Was it locked or bolted from the inside?"

"I didn't notice, Papa," she said dejectedly.

John was questioning her like it was a police interrogation, and realized he was upsetting her.

"I'm sorry if my questions made you nervous sweetie, but it is important that we get to know everything about this place as fast as we can so we can be ready for anything that might happen," John consoled.

It was the end of day one, and so far John was unsure of what was happening. He supposed that it was a kidnapping, but wondered why it was him and Priscilla, and why it had taken so long to develop. He thought that bagging a prize like himself would surely be enough, so why take little Priscilla as well? It was another mouth to feed and deal with.

It could be a sympathy factor, he thought. Taking the little girl as well might give the family more incentive to follow his orders and pay up. John tried to listen intently for any conversations that Brad might be having with anyone outside the apartment. He heard nothing except the television set. He faintly heard a news report that said shipping magnate John Wingate and his granddaughter had gone missing.

"Sweetie, are you still awake?" John whispered.

"Yes, Papa."

"Before you go to sleep, do some leg lift exercises and sit ups. Be careful not to make any noise," John said.

She did as she was told and John could hear her moving quietly on her mattress, as he did the same.

"Any exercise, or quiet and repetitive flexing of any muscles you can think of, especially leg muscles, will be helpful, and you should do it throughout the day when we are alone. Do you understand?"

"Yes, Papa."

John was concerned that if he went to sleep before Priscilla, he might wake her up with his loud breathing. He decided to wait until he was sure that she was asleep before he attempted to sleep himself.

Fortunately, her young body went into sound sleep almost immediately after their goodnights. John had consoled her and blew her a kiss before she put her head down.

At seven the next morning, Brad came into the room and kicked both of the mattresses. John was already awake, and Priscilla quickly awoke with a start.

"Alright, you first," he said to John as he bent down and unlocked the chain. He relocked the chain, shortening the links between his hands, making it more difficult for him to do anything physical. John was led to the bathroom where there was toothpaste, a tooth brush, a razor and a towel.

"You have fifteen minutes to get it together, and no funny business, or the brat pays. Am I clear?" Brad threatened.

"Yes," was John's reply. He now understood that taking Priscilla was this man's way of keeping John in line.

Brad left the door ajar so he could hear what John was doing from his couch, about ten feet away. John finished his ablutions on time and was led to the kitchen where a bowl of cereal with milk and a cup of coffee awaited him. He sat and ate quickly and waited for the next move, which came almost immediately.

He was brought back to the bedroom and re-chained to the floor. Then it was Priscilla's turn. He nervously awaited her return.

"Are you okay, sweetie?" John asked when Brad left the room.

"Yes, Papa," she answered. "He didn't touch me."

John was relieved. He began to think that Brad was going to play the game straight, and maybe there was light at the end of the tunnel.

John and Priscilla spent a long and boring day together in the dim bedroom. John whispered to her and they played word and trivia games to keep themselves mentally occupied. Often John would console her and offer her advice to deal with the isolation and fear she was experiencing for the first time in her young life. John hoped it would be the last.

"Our eyes are heavily dilated, you understand, due to fact that we are in such dark, dim surroundings. That means that if you were to go directly from here into a bright environment, you would be temporarily blinded," John told her.

"Why does that matter, Papa?" she asked.

"It means that if we were able to get a chance to run for it, we would use precious seconds getting used to the glare and possibly lose our opportunity," John said.

"I see," she replied.

"It's a good idea that you squint sharply when you first leave this room, and slowly acclimate to the light differences. You can move quickly and still see through squinted eyes until they adapt. You can practice when he takes you to the bathroom," John said.

Priscilla was a quick study and was looking forward to the next time she would be led out of the room. Priscilla wanted to please John by remembering all of his comments and warnings, but most of all understood that he was giving her this information so that she could survive. She knew that stealth, not strength, would be her best ploy.

John thought he heard the apartment door open and close. He listened for signs of movement in the other rooms and heard nothing. He waited and listened.

"Hey Brad, I have to use the bathroom," John called and waited.

"Hey Brad, I really have to go, give me a break here," John shouted loudly. There was no reply. Suddenly the door opened wide, letting light into the room. A disheveled young woman wearing only her panties stepped into the room in a stagger, holding the door jamb for support.

"Who's in here?" the woman slurred.

John and Priscilla were silent. The woman came closer to them, teetering slightly.

"Melany, what are you doing here?" Priscilla burst out.

"Who are you?" the woman said.

"It's me, Priscilla, Priscilla Wingate."

"I don't know anyone by that name," she said indistinctly and turned to leave.

"Melany, please help us," Priscilla pleaded.

"I don't know any Priscillas," the woman insisted and staggered out of the room, leaving the door ajar.

John heard the door to the bathroom open and close. He waited and listened. He heard the toilet flush and the door open and close again. He saw the woman lurch past the door, hitting it with her shoulder.

"Goddamn door," the woman screeched as she slammed it closed. They were in pitch darkness.

"Papa, that was Melany, my first ballet teacher, I'm sure of it," Priscilla whispered.

"She is either very drunk, or on drugs," John said. "She didn't seem to or didn't want to recognize you."

"I'd know her anywhere, we were very close," Priscilla murmured.

"How the hell did this door get closed?" Brad barked at John.

"Some woman came into the room earlier while you were gone. She asked us what we were doing and then turned and staggered to the bathroom. She seemed drunk and bumped into the door and it closed," John offered in answer.

Brad turned and walked to the other bedroom where Melany lay sprawled across the bed, untethered, completely naked and sound asleep. She looked very enticing, but his disgust for her quashed any feelings he might have had. *Wonder what she did with her panties,* he thought. She was hooked, she wasn't going anywhere.

That evening, Brad took Priscilla to the bathroom.

"Time for a shower, brat, take off your clothes and stand in the middle of the tub," he ordered.

There was a spray hose connected to the tub fill faucet. He ordered her to stand still in the middle of the tub while he sprayed both front and back of her body. He handed her a bar of soap and a wash cloth and told her to clean herself. Embarrassed and nervous, she scrubbed her young body while he stared at her with a leering smirk.

He got her head wet and she soap scrubbed her hair and face. He took the soap and washcloth from her and rinsed her completely, removing the soap suds.

"Turn around and bend over," he ordered.

He sprayed between her cheeks and legs, removing the last of the soap.

"Okay, you can get out," he said throwing her a towel.

"You have fifteen minutes to finish cleaning up and getting ready for bed," he demanded.

Shaking from the cold water, scared, and angry, she completed her cleaning and walked out into the living room in her panties and camisole. He had taken her clothing. He threw her a pair of gray sweatpants and a white sweatshirt.

"Put those on and go into the bedroom," he ordered.

He locked her into the restraining bolt and unlocked John's chains.

"You have twenty minutes to take a shower and get ready for bed, no funny business."

John willingly got into the tub and showered. It had been nearly a week, and he needed it badly. There was only cold water, which reminded him of his Navy days. Halfway through, Brad came in and took his clothing and dropped off a pair of sweatpants and a sweatshirt. It actually felt good to be clean. Brad unlocked John's chains at gunpoint to allow John to dress. When John was finished dressing, he told John to chain himself.

"Did he touch you in the bathroom while you showered?" John asked Priscilla after Brad left the bedroom.

"No, Papa," she said. "He did look at me funny though."

John seethed at the thought of Brad ogling her, an eight-year-old child.

"I'm sorry that had to happen, sweetie," he said. "Do some exercises and then go to sleep. Everything is going to be fine."

John laid there thinking and waiting for his turn to sleep. He wondered what was going on with negotiations with his family. He hadn't heard Brad speaking with anyone, but Brad left the apartment during the day, and could have been making his calls at that time. He wondered what the ransom amount would be. He knew the family would pay it, no matter what the cost. He drifted off to sleep with that thought on his mind.

25

CONTACT

Carrie and JT paced around their living room, first looking out the window, then the walls, then the floor, and finally at each other. Jennifer sat calmly reading the morning paper. It had been six days, and still no word.

"If they are trying to sweat us out, it's working with me. JT, I'm starting to get scared," Carrie said.

"It's hard on all of us sweetheart, but just like Hobyo, we have to keep our cool, stay focused, and be ready for anything that happens," JT consoled, walking up to her and putting his arms around her. Jennifer looked up at the couple with understanding, apprehension, and sadness. She too was beginning to worry about the silence.

"Whoever has them must be getting tired of maintaining them by now," Carrie said.

Carrie pictured John and Priscilla in a cage somewhere where someone would throw them some food every so often. John with a beard and rumpled hair and Priscilla with matted hair, her face smudged and pale. She shuddered at the pictures she sketched in her mind.

"I was talking with Vince Packard this morning and he is convinced that they are winding us up for a bigger pay day and one hundred percent cooperation," JT told her.

When Trent McSpadden and the family negotiated with the NYPD over protocols, Trent had insisted that the voice at the family's end of the phone be Vince Packard. JT and Carrie were insistent as well, recalling the fantastic job Vince did for them during the Hobyo affair. Vince's experience as a hostage negotiator was well known by the NYPD, and even welcomed.

I know in my heart of hearts that they are alive and well, otherwise this would all be for naught. If whoever it is wanted to kill John and Priscilla, they would have done so at the offset, Carrie thought to herself.

The team had just finished their breakfast when JT, Carrie, and Jennifer joined them in the makeshift operations room in the dining room/kitchen area.

"Good morning, fellas," JT said to the group of three: a uniformed policeman, Detective Johnson and the day shift negotiator, Vince Packard.

"Good morning, Sir," Detective Johnson said, sipping the last of his coffee.

"Got a good feeling that today is the day we get started," Vince said smiling broadly. "Seven is my lucky number as well." He was trying to thin the dense atmosphere in the room.

"Should we stay home today?" JT asked.

"Not necessary," Vince said. "We'd rather keep you out of it if we can. If he or she insists that you be on the phone, that's a different matter, and we will send for you."

Vince had already discussed his strategy with the group. He was going to say that he's JT Wingate, the senior member of the family, and the only one qualified to negotiate. Because of the two initial murders to pull off the kidnapping, Vince felt that the perpetrator was not a skilled kidnapper. Kidnapping is the lowest on the list of violent crimes. It ranks with extortion and harassment. Professional kidnappers are smart and well prepared, and probably would have tased or gassed Charles and Eric. Vince was sure he was dealing with a hot-headed amateur, his favorite kind of perp.

They all began the long day of waiting. Vince was reading a book entitled *The Mind and Heart of a Kidnapper,* by Anson Berman, famed hostage negotiator. Detective Johnson was writing in his journal and the uniformed officer was looking out the window at the city below.

Suddenly the hostage phone rang. Vince calmly put down his book and began counting rings with his fingers for all to see. The ringing got to five and Vince picked up the receiver.

"Hello," Vince said in a clear firm voice.

"Who am I speaking to?" a deep, slow, telephone voice-changer voice said eerily.

"This is JT Wingate, and I am having a little difficulty understanding you."

"Get over your difficulty and listen asshole, or you'll never see the old man and the brat again," Brad threatened. "Now let's get down to business."

"Certainly," Vince said.

"I want five million dollars in unmarked bills. Five satchels, one million each, all one hundred dollar bills or less in denomination. You have five days to get it together, and I will call you again at that time with further instructions."

"We will need proof of life before we do anything," JT said.

Brad got up, walked to the bedroom, put the phone in front of Priscilla and switched off the voice changer.

"Daddy, I'm so scared, please come get me," Priscilla said shakily.

Brad put the phone in front of John.

"JT, we're okay," John said into the phone.

Brad flipped the voice changer back on.

"That good enough for you?" Brad's eerie voice asked.

"As a matter of fact, it is not," Vince said. "We require a video of both John and Priscilla together with today's paper in front of them. For all we know, you just played us a recording."

Brad seethed. *Who is this asshole to ask for shit when it's me who holds all the cards? The guy seems awfully calm for a father with a kidnapped daughter,* Brad thought.

"How do I know I'm talking to JT Wingate and not some cop?" Brad asked.

"I'd be happy to send you a video if you like," Vince said with a smile.

"Right, funny man. Why aren't you more nervous and upset? I've got your fucking kid for Christ's sake," Brad asked.

"I'm the President of one of the world's largest shipping companies. I've learned to control myself in any given situation," Vince said. "And, by the way, I can assure you that I am very upset."

Brad bought the explanation, and realized the call was taking more time than he wanted it to go.

"You have five days," the eerie voice said and was gone.

Vince got on his cell phone immediately with JT. He ran through the kidnapper's demands and related the gist of the conversation.

"I suggest that you put the money together as soon as you can, at least get someone working on it now," Vince advised.

"Very good Vince, I'll get someone on it immediately," JT said with a firm voice.

"As soon as the proof of life video comes through, I'll get it to you," Vince said to JT and hung up.

Vince's next call was to Trent McSpadden to give him an update.

"So do you still think he's an amateur?" Trent asked Vince.

"I do, even more so," Vince said.

Vince explained that almost every kidnapper he had ever dealt with in the past had been polite, firm, and professional at the offset of negotiations. Only if things start to go bad for the kidnapper did they morph and become confrontational. Typically, a kidnapper does not want to upset their victims. They want them to believe that if they follow the kidnapper's demands, their loved ones will be returned.

"He called me asshole and threatened me in the second sentence out of his mouth. It's not the norm for a professional, but it is for an amateur. I've heard it several times before," Vince said.

"That bothers me a little. If he is brusque and threatening, that means he is defensive and scared. I'd much rather he was cool and calm and more predictable," Trent said.

"You and me both,"

"How is the family doing?" Trent asked.

"Talk about professionals, what a pleasure it is to work with them," Vince answered.

"That family has been through more than you can imagine. You know, you were with them during the Somalia ordeal."

John heard only bits and pieces of Brad's conversation with Double O's negotiator. He heard Brad's demeanor, however, and wondered how JT was taking that. He heard Brad walking toward the bedroom again.

"On your feet, both of you," Brad ordered, pointing his gun at Priscilla.

He unlocked the chains from the restraining hook, and re-cuffed their hands in front of them. He brought them into the seedy living room and sat them down together on the couch. He gathered up the morning New York Times and handed it to Priscilla to hold up in front of her.

"Alright, we're going to make a movie called 'see, I'm alive,'" Brad said with a smile.

He sat in a chair in front of the coffee table that separated them.

"Okay, no funny business now. I'm going to ask you questions and you will answer them yes or no. I don't want to hear any pleas for help, or cryptic sentences that only you and the other guy understand. Do I make myself clear?" Brad said sternly.

Both John and Priscilla nodded their heads. John looked at Priscilla to see if she was okay and ready for the ordeal. She seemed fine. John smiled and winked at her.

"Okay, here we go," Brad said, aiming his cell phone camera, "Mr. Wingate how are you feeling today?"

"Fine," John answered.

"And you, Miss Wingate, how are you feeling today?"

"Okay," she murmured, voice weak and shaky.

"Miss Wingate, are you being treated well?"

"Yes."

"Are you getting enough to eat?"

"Yes," she said, head down, eyes closed.

"And Mr. Wingate, you appear healthy, is that the case?"

"Yes," John answered.

"Both of you stand and slowly turn around," Brad ordered.

John and Priscilla did as they were told and sat down again.

"I assume that anyone watching this will see that both these people are in good physical condition," Brad said loud enough to be recorded clearly.

He shut off the phone and laid it on the coffee table. He ordered John and Priscilla back to the bedroom where he restrained John first and then Priscilla. He walked back to the living room and sat down on the couch. He sipped a beer and watched the video he had just taken. He was proud of his efforts and sent it off.

"That should hold the bastards," he said aloud.

Brad had five days now to concentrate on the one person he most wanted to hurt. He wasn't sure of what he was going to do or how he was going to accomplish it. He knew Jake was surrounded by goons all the time, so he had to either entice the goons away, or deal with Jake at a distance.

He was up in the air as to whether he wanted to kill him or just hurt him badly, an eye for an eye. As he thought the situation through, he realized that a well-placed, 130 grain soft point .270 Winchester Rifle bullet in the small of the back, should *fuck him up pretty good*.

A month ago, Brad had purchased a Mossberg 100 ATR bolt-action .270 Winchester with a cheap but reliable scope from an online arms dealer for three hundred and twenty five dollars. The rifle was affordable and packed a wallop. He practiced at a rifle range on 20th Street, not far from his apartment. He zeroed in the scope, and put it in his car trunk with nearly a hundred rounds of ammunition. He was ready.

26

THE PARTY'S OVER

It was seven PM and Jake was sitting at the Pussy Cat Club bar with his bouncer Phil. One of the girls was doing her best to wind up the few customers, but the night was slow and the interest level low.

"Shit Phil, if things don't pick up, we're in trouble," Jake lamented.

"Where is the caterer? I'm hungry," Phil said.

"He told me last night that he was going to cut back, and open the kitchen on Fridays and Saturdays, only until things got better," Jake answered, "Why don't you go and get some Chinese takeout and come back, we'll eat in the office."

Jake walked Phil to the door and stood at the doorway looking for customers, breathing in the cool evening air. The street was empty.

"Where have all the horny bastards gone?" Jake said to the front door bouncer.

"Don't know Jake, it's like you can fire a cannon down the middle of the street and not hit a soul."

Across and up the street, Brad crouched behind a car looking through the window at Jake and his bouncer. He looked around at the store fronts facing the Pussy Cat. The one directly across the street, a three story office building with a Mongolian BBQ restaurant on the first floor, looked like the likeliest spot to set up, but it also looked like the most difficult to get away from. There were wide alleys on both sides making it impossible for him to leap from building to building if he had to run for it. He decided to climb the fire escapes on the buildings next door on either side and determine which would be best.

He limped away, in a crouch, into the alley. The fire escape to the building left of the Mongolian restaurant was located at the rear of the building, and it couldn't be seen from the street. *So far, so good,* Brad thought. There were several good parking areas close to the fire escape as well.

He climbed the ladder and began his way up the stairs to the roof. On the roof he crouch-walked to the front of the building. He carefully peered over the low parapet wall toward the entrance to the Pussy Cat. There was a tree branch that slightly obscured the entrance, but there was at least a three foot clear area between Jake's SUV and the front steps. If he was fast enough, he could get off a shot. There was also an architectural feature at the front corner of the building that would obscure him from onlookers below. However, he would have to kneel while he waited for a shot, a situation he didn't like.

He climbed down the fire escape to his waiting car, and drove around the block to the alley on the right of the Mongolian restaurant. The fire escape was right on the alley, about halfway back from the street. Brad would not have as much get away time as he would have liked.

He climbed the second fire escape and stepped onto the roof. The parapet wall was higher on this building. He could stand at a crouch, rest his rifle on the parapet wall, and have a clear shot. He judged the clear distance from Jake's SUV to the door from this vantage point to be about five to six feet, giving him plenty of time to get off a shot.

Brad walked to the far side of the structure and noted that the next building abutted. He shinnied over the parapet and dropped down four feet to the roof. He noticed that the fire escape was at the rear of the building. There was a narrow alley and he climbed down to have a look around. He walked back to his car.

Brad was satisfied that he had found his sniper's nest.

Brad drove back to his apartment and walked up the stairs to the second floor, passing the third floor visitor along the way. It was ten after eight.

"Evening," Brad said with a mustached smile.

"Evening," the man said without stopping or looking at Brad.

Brad unlocked the door to his apartment, and something didn't feel right. He walked in carefully and first looked into the hostage room. Both John and Priscilla lay on their mattresses, both awake, hungry, and in need of a trip to the bathroom.

"I'll be right back," he said and turned to the front bedroom.

He cracked open the door and saw that Melany had forced the lock on the nightstand drawer. She was out cold on the floor.

"Pig," he said as he turned and closed the door.

He went back to the other bedroom and relieved his hostages one at a time, Priscilla first. When John was done, Brad marched him to the kitchen table where Brad had fixed him a peanut butter and jelly sandwich, a glass of water, and an apple.

"Do we have anything other peanut butter and an apple?" John asked.

"I'm not into haute cuisine, asshole," Brad said. "Shut up and eat. I'm not in the mood for you tonight."

John quietly finished the rest of his meal and Brad took him back to the bedroom.

Later, as he was doing his exercises on the mattress, Priscilla called to him.

"Papa, Papa," she whispered.

"What is it sweetie?"

"I can wiggle my hand out of the handcuffs," she said excitedly. "Look." She sat up on her mattress and waved a free hand at him.

"Oh, wonderful sweetie," John praised. "Now put it back on, quickly."

He asked if it hurt to do it and she said no, if he doesn't tighten them too much. She explained that she had complained to Brad about circulation when they were in the bathroom together and after that he loosened them for her and it was just enough.

"You are a brave, smart girl. Now we don't want to do anything to cause him to tighten them again. I have a plan," John said.

She quickly put her hand back in the cuff, and giggled a little as she did. John was amazed by her bravery and her ingenuity.

"Can you get them both out sweetie?"

"Yes I can, Papa," she said.

They talked a little longer, did more exercises, and John blew her a kiss as they went to sleep. While John waited for Priscilla to fall asleep, he thought out the details of his quickly hatched plan now that Priscilla had become a Houdini all on her own. He thought about just having her run the next time Brad announced he was going to be out for the evening but then thought better of it. *What if he has someone watch the apartment while he is gone,* he mused. Tomorrow he would have to study the front door to see what it would take to open it.

Brad finished his sixth beer of the night, made up his bed on the sofa, and went to sleep. He was tired of the babysitting and wanted an end to this game, but knew that there was a minimum of twelve days, maximum two weeks before he could conclude his dealings.

"Rise and shine," Brad said, kicking the mattresses.

John was already awake and watched every move that Brad made. He noticed there was a brief moment between the time Brad unchained their hands and when he relocked the chains again. It was seconds only. Sometimes he was armed and pointing his gun at them and other times he wasn't.

John also saw for the first time the straight blade knife Brad had sheathed at the small of his back. He saw it as he squatted to release Priscilla for her morning routine. He also noted that Brad had a little difficulty getting up from the squat position. He wobbled slightly on his bad leg, taking full seconds longer to right himself and get his balance. Once he took a few hopping steps backward trying to gain control.

When John was finished with his morning routine, Brad walked him back to the bedroom and locked his handcuff chains into the restraining ring.

"Tomorrow night I'm going to be out a little later than usual. I'm going to leave you with food and a bucket, in case you have to go," Brad said.

"What if something bad happens and we need attendance or a doctor, or the place goes up in smoke? What do we do then? I assume the person in the other room is no help to you," John said.

"You assume correctly, and nothing is going to happen," Brad snapped. "So don't worry about it."

John was concerned about being left alone, but saw it as a good thing. If Brad was gone for a period of time, Priscilla could get up and check out the front door and see what it would take to open it. It was very important that she get the chance to study the locks. John thought he remembered that he saw only one dead bolt and one security chain lock. If he was correct, it would take no time to open the door.

"I'll be back later this afternoon for your piss break," Brad said before he turned and left the room.

"Hey Brad, can you leave the light on during the day?" John asked.

"What the fuck," Brad said, flipping the switch as he left the room.

During the day, John talked with Priscilla about the following night. He wanted her to be fully prepared for what he wanted her to do. He explained the two locks and told her to verify that. He told her that the security chain wouldn't be on, but she was to practice locking and unlocking the chain and the dead bolt.

"If you hear anything in the hall, make sure the security chain is unlocked, run back to the room, and get back into you cuffs. Do you understand sweetie?"

"Yes, Papa. Why are we practicing that?" she asked.

"I'm not saying we are going to do it, but it might come to the point where we have to make a run for it," John explained.

He explained that if it came to it, she would have to open the door, run down the stairs and run as fast as she could toward any sign of life. If it was nighttime, she should run toward any store light she could see, give her name to whoever she came in contact with, and ask for their help.

"Our pictures have been on the TV news since this all started, I have heard bits and pieces of the broadcasts. People will probably recognize you," John said. "The picture they show will probably be one where you have a smile on your face, so you don't want to look too bewildered and frightened."

"Oh Papa, it scares me when you talk like this," she said shakily.

"I know sweetie, but we need to have plans. This one we will call Plan One. If the situation arises, I'll say 'plan one' and you can swing into action. It will probably take me some time to deal with Brad, so I'll be along behind you. Don't wait for me, run as fast and as far as you can."

John went over the plan step by step, over and over again until he was sure that Priscilla got it. He knew that she was more than capable of understanding the plan, but was concerned that her fear might be blocking her ability to commit it to memory.

27

READY, AIM, OOPS

JT walked past Jennifer's room and heard sobbing. He hesitated for a moment, not sure if he should knock on the door. After a full thirty seconds, he lightly rapped on the door. Jennifer opened the door, sniffling and wiping her nose.

"Is everything okay?" JT asked.

"Oh, JT, I'm so worried. It's been ten days. I have visions of John and Priscilla that aren't pretty," she said, choking back tears.

She backed away from the door and JT entered. He sat on a large sofa and Jennifer joined him. She was still in her work clothes. She had dismissed Franklin since she wasn't going anywhere tonight, or any night, until John was safely home.

"What must it be like for them?" she asked.

"Judging from the first video we received, they looked rumpled, but fine. Little Priscilla looked scared, and that is to be expected. John looked properly contrite, but I know that brain of his, he's thinking all the time. He blinked a lot, must have been the lighting."

"He blinked a lot?" she asked.

"Wait a minute, he wasn't blinking. He was communicating. Let's look at that video again."

JT took out his cell phone and found the video. He looked at it closely, over and over, with Jennifer watching at his side. He knew

John would not sit idle, and wondered why this hadn't dawned on him sooner.

"Yes," JT blurted out with excitement.

"What is it, JT?" Jennifer asked.

"He spelled out BRADMEL."

JT jumped up and bolted toward the door with Jennifer close behind. They went downstairs to the operations area to talk with Vince. He knew Vince could make good use of the new information. JT excitedly blurted out the news.

"Our suspicions are confirmed. I'll let Trent and the detectives know. They'll know what to do," Vince said.

Pictures of Brad and Melany filled the TV screens on the ten o'clock news. The news anchor was calling Brad the number one suspect and Melany his accomplice. Rewards, hotlines, and more pictures came on the screen.

Brad brought food, water, a bucket, and a roll of toilet paper into John and Priscilla's room. He let out more chain to allow them to reach the bucket. John noted that the food was peanut butter and jelly sandwiches.

"I was going to get you take out, or a pizza, but payday hasn't arrived yet," Brad said with a chuckle.

"Are we going to get a chance to clean up tonight?" John asked.

"No. I won't be getting back until later tonight. I'll give you an extra five minutes tomorrow night. How does that sound?"

Neither John nor Priscilla answered.

"Hey Brad, leave the light on when you go, will you please?" John asked. "You can turn it off when you get back."

Brad agreed, turned and left the room. John heard the front door close, and the dead bolt slide into place.

"We'll wait an hour or so to make sure he's gone," John said.

They both did leg lifts, various muscle stretches, sit ups, and breathing exercises. They didn't care if they made noise or not. Apparently Melany was out cold again.

"Okay sweetie, are you ready to go?"

"Yes, Papa."

Priscilla folded her palm together lengthwise and easily slid out of the cuffs. She smiled at John as she got to her feet. She went to the door, slowly pushed it open, and looked around. There was no one there and Melany's door was shut.

She tiptoed out to the front door and set the security chain in place. She left one hand on the security chain and one on the dead bolt thumb turn. She counted to three and opened both locks simultaneously. She opened the door and looked out. It took less than two seconds. She did it again and again and again until she was satisfied she knew what she was doing. She closed the door, set the dead bolt, and left the security chain dangling. She turned to head back to the bedroom.

Suddenly Melany's door came open. Priscilla froze. Melany stumbled out, sliding her hands along the wall to keep herself upright. She had her back to Priscilla most of the way to the bathroom. As soon as the bathroom door closed, Priscilla raced to the bedroom, put the cuffs on, and laid down on her mattress.

"Phew, that was close," she said to John.

"What?" he asked.

"Melany came out of her bedroom while I was at the front door. She was so far gone that she didn't notice me."

"You are one brave little girl, sweetie."

She told John what she had done, and how fast she had done it. She told John that she peeked out in the hallway and saw the way to the stairs and told him she could get there in the dark if she had to. John was proud of her and felt better now that he had a viable plan to get Priscilla out in one piece. It was like a weight had been lifted from his shoulders. John wasn't concerned for himself. He had to reunite

Priscilla and Carrie. He couldn't stand the thought of Carrie losing two such beautiful and talented daughters.

Brad drove around the block at the Pussy Cat Club and noticed that Jake's SUV was not at its usual parking spot. He parked in the right hand alley of the Mongolian BBQ restaurant, well back from the street. He parked facing in the same direction as he drove in. He pulled his black rib-knit, three-hole balaclava down over his face, slid on his black leather gloves and got out of the car. He unlocked his trunk to remove his rifle and strapped it over his shoulder. He reached for a small bag of ammunition and removed three shells, then put them in his pocket. He took out his stick seat as well.

Brad limp-walked the one hundred and twenty feet to the fire escape of the second building, to the right of the Mongolian BBQ. He climbed the ladder and then the stairs in the cool New York City night air. He walked to the front and climbed over the four foot parapet wall to the adjacent building.

Brad shrugged the rifle from his shoulder and placed it on top of the wall. He crouched and sighted in the front doorway of the Pussy Cat Club, and imagined the shot he would take later tonight. Through the scope, he could see the advertising poster of nearly-nude Melany hanging prominently at the entrance. He sat back on his stick seat, resting his arms on the four foot parapet wall. His position gave him a full view of the street and the Pussy Cat in his 180 degree field of vision. He sat there, not knowing how long it would take.

Brad looked at his watch; it was eight PM. He had smoked nearly all of his cigarettes, one after the other, and when he glanced at his watch again, it was nearly nine thirty PM. From the corner of his right eye, he saw lights coming down the street. It was Jake's SUV. He quickly looked right, and positioned himself to aim the rifle. He picked it up and sighted it in on the doorway as Jake's driver pulled into his reserved parking spot.

Jake exited the car on the passenger's side and jauntily rounded the front of the vehicle, heading for the entrance.

Brad took deep breaths and followed Jake with the scope.

"Hit him between the L5 and S1 Vertebrae," Brad said to himself as he began his squeeze of the trigger.

The instant before the oblique shot was fired, Jake hopped up, as usual, from the sidewalk to the first step of the entrance to take the stairs two at a time. He heard the shot and instantly felt the hot lead rip into his body. His signature hop to the first step had raised his body six inches higher and the bullet tore into the fatty flesh of his right buttocks, completely missing bone. He fell forward, out of sight.

Brad wasn't sure if he had hit his mark or not, and reloaded his rifle. He carefully looked out over the parapet and saw Jake's goons looking up and down the street, not sure where the shot had come from. He couldn't see Jake and decided that his shot was a success. He dropped down, pulled the rifle down from the wall, and dropped it on the roof, where he left it along with the stick seat and the remaining rounds of ammunition. He did not want to be encumbered trying to flee.

He crouched and ran along the four foot wall to the back of the building. He quickly climbed down and dropped to the alley below. He ran as fast as he could to his waiting vehicle, got in, and drove off, looking back in his rear view mirror. No one came.

Jake's men called 911 and waited for the police and paramedics. The first detective to arrive cordoned off the area and closed the entrance. Brad was long gone.

"What happened here?" the officer asked the waiting men.

"The boss was coming in for the night, and a shot went off and hit him in the ass," one man said.

"Where did it happen?"

"Right there at the first step. You can see the blood spatter, and there's the spot where the bullet hit the wall."

The detective looked at the concrete spalls and the chip in the wall. He also noted another fresh chip out of the first step where he assumed the bullet ricocheted a second time. He looked all over the area and finally found the bullet resting on the sidewalk, up against the first step. He photographed it and placed it in an evidence bag.

"No one is to use these stairs until I say so, understand?" the detective said to the uniformed officers on the sidewalk and the bouncers at the top of the stairs.

"Have everyone use the back entrance. It's probably a good thing for you to give everyone a free drink, they're going to be here for a while. Start getting names and addresses," the detective ordered. "I'll be in soon to ask questions."

Brad walked into his apartment, turned on the ten o'clock news and went to the kitchen to get two beers. He came back and sat down to watch the news. The station had Brad and Melany's pictures full screen.

"What the fuck?" Brad gasped. "How the fuck did they get her name?"

"Brad Waterman, aka Waters, aka Watson and his accomplice Melany Barton are still assumed to be here in the city. If you have seen either of these people in the last week, please contact police. Do not approach them, they are presumed armed and dangerous," the news anchor said.

Brad's heart raced for a few minutes, and then he calmed down. As far as he could remember, no one saw him bring Melany into the building and she hadn't been outside since she arrived. *They probably put two and two together because Jake had most likely reported Melany missing,* Brad thought to himself.

Brad finished his beers and went in to look at his hostages. Both were asleep with their backs to the door. He turned out their light and went back to the couch.

Nothing on the news about Jake's shooting, Brad thought to himself. Brad thought it was probably too soon, or not important enough to make the news.

※

"Detective, I found these on the roof of that building," the uniformed officer said, pointing and handing over Brad's rifle, stick seat, and ammunition.

"Good work, Officer."

"I also found this cartridge and some cigarette butts," the officer said, holding out several evidence bags.

A forensics team finished photographing the scene and collecting what little evidence they could find. The officer began taking down the security tape as the detective went up the stairs to speak with Jake. The paramedics had finished their preliminary preparations and were taking Jake out the rear entry to a waiting ambulance.

"Can I ask him one or two questions before you take him out of here?" the detective asked.

The paramedic looked at Jake for approval, and he nodded his head.

"I'll get your personal information from your staff, but do you have any idea who might have done this?" the detective asked.

"Yes, that asshole Brad Waterman, the same guy who killed the two men and the girl last week, the kidnapper," Jake said emphatically.

"Do you have any idea where he lives?"

"I used to, but he moved recently. I've had my men out looking for him, but no luck yet."

"How bad were you hit?"

"Damn near shot my ass off, but no real damage. The bullet was through and through, gonna take a few stitches. Hurts like hell, but they say I'm gonna live," Jake gamely answered.

"Thank you, Sir," the detective said, nodding to the paramedics.

28

IT'S ME AGAIN

Vince was expecting contact again, and told everyone to be alert.

"The delivery date is tomorrow, he will definitely be calling with the instructions," Vince told everyone in the room.

Not more than half an hour later the phone rang. It was ten thirty AM.

"You know who I am," the eerie voice said. "Let me speak with JT."

"This is JT Wingate."

"Listen closely, I will say this only once. If you fuck up, one of the hostages gets hurt, badly. I want you, JT, personally to take one of the bags to Grand Central Station, Main Concourse, 6PM, alone. A man in a motorized chair with a red ball cap and a cell phone will approach you. Give him the bag. He will let me know immediately that he has the bag, and then when he is free and clear of the terminal. If all goes well, I'll call you again. If not, one of your little ballerina's toes gets cut off. Ouch," the voice said.

"We will need proof of life today," Vince said hastily.

"Okay," the voice said and hung up.

Carrie hugged JT tightly, concerned about the voice's threats.

"The man is diabolical," JT said.

Everyone looked at each other and wondered why only one million was asked for. Vince explained that he had seen the same thing happen once before in a negotiation he headed. He told the Wingates that it was a ploy to ensure the kidnapper's safety.

"He receives four of the five bags, gives instructions for the last bag and the hand over, and takes off long before the deal is to go down," Vince explained.

"You mean he settled for four million?" JT asked.

"No, that's all he wanted in the first place," Vince answered. "The last million bought him twenty four hours of getaway time. Cheap price to pay, especially when it's someone else's money, although that was back in the 80's, when a million was a million."

"That's pretty cagey," Detective Johnson said. "I've never heard of that before. This guy might be a little smarter than we thought."

"Actually, the kidnapping was made into a movie, *Easy Come, Easy Go*, starring William Townsend. I was called in to help with the accuracy of the case portrayal. Our genius probably saw it. Come to think of it, cutting off digits was in the movie, too."

"So Brad, how much longer is this going to go on?" John asked on his way to the bathroom that evening.

"After dinner tonight, when you are all cleaned up, we're doing another proof of life video. Things are starting to move."

At eight thirty PM the proof of life video arrived, and JT shared it with everyone. John and Priscilla, wearing the same clothes, sitting on the same couch, holding today's newspaper filled the screen. The voice did roughly the same banter.

JT watched John's eyes intently and picked up on the increased flutter. He played the video over and over until he deciphered John's message, GETGNERV. JT told the group that John spelled out Getting Nervous.

Carrie and Jennifer hugged each other.

"Is this a good sign that he wants to let John and Priscilla live?" Jennifer asked.

"It might be," Vince said. "Most kidnappers don't want murder on their arrest warrants, but this guy already has several to his account, so it's a mixed message thing for me. Eric and Charles were an immediate threat and had to be dealt with quickly. Audrey was an eye witness that had to be dealt with."

"John and Priscilla are eye witnesses as well," Carrie said.

"That's true, but he now knows that we know who he is, and just wants more time to run. I don't think he has anything against John and Priscilla, and they certainly don't pose a threat."

The following day, JT got ready for the trip to Grand Central Station. His new driver picked him up at five forty PM as agreed. The station was only five blocks away. JT got out of the limo, retrieved the bag, and walked to the terminal. He looked up at the Grand Terminal Clock, and it was five minutes to six.

He walked with the heavy bag to the center of the main lobby and placed the bag on the floor between his feet, where he waited. Six PM came and went, but there was no one in a motorized chair, just the milling crowd. At ten after six, someone kicked his leg from behind. JT twisted around and saw the man in the red ball cap.

"Don't turn around, just kick the bag backwards toward me," a voice said.

JT did as he was told and stared straight ahead. He heard the man say, "I have the bag." He then heard a motorized chair move away. One minute later, JT turned around to see if he could catch sight of the man and saw what he thought was a man in a wheelchair rounding a corner and moving out of view. He thought about running after the man, but decided not to, sensing there might be a second man watching him.

He walked back to the terminal entrance where his driver was waiting for him.

"Is everything okay, Sir?" the driver asked.

"Randy, did you see a man in a motorized wheel chair, wearing a red ball cap, come out here?" JT asked.

"No, Sir."

"Let's go home," JT said dejectedly.

"Yes, Sir."

Back at JT's apartment, everyone gathered for a briefing.

"I really can't tell you much. He came up behind me, I saw his red ball cap, but the brim covered his face and I didn't see anything," JT said, with exasperation. "I heard him tell someone on the phone that he had the bag and then he was gone. I had the feeling I was being watched, and acted accordingly. Randy said he didn't see anyone in a red ball cap and wheel chair come out of the station."

Brad returned to the apartment, heart beating a million miles per hour, dropped the bag on the coffee table and went to the refrigerator for a beer. He returned back to the living room, sat on the couch, leaned back and admired his haul. He finished his beer in three pulls, sat up and dragged the bag to him. It was heavy. He opened the bag and rummaged through the contents. He dumped the contents on the table and checked the bag for bugs, wires, and hidden electronics.

"One million fucking dollars," he whispered aloud to himself.

He stacked the strapped packets. Seventy five packets of mustard-strapped $100 bills, seventy-five packets of violet-strapped $20 bills, seventy-five packets of yellow-strapped $10 and fifty packets of red-strapped $5 bills filled the bag. He did the math by hand, and it totaled one million dollars.

He fell back against the cushion and stared at the ceiling. He had never seen that amount of money in one place ever in his life. He went to the kitchen for another beer and returned to the living room.

He sipped his beer and absentmindedly began thumbing several of the $100 bill packets of used currency.

"Fucking beautiful," he said aloud. He took out one of the mustard-strap packets and two of the violet-strap packets, loaded the rest back into the duffle bag, and put it under the coffee table. Brad had a phone call to make.

"This is JT," said Vince, answering the eerie voice on the phone.

"I'd like to compliment you on a job well done, JT. My cohort and I are very pleased with your performance," Brad said through the unnerving voice changer.

"Thank you," Vince calmly answered.

"Day after tomorrow, JFK Terminal 1, Lufthansa ticket area, 6 PM sharp, one million dollars, got it?" Brad ordered.

"I understand, but I want proof of life again at least three hours before six PM," Vince sternly replied.

"You'll have it," the voice said and hung up.

Pleased with himself and his success, Brad went into John and Priscilla's bedroom. John had heard mumbling in the living room, but couldn't make out what was being said. He was frustrated with his lack of control.

"Okay brat, the usual drill, you first," Brad said as he unlocked Priscilla's chains from the restrainer bolt.

John waited patiently for twenty-five minutes for Priscilla to return. She sat down on the mattress while Brad set the chains. She stared at the floor, she had been crying. *Something is wrong*, John thought as he got to his feet to make his way to the bathroom.

The whole time he shaved and brushed, he thought about Priscilla. What happened? He knew it was something.

He walked from the bathroom to the kitchen. He noticed the Double O Shipping sea bag sitting under the coffee table. One and one half feet by one and one half feet by three feet long, the navy blue bag with the Double O logo was unmistakable. John had them made for his crew personnel over twenty years ago. He had them made in four different colors, navy blue, gray, dark green and black. The company had given out thousands over the years. John knew Brad had received his ransom money, and a substantial amount. The bag looked like it was stuffed full.

He sat and ate his peanut butter and jelly sandwich and glass of milk.

"Alright, that's enough, off to bed," Brad said with a slur. He was on his fifth beer. He made John set his own chains at gun point, rattled the chains as a security check, turned and walked out of the room, turning off the light and closing the door.

John thought for a moment that Brad was getting a little sloppy.

"Are you alright, sweetie?" John immediately whispered to Priscilla.

"No, Papa."

"What's the matter?" he asked, with tenderness in his voice.

"He touched me from behind while I was brushing my teeth," she said and started to cry again.

John's biggest fear was realized. The no-good bastard had stolen her youth and naivety. The family had sheltered and protected her from this sort of thing, and now in a drunken needless act, the low life bastard takes it all away. John was not a hateful man, but he loathed the scum that committed senseless acts that caused so much pain to others for a moment's satisfaction. Rapists, molesters, and perverts were of the lowest on John's human scale.

"Oh sweetie, I'm so sorry. I've let you down," John said, trying to absorb the blow for her.

"He didn't do anything really bad Papa, just touching," she said, feeling his concern.

"Please try and put it out of your mind, this is the type of human being you won't ever have to deal with again, I promise you," John tried to reassure her.

"Papa, I know there are bad people in the world, and I also know that there are more good than bad. It was just such a shock to me that someone would do something like that to someone else."

"I understand. If you're okay, let's try and get some sleep. Don't forget your exercises."

"I'm okay, Papa."

"I love you sweetie. I wish I could give you a big hug right now."

"I love you too, Papa."

John heard Priscilla quietly doing her exercises. She was such a strong and determined little girl. He knew she would survive this, and he knew it was up to him to make sure she did.

He could not think of a single reason why Brad would let them live. He guessed that he already had two murders to his credit with Charles and Eric, what difference would two or three more make?

He couldn't understand the Melany situation. She was just wasting away in the other bedroom, what is that gaining him? She's is an attractive woman and yet he fondles Priscilla. John was confused.

Why, if Brad has received his ransom, was he still toying with them, why hasn't he killed them or let them escape on their own while he fled?

Too many questions, too many incongruities, too much confusion.

29

ROUND TWO

JT prepared for the trip to JFK.

"Are you sure you don't want us to have your back on this one?" Detective Johnson asked.

"Positive," JT answered. "I don't want to do anything that might put my daughter and my uncle at risk."

"Fair enough, but how about if we just observe, and not engage, unless, of course, something goes wrong and you need our assistance?" Detective Johnson urged.

"Maybe on the next one," JT said. "I want him to develop confidence to the point where he might let his guard down. We're guessing there will be two more bags after this one. When it's time for the fourth bag, we'll talk about it."

JT was adamant about his position. He also wanted to give John more time to develop whatever plan he might have. JT had no idea what John's plan might be, but he knew absolutely that John had one.

"Randy, what route are you taking this evening?" Vince asked JT's driver.

"The I-495 to the I-678. If we get bad traffic reports, we can always switch to the 878 and Belt Parkway. We're leaving early enough to make sure that we won't be late," Randy said.

JT sat in the back of the limo, staring out at the late afternoon sky. All he could think about was his daughter. He prayed that nothing bad would happen to her, or to John. *Wealth is a blessing and a curse,* he said to himself. There were times that he wished life was simpler. He snapped out of his thoughts as soon as Randy pulled over at the limo waiting area.

"We're a little early, Sir, do you want to wait here in the car?" Randy asked.

JT looked at his watch and saw it was five forty PM.

"No, I'll get out now and it will give me a little more time to look around."

Standing in the busy international check-in area, he watched the crowd moving around him. JT noticed all sorts of people; Chinese, Japanese, Turks, Mexicans, milled around, all with their own course to follow. He saw people pushing carts, carrying babies, children running, mothers and fathers chasing, a typical assemblage in an international air terminal that he was all too familiar with.

It was six fifteen, and a tap on his leg brought him back. He turned quickly and saw the red ball cap. He handed the sixty-five pound duffle bag to the seated man and quickly turned back. This time he noticed a corner of the man's moustache sticking out from under his pulled-down hat brim. Within seconds, he heard the man say that he had the bag and was leaving the terminal. Again, JT waited to turn to see the man leave. Nothing. This time the man disappeared into thin air. He saw two policemen on the mezzanine level who he thought were looking down at him.

Johnson had better not have gone behind my back on this, JT thought.

JT made his way back to the sidewalk and the limo waiting area. He got into the back seat.

"Did you see anything, Randy?" JT asked his driver.

"No, Sir, I'm sorry. I stayed riveted to the door you entered. He must have gone out a different exit."

Back at his apartment, JT again briefed the group.

"It was the exact same set up, wheelchair, red cap and phone call to his accomplice. I noticed, this time, however, that he has a reddish brown moustache. He vanished before I could turn around to watch him leave."

"There was nothing else?" Detective Johnson asked.

"Well, there was something," JT said.

"What was it?" the detective asked.

"We made an agreement before I left tonight, didn't we?" JT asked Detective Johnson.

"Yes, we did," was Johnson's answer.

"There were two uniformed police officers on the mezzanine level that appeared to be looking down at me."

"JT, they were not my men, and I will find out right now what that was about," Detective Johnson said as he left the group to make phone calls.

Brad finished counting all of the money and placed the second bag under the coffee table. He made his phone call to JT and gave him the instructions for the next delivery.

"By the way, I saw the two cops on the mezzanine floor and I sincerely hope they weren't there for you. One false move, and it's over. Do you understand me?" the kidnapper threatened.

"They had nothing to do with me, and I understand," JT answered firmly.

With his newly-earned wealth, be purchased four new burn phones and threw his old phone in a trashcan at JFK Airport. He had no idea if JT was having his phone traced or not, and he wasn't going to take any chances that he might.

During the evening clean-up and dinner routine, John noticed the gray bag with the black-stenciled letters, *Double O Shipping*, where a blue one had been the night before. As casually as he could, he looked around the room for the other bag, but couldn't find it.

"How come we are having pizza tonight?" John asked Brad.

"Well, I just came into a lot of money, and I thought I'd give you a treat," Brad said sarcastically.

As he talked, John noticed that the gray bag was stuffed full, and wondered just how much money Brad was getting. John noticed that Brad was wearing new clothes and shoes.

"I'm going out to do a little celebrating tonight, and I don't want any funny shit happening while I'm away," Brad announced.

Brad left John and Priscilla in the darkened bedroom, grabbed ten hundred dollar bills and left the apartment headed for one of Manhattan's many strip clubs. *I have earned it*, he thought.

While Brad was gone, John had Priscilla practice leaving the apartment again. She went through the paces, and from the time he said 'Plan 1' to the time she was ready to leave the apartment was two-plus minutes. Removing the handcuffs took two minutes, and getting out of the front door took about one minute. John knew that he had to hold Brad down for at least ten minutes for her to get completely away from the apartment, out of sight and safely on the run. He could cut that to eight if she freed herself from the cuffs before John attacked Brad. Eight minutes was a long time, and John was unsure he would be able to subdue Brad for that length of time.

Brad was strong, armed, and volatile. He had a knife and a gun. He was also a drinker and was now becoming over confident with success and drinking even more. He also had an infirmity that John thought he might possibly use to his advantage. Did these two weaknesses outweigh the strengths? John knew he was still in reasonably good shape, but he remembered Eric's comment about quickness when Eric tried to stop Brad at Henri's restaurant. Brad's left hand was nearly in Eric's face before he could react.

"Wonderful, sweetie, now put the cuffs back on and let's do our exercises and get to sleep," John said.

John laid on his mattress, deep in thought. If he could somehow remove his own cuffs before trying to restrain Brad, he would have a much better chance. If his hands were cuffed close together, Brad could hold them in check easily while he reached for his knife.

John concluded that there was no way he was going to get out of the cuffs before jumping Brad. He would have to come up with another solution.

John finally heard the steady deep breathing of the sleeping Priscilla. He decided to revisit his problems tomorrow and go to sleep. It was a welcome sleep. Even though he had been laying on a mattress for most of the day, he welcomed the chance to sleep and clear his head.

John slept soundly throughout the night and was awakened by Brad's kick the following morning. He was a little surprised, and he felt well rested.

"Get up and get started, no noise, don't even speak. I have the mother of all headaches this morning, and I don't want to hear a thing from either of you."

Brad threw John the keys and told him to unchain himself and lock his wrists closer together. John did what he was told, and realized he must have missed an excellent chance last night when Brad came home in a drunken state. It would probably have been too late at night though, and he had to get Priscilla out while corner grocery stores, bars, and liquor stores were still open or about to open for her to have a chance to get help. *Bide your time John*, he said to himself.

John completed his morning routine and walked back to the bedroom. On the way back, he again noticed a gray Double O duffle bag under the coffee table. He also noticed that the blue one was either gone or somewhere out of sight. Two duffle bags in three nights. He got to the bedroom and Brad told him to lock himself into the restraints.

It was Priscilla's turn. He unlocked her chains from the restraints and walked her to the bathroom.

"I'd like some privacy if you don't mind," she said to Brad.

"Don't worry brat, I was with a real woman last night. You and your boy body don't interest me," Brad said hurtfully.

John laid thinking about the second bag. He knew that Double O had four different colors of bags, and maybe it was a message from JT so John could keep track of the amount of money being sent. The trouble with that was he had no idea how much ransom was requested, or how much money was in each bag. No, there was some other reason for using the different color bags.

Priscilla completed her clean-up and breakfast and was taken back to the bedroom. Brad locked her chains and rattled both hers and John's, checking for security. Satisfied everything was in place, Brad left the room.

Priscilla explained to John that Brad had told her he wasn't interested in her 'boy body' because he had been with a real woman last night.

"I don't know what he is talking about, sweetie," John lied, saving Priscilla further embarrassment.

"Papa, let's play trivia again," she said with a big smile. The game was an excellent way to pass time, but also to sharpen the mind and keep it working. Each of them had to think of questions and answers and keep score in their heads. They decided that John would keep her score and Priscilla would keep his.

They played for two hours and John asked what his score was and she told him one hundred and fifty points.

"What's mine, Papa?" she asked.

"One hundred and twenty-five," he said.

"No, Papa, it's one hundred and seventy-five. I won seven games, and you won six."

"You're right sweetie, I was just testing you," he said with a big smile.

John thought he heard the front door close. It was two PM.

Brad carried the Gray Double O bag to his car and placed it in the trunk. He drove to the nearest mailing service and brought the bag in with him. He selected a box and placed the bag inside.

"Anything of value, Sir?" the clerk asked.

"Some clothing, a few books, stuff I'm sending to my sister for storage until I can get back from Iraq to retrieve it," Brad lied.

Brad was sending the package to his sister, but the contents did have value. The address on the package read Scottsbluff, Nebraska. In his conversation with his sister, five days ago, she agreed to receive the packages and send them to him as soon as he could set up a new address. He sent her a separate package with two hundred and fifty thousand dollars as incentive. He told her that if he did not contact her within the next ninety days, she could keep all the packages. He sent the first package from a facility downtown. *Three more to go,* Brad thought, *before this part of the venture is over.*

30

ROUND THREE

The trip, three blocks west to Lexington Avenue, eight blocks south to E 37th Street, five blocks west to E 34th Street and four blocks south to 34th Street Penn Station, took Randy twenty-two minutes. Randy parked at the limo wait area just up the street from the 34th Street and 7th Avenue entrance. It was five fifty PM, a comfortable ten minutes early. JT looked out of the rear-tinted window at the crowd of people entering and leaving the station. It was rush hour and hundreds of passengers scurried in and out. He looked for a man in a wheelchair, but saw no one.

JT got out of the car and disappeared into the main lobby area. He found a suitable place to stand, put the bag on the floor between his legs, and waited. At ten minutes after six, he felt the now-familiar tap on his leg. He picked up the bag, turned just enough to identify the red ball cap, handed over the bag and turned back, looking forward.

"I've got the bag," the man said and took off toward the opposite side of the building.

JT turned just in time to see the red cap disappear into the crowd. He waited two or three minutes, and walked back to the waiting limousine.

"I don't suppose you saw anything, did you, Randy?"

"Actually I did, Sir. A man in a wheelchair and red ball cap went out the far side of the building at the 33rd Street Entrance. He was moving pretty fast. I lost sight of him when the doors closed."

"Three million out the door, and we don't know anything more than we did with the first million," JT lamented. "Let's go back to the apartment."

"Same scenario, different place," JT said to the waiting group as he walked in the apartment door.

"Didn't the man say anything?" Jennifer asked.

"No, he didn't, and I'm starting to worry," JT said.

Detective Johnson and Vince looked at each other, both wondering what the kidnapper's next move was going to be. He was brazen enough to meet three times in the open so far. He was obviously confident in his plan. He was holding all the cards as long as he had John and Priscilla, but that didn't mean he couldn't be pursued and caught.

"What do you think Vince, where do we go from here?" JT said.

"We are thinking that the pick-up man is an accomplice, and our kidnapper is on the phone with him after each delivery," Vince said to the group.

"That's right," Detective Johnson said.

"What if the pick-up guy and the kidnapper are one in the same? What if his phone call is just a ruse to have us believe he isn't working alone?" Vince offered.

"Boy, that would take major balls," Johnson said. "The game would be over if we nabbed him. If he is working alone, who is looking after John and Priscilla when he is making a pick-up?"

Carrie reminded everyone that the girl Melany was thought to be with him, but said that from what she knew of Melany she doubted that Melany had the stomach for cutting off toes or fingers, much less killing someone.

"I don't think that Melany is the killer type either," JT said. "She couldn't harm anyone."

"Don't be too sure of that," Detective Johnson said. "We don't have any idea what the situation is, or what the kidnapper is doing to keep her with him. Didn't that bar owner say that Brad was supplying her with drugs at one time?"

"I think you're right, Detective. She was also prostituting herself in order to get drugs," Vince said.

"I think we need to talk to that man again. I'll get Detective Brady to go over to the Pussy Cat Club and see what he can find out," Johnson said.

They all began the boring wait for the phone to ring. Vince was reading his book, Detective Johnson was talking with someone on his cell phone, Jennifer and Carrie were in their bedrooms, and JT was going over the day's Double O correspondence.

The phone rang at nine PM. Vince put down his book and began counting the rings. At the fifth ring, he picked up the phone.

"Hello, this is JT," he said.

"Another successful meeting, JT, don't you think?" the eerie voice said.

"Maybe from your point of view," Vince returned coldly. "When do we start getting some information?"

"In due time." The voice went on to say that he was changing things up a little, and he was altering his plan for the handover of the fourth and fifth bags of money.

"I'll be calling you day after tomorrow. Be ready to go. Give me a cell phone number to contact, you'll be on the move."

Vince snapped his fingers at JT, motioning him to write down the phone number. JT quickly jotted it down.

"Alright then, until day after tomorrow," the voice said.

"I want proof of life tonight, and a second one, one hour after I hand over the fourth bag," Vince hurriedly said into the phone.

"Okay," the voice said. "But probably two or three hours after." He hung up.

The next morning, John noticed that the gray bag had been replaced by a green one. John was getting nervous. Three bags negotiated and delivered over a six day period had to be risky, and he wondered how Brad was getting away with it. He wondered if Brad had any help, or if he was boldly alone.

Four bags had to be the end of things, John thought. Either there was going to be a hostage exchange soon, or there was going to be two dead bodies. As he waited for Priscilla to finish her morning routine, he pondered what and when his next move should be.

"Papa, we've been here for nineteen days now. How much longer do you think it's going to be before we can go home?" Priscilla asked naively.

"It should be soon now, sweetie," John said. "It should be very soon now."

The day wore on slowly. Brad had left the apartment and was gone for around two hours. What was concerning John was the time that was passing by. Sooner or later, there was going to be a mistake and Brad was going to finish his game well or badly depending on the severity of the error. John heard the front door open, close again, latch, and then silence. He stretched on his chains as far as he could to look out of the crack in the door. He could just see the corner of the coffee table, and he saw that the green bag had been removed.

Putting two and two together, John surmised that Brad was dealing with the money. He made a mental note to verify that this evening.

John heard Brad return to the apartment that evening. Brad had his evening beers watching the local five o'clock and five thirty news programs. John faintly heard his name mentioned one or two times in each broadcast.

"What the fuck," Brad bellowed. As he watched the program, the station flashed side by side pictures of him, one with a moustache, the other without. The broadcaster continued with the usual *armed and dangerous* announcements and the police phone numbers. John was unable to make out any of the broadcast, but he got that something had disturbed Brad.

Brad got up and went to the bathroom. Long minutes passed and John felt Brad had been in the bathroom an unusually long time. Finally Brad returned and came into the bedroom to give John and Priscilla their clean-up time and evening meal of fast food burgers, fries, and cokes with no ice. When it was John's turn, he immediately noticed that Brad had dyed his hair jet black, and that the third bag was no longer to be seen in the room.

"Your asshole nephew wants another proof of life photo tonight," Brad announced to John. Brad gave John the keys and at gunpoint had him unlock Priscilla's restraints. The two then paraded out to the living room couch and sat down as Brad sat across from them. They did and said as they were instructed and escorted back to their bedroom.

John sat on his mattress, smiled at Priscilla and reassured her again that everything was going to be all right. He didn't want to tell her his plans just yet. He knew she would worry. He decided to let her know minutes before he was going to attack Brad. She had very quick reactions and a certain calm that came over her just before it was time for her to perform.

"PGOSA4," JT said. "What do you suppose that means?"

They all sat quietly thinking as JT wrote out the cryptic alphanumeric on the easel flip chart pad that John had blinked out in the video. He wrote out the letters with a space between each one.

"A, in code, usually means 'after' or 'ante,'" Vince offered.

"P could be 'plan' or 'Priscilla,'" JT said.

"That leaves G, O, S and 4," Carrie chimed in.

They sat, foreheads furled, hands to their heads, or eyes staring up at the ceiling.

"It could be very simply, 'plan goes after 4,'" Detective Johnson said. "Or Priscilla goes after 4."

"4PM?" Carrie asked.

"4 days, 4 hours?" Detective Johnson added.

"4 bags of money," JT added with a eureka-flare to his voice.

"Priscilla goes after the fourth bag of money," Vince said with a smile, patting JT on the back. "That has to be it."

Heads nodded and smiled at their decryption prowess. Everyone knew that John would have some sort of plan brewing in his never-resting brain. That was a given. Somehow or another, he had figured out a way to get Priscilla free and on her way home.

"Boy, I don't know if that is such a good idea," Detective Johnson said, face knotted, pacing in front of the group.

"Why is that?" JT asked.

"We're so close to the end. If John screws up, it may jeopardize the outcome," Johnson clarified.

"Obviously John knows something we don't," the previously quiet Jennifer said firmly. "John doesn't do anything unless he has thought it through from beginning to end. He weighs everything before he acts."

JT nodded his head, as did Carrie. Joe and Pat had knowing looks on their face.

"I'm sure that it was lack of time that kept him from saying more, but if we buy our decoding, there's nothing about what's next for him," JT said.

"There is still one more proof of life before he puts his plan into action," Vince interjected. "Maybe then we will have a better idea of what he is planning."

31

READY, SET, ...

"Good to see you again, boss, how are you doing?" Jake's bartender asked.

"Everything seems to be healing just fine," Jake said.

It had been just over a week since the shooting. Jake knew he had been very lucky to have gotten away with a flesh wound. One or two inches further up and to the left, he may have been in a wheelchair for the rest of his life.

"Where are the fellas?" Jake asked.

"Phil is out looking for that asshole, and your driver's with him," the bartender said.

Jake couldn't understand why he wasn't hearing anything on the grapevine about Brad. Somebody always knew something, but for the last several weeks, nothing. That had to mean that Brad was laying very low and wasn't up to his old tricks.

Jake was very concerned about Melany. He knew in his heart that the bastard had gotten her hooked again, otherwise she would never have stayed with him. She was weak, but not that weak. When it was all over, Jake would have to get Melany back on track. He vowed to take the responsibility. Since she had been gone, he realized that he actually missed her and wanted her company. He wasn't sure if he was in love or not, but he did know that he had feelings for her.

Jake decided to step up his search. He felt well enough to join the hunt, and he would pay others to help him.

"Phil, any luck? Anything?" Jake asked as Phil and the driver walked into the Pussy Cat Club.

"Nothing, Boss," Phil said. "We've searched every one of his old haunts and hangouts a half dozen times at all hours of day. We've harassed junkies he used to sell to, the bums he used to roll, and they all swear they haven't seen him for two or three weeks, and they're all happy for that. They have no idea where he is, and said they would get in touch with me if they heard anything."

"Have you looked in any new places?" Jake asked.

"Like where, Boss? Manhattan is a big place."

"I know, smart ass, but you could start by branching out away from his last known address, and work your way from street to street. By the way, did you speak to his last land lord?"

"Yeah, he's pissed. Brad skipped on his last month's rent and left the place in a real mess," Phil said.

Jake explained that he was going to hire a few more guys to help with the search temporarily. He gave them a search method and a plan of attack and told them he wanted them on the street all day and all night until they found the bastard.

"My guess is that he's still fairly close by, and is probably out watching us right now. He's staying to the shadows, no doubt, but he has to make an appearance sometime. Phil, you knew him the best. Just keep cruising up and down the streets, especially at night. You might get lucky. The rest of the guys can put in the legwork and canvas the markets, restaurants, and bars, showing people pictures and asking questions. If we get a hit, we can concentrate on that area."

"Okay, Boss," Phil said. "What do we do if we run into the cops?"

"Don't seek them out, but if you encounter them, be open with them and share any information you have. We have a mutual goal here, and we want to appear as cooperative as possible."

Detective Johnson met Detective Brady at Flanagan's, a cop bar near the precinct house. Brady was overseeing the street cops assigned to them while Johnson was with the Wingate family and the negotiator.

"Any progress?" Johnson asked his partner.

"We had a hit from a guy who owned a gun shop over on twentieth. He said a guy that looked a lot like our guy shot several times at his rifle range about a month ago. He said he came in, kept to himself, fired probably twenty-five rounds each time, and left."

Brady continued to say that the man didn't try to engage anyone, that he was a loner, and that he seemed to know what he was doing.

"Other than that, nothing. He seems to have gone way underground if he's still in the area," Brady concluded.

"Well, we do know he is still in New York, he's keeping us going with the ransom drops," Johnson said. "Our guess is that he is going to bail before we deliver the fifth and last bag, which if he holds to his schedule, is only a few days away," Johnson continued.

"You know, Johnson, we really need to work on Wingate to let one of us go with him on the next drop. Had we been with him on the first three, we'd have the guy by now."

"I agree, but we need to respect his wishes, whichever way he chooses to go."

The two men finished their drinks and left the bar. Detective Johnson went back to the Wingate apartment and Brady back to the precinct. He had some paperwork to complete.

The next day, the call came in around four PM. The eerie voice asked for JT, as usual.

"This is JT," Vince said.

"Are you ready to go?" the voice asked. "I want you to drive to the Roosevelt Island Bridge on-ramp on Roosevelt Island. When you get there, find a place to park and wait for my call."

Randy drove as quickly as it was safe to do so and found a parking space on Main Street near the on-ramp to the bridge. They waited approximately twenty minutes for the phone to ring. The voice was unchanged and Brad spoke in a clear voice.

"When I hang up, drive onto the bridge and slowly cross. At the far end of the bridge, you will see a white flag on your right. Try to hit the flag with the bag. Keep driving straight on Thirty Sixth Avenue to Northern Boulevard. Return to your Manhattan apartment on the Ed Koch Queensboro Bridge. You will be followed. Any deviations and the brat pays."

Brad hung up the phone and grabbed the flag pole. Standing on the top of the red fence, he held it up two feet above the railing and waved it one foot to each side. He didn't want to raise too much attention. The bag actually hit the pole and dropped to the roof of his vehicle with a loud thud. He quickly grabbed the bag, threw it on the front seat, and drove in the same direction JT and Randy were taking. He saw JT's car four or five ahead of his and smiled.

"The perfect direction follower," Brad said aloud to himself.

Brad followed at a safe distance behind and made sure he was not followed to his apartment.

He enjoyed counting out the packets of bills again. He checked off each denominations packets that added up to the million dollars. *Four million dollars,* he thought. Enough in itself, but he was greedy and wanted it all.

His final delivery scheme, he felt, was foolproof, and had no fear that it would be foiled or that he would be caught. Once he received his last bag, he was on an eighteen-minute direct driving route to La Guardia and a First Class flight to financial freedom.

He returned to his apartment and made a phone call to JT.

The phone rang, and Vince again counted the rings with his fingers. At six rings, he picked up the phone. "This is JT."

"Great toss, JT, you actually hit the flag, perfect delivery. By the way, JT, I want you to know how great it makes me feel that I have a giant corporation exec making deliveries and waiting for my phone calls," Brad said.

"Well, I'm happy for you," Vince said. "But this is where the rubber meets the road. We have one more delivery to make, but I'm not going to do it unless I have assurances that my family is alive, and that I'm going to get them back once I live up to my end of the bargain."

"I guarantee you that you will have your assurances. I have no desire to harm your family, especially that adorable little brat, I mean princess, of yours," Brad said with a laugh.

"You see, Brad, when you say things like that, you give me cause to disbelieve you."

"Lighten up, JT, I was only having a little fun with you," Brad said.

"I want a proof of life now, and first thing tomorrow morning. I want one tomorrow night, and one before I have to leave to deliver the last bag. They all must be videos."

"Okay, I'll see what I can do," Brad said.

"No, Brad, you'll do it or we will have problems with the last bag," Vince said.

"Fine," Brad said and abruptly hung up.

Brad gathered John and Priscilla to the living room for the proof of life JT had asked for. John saw the fourth black bag under the coffee table.

"Your pushy nephew wants a proof of life tonight, and one in the morning, so let's get started," Brad said, sipping his beer.

"Mr. Wingate, are you feeling okay?" Brad asked.

"Yes, I'm fine," John answered.

"And you, Princess, how are you feeling?"

"I'm fine as well," she said, eyes looking at her knees.

"Tonight, your father got very upset with me when I called you brat, so from now on you are princess," Brad said with a sneer that could be heard but not seen on the video.

"All right, that's it for tonight," Brad said as he stood and followed them back to the bedroom. Brad locked Priscilla in her bed first, and threw the keys to John to lock himself in. Brad held his gun steadily pointed at John's head as John knelt to lock his chains.

"Sleep tight," Brad said and turned out the light.

JT wrote out the letters John had transmitted, P O U T M O R N, on the easel chart pad. Everyone was tired, but they wanted to get the translation before they went their way for the night.

"P is Priscilla," Vince offered.

Everyone sat staring at the pad. Each person went through their individual iterations to try and break John's code.

"What if it's not code?" Vince offered. "What if it is simply "out morn," or in other words, out in the morning."

"It seems too easy, but maybe that is all John had time for," JT said.

"Man, I hope this doesn't screw things up," Detective Johnson offered. "We have no idea what the kidnapper is planning or what he will do. Let's hope for the best."

For the next hour, they talked about various scenarios that might play out. If Priscilla was successful in escaping, could she get to a phone and contact them?

If she was caught trying to escape, what would the kidnapper do to her? What would he do to John? Both of them represented the prize, but if one of them were killed, they would still have to pay the final ransom to have the other released.

What if both of them were killed and the kidnapper tried to fake his way through to the end? He still had the obligation to provide the proof of life videos.

John laid on his mattress looking up at the dark ceiling. It was his duty and obligation to see that Priscilla survived this ordeal. He had gotten her into this situation, and it was up to him to get her out. He debated whether to tell her now or wait and spring it on her in the morning. He asked what he would have wanted if the situation were reversed. He recognized what he had to do.

He knew that when he talked with her that she would start to get nervous. He had to make sure she stayed calm and on track. A flickering light showed at the bottom of the door which meant Brad was still awake, watching television.

"Priscilla, are you still awake?" John whispered.

"Yes, Papa," she whispered back.

"Tomorrow, you're going to escape from here."

"Oh, Papa, that scares me so much," Priscilla said in an excited whisper.

"I know, sweetie, but it is what has to happen."

He explained to her that he thought there might be one more bag of money to be delivered, but he wasn't sure. If there was another bag of money to be delivered, then it would be two more days before a hostage swap would be made. He told her that Brad was very confident of his work so far, and if he was going to make a mistake, it would be now. He talked on for another ten minutes.

"How do you feel now, sweetie?" John whispered.

"Papa, I know we have to try this, but I'm afraid of what will happen to you if I'm gone."

"You will be successful, and when he finally realizes that he's lost you as a hostage, he'll have to be very nice to me because I'll be the only one left. I wouldn't worry about that at all. He'll be mad as hell, and he'll probably beat me up a little, but he isn't going to kill the goose that lays the golden egg."

John heard her audible, deep sigh.

"We'll get this done in the morning, just follow my lead. Sleep well princess, I love you with all my heart, and I know you'll be successful tomorrow."

"Goodnight Papa, I hope so and I will do my very best. I love you too."

John turned on his side as he felt tears come to his eyes. She was a very brave little girl. He waited until he heard her rhythmic, deep breathing telling him she was asleep. He was having trouble getting to sleep, but half an hour later he finally succumbed.

32

RUN FOR IT

John's internal clock woke him at four thirty AM.

"Wake up, sweetie," He whispered to Priscilla.

She groaned herself to wakefulness.

"Sweetie, get your shoes on, take your hands out of your handcuffs, and lay there with the blanket covering the chains and your hands like we practiced."

She worked diligently at freeing her hands and putting on her shoes. When she was done, she got into position under the blanket.

"Are you awake? Are you ready to do this?" John asked her.

"Yes, Papa, I'm ready," she said.

"As soon as I knock him down, you get going."

"Okay, Papa, I love you."

"I love you more, sweetie."

John pushed his covers off and moved to a sitting position on his mattress.

"Hey, Brad, I have to pee, and bad!" John yelled.

"What the fuck," Brad said as he swung his legs off of the couch and started to stand. He reached for his gun, and clad only in his boxers, walked to the bedroom and turned on the light.

"Sorry to wake you, but I have to pee really bad."

Brad threw John the keys and stood back, pointing his gun, yawning and rubbing his eyes with his free hand. John, kneeling on one knee, leaned forward to unlock his chains. He fiddled with the lock for a bit and looked up at Brad.

"I don't know what's wrong, but I can't seem to work the lock."

"Oh for fuck's sake, back away." As John backed off, Brad knelt, placed the gun at his side and reached forward to deal with the lock.

A soon as the lock was free, John sprang at Brad from his kneeling position. Brad tried to stand, but fell backward when his bum leg failed him, hitting his head hard on the wall behind him. John wrapped his chains around the temporarily stunned Brad's neck, and held on for all he had.

"Now sweetie, go," John groaned at Priscilla under the strain of his neck hold.

Priscilla sprang to her feet and jumped over the two fighting men.

"I love you, Papa!" she said as she went out the bedroom door. Within seconds, she was out the front door and running down the dingy, ill-lit stairs. Sure-footed, she reached the bottom and ran to the front door. She looked up and saw the numbers 08632, backwards painted on the transom window. She threw open the door and ran down the eight steps to the sidewalk.

She looked up and down the street, and decided to run toward the only light other than street and house lights that she could see.

John was struggling with everything he had, and Brad began to pummel his back, ribs, and head. John pulled the chains as hard as he could and Brad was beginning to choke and cough. It wasn't enough though, and John held on as best he could. Brad hit John with a forceful blow that bruised one of his ribs. John winced, and the choke hold loosened more. He figured he had been holding Brad for about five minutes.

Priscilla ran to the first corner and looked at the street sign as she crossed the intersection. *I'm on Madison Street,* she said to herself as she ran ahead as fast as she could. The light was still three long blocks ahead of her. She ran and ran, concentrating on the light and the sidewalk beneath her feet. As she got closer, she could make out a sign that was written in a foreign language. She was nearly there when she noticed a body, a man, laying on the sidewalk ahead of her. Like a hurdler, she leapt over the sotted figure and sprinted the last twenty yards to the shop door.

When she got to the door of the small mom-and-pop Lao Asian grocery store, she saw a man inside preparing his shop for the day.

The door was locked so she knocked calmly. The man turned and looked at her. She smiled and pulled back her hoodie so that he could see her blond hair. The man walked up to her, almost as if he knew her and unlocked the door.

"Please help me, I'm the little girl you've seen on the news recently, and I've escaped my captor."

He mumbled something in a language she didn't understand, and motioned her inside and away from the front door and locked it again. He walked her back behind some shelves so she could not be seen from the street, and motioned her to stay put and he scurried to the back of the store. Several minutes later he returned, shuffling, with a little girl in tow, not much older than Priscilla herself.

"What do you want?" the little Asian girl asked in perfect English.

"I'm the girl you have seen on the news recently who was kidnapped and I've just escaped from my kidnapper," Priscilla said.

The sleepy Asian girl's eyes opened wide in recognition, and she quickly ushered Priscilla to the living area in back of the store.

"Is he chasing you?" the girl asked.

"He could be, but I don't think so yet, I got a good head start and I ran pretty fast," Priscilla said with a weak smile.

The Asian girl quickly explained to her father what was going on. He quickly switched out the light at the front of his store, and turned off the store lights. He shuffled up to the cash register to retrieve a loaded shotgun, and stood firmly watching the front door.

John was fading and he didn't know how much longer he could last. He figured it had been about seven or eight minutes that he had been holding on to Brad.

Two more minutes, just two more minutes, John moaned to himself.

Brad flailed and pummeled, and John was no longer able to keep a strong choke hold, but he still held the upper hand, and his weight and size pinned the slightly smaller man to the floor.

John's head was almost cheek to cheek with Brad's. Brad's fist came up and hit John in the temple with such force that he swooned from the blow. The next thing he knew, he felt himself being pushed off the younger man beneath him. When he rolled over and hit the floor, his head hit again, knocking him out cold.

Brad leapt to his feet and locked John's chains into the restraint. He threw on some clothes and shoes and ran out of the open door to the apartment. He ran down the brown stone stairs to the street, and looked both ways. He looked east on Madison and saw only the changing street lights and the sun's first glow on the horizon. As he turned his head to look west, he noticed a light go out about four blocks away, catching his attention.

He stopped to think for a minute. The brat had probably made it to a safe place and by now had made a phone call to her parents or the police, or both. That meant there was a chance that the police could be arriving shortly. He started to run toward the extinguished light and stopped. He knew that with his bad leg he wasn't going to get there in time to return, grab John, and leave. He knew that there was no guarantee he would be able to retrieve the child anyway.

John was Brad's only hope for the final million. He ran back inside and got his knife, phone, wallet, and gun, and to administer one last insult to Melany before he left for good. He then went in to revive John who was sitting slumped on his mattress, head down, moaning and bleeding from his left eye and nose. Brad roughly grabbed him, got him to his feet, and headed for the front door.

"What's all the noise?" a slurred voice called out, almost incoherent. She closed her eyes and passed out.

"Nothing, Melany, go back to sleep. I have to go out for a minute, and I'll be right back," Brad lied and closed the front door behind them. Melany didn't hear his reply.

Brad shoved John into the car and secured his chains to the passenger side armrest. John leaned against the cool window and closed his eyes. He was in pain.

"Daddy, I'm at a grocery store, on a street called Madison, and one of the cross streets is Throop Avenue," Priscilla told her father and spelled out T H R O O P.

"Are you okay?" JT asked.

"Yes, Daddy, but I'm very worried about Papa. He was fighting with the bad man and I'm not sure he is going to win the fight. The number of the building he is in is 23680 and he is on the second floor."

"Where are you now?" JT asked.

"I'm at 23210 Madison Street," Priscilla said. JT was amazed at his daughter's calm and thorough demeanor. She knew exactly what she had to tell her father and was prepared.

"What part of town are you in, do you know?"

"Wait a minute, I'll ask Adriana," she said.

She looked at the little Laotian girl and asked what district she was in.

"This is the Bedford-Stuyvesant district," Priscilla told her father.

"Are you sure you're safe, Priscilla?" JT asked.

"Yes Daddy, I think so. Someone would have come by now I think, but these people are very nice and protecting me, the man has a gun and he's standing guard by the door."

At that moment Brad slowed down and passed the shops on the 200 block. There were a few with lights on above the stores, but the stores themselves were all still dark. He spat out the window and drove on. He still had one live Wingate left and that had to be enough. He pondered what he was going to do with Mr. Wingate for the remainder of the day. His flight wasn't until six thirty PM.

⚬

JT and his group were elated by the news of Priscilla's escape. They all hugged each other and breathed sighs of relief. They gathered around Jennifer to let her know that they were all with her.

Detective Johnson called his team into action and sent a team to both the 23680 address and the 23210 address. He contacted the Bed-Stuy Precinct and told them what he was doing and why, and asked for back-up. The Bed-Stuy police were very cooperative, and said they would secure both sites immediately, check for safety and security, help anyone in need, and wait for Detective Johnson's men to arrive.

"This still isn't over, we haven't brought John home yet," Vince soberly reminded everyone. The jubilant crowd calmed down and looked at him.

"How do you propose we proceed from here?" JT asked.

"It's business as usual," Vince said. "He's still calling the shots, and it's looking like he wants the last bag of money."

⚬

"Jake, Detective Brady called me and said that they found Brad's hiding place, and that he and some uniformed police are on their way there now," Phil reported.

"Where is the place?" Jake asked.

"Bed-Stuy. He said it was 23680 Madison Street."

"Where are you now?"

"About three blocks away from the Pussy Cat," Phil answered.

"I'll meet you out front."

Jake grabbed his medical pillow and hobbled to the door. He told his bartender to hold down the fort until he got back. Jake had to know what was going on.

"Phil, you stay here and look after the place, we'll be back soon," Jake said to his trusted bodyguard.

"Okay boss, but don't do anything foolish, the place is probably surrounded by police," Phil said.

Jake and his driver set the GPS and drove as fast as they could given the traffic and the laws.

33

RESCUE ME

Two Bed-Stuy squad cars, sirens blaring and lights flashing, pulled up to the 23210 Madison Street address with a screech of tires. Two policemen jumped out and started to cordon off the front of the building.

"I'll go around back to make sure there aren't any issues there," one of the officers said.

One officer knocked on the front door of the grocery. The Laotian proprietor immediately let him in and led him to the back where Priscilla was sitting, shaken and scared.

"Are you Priscilla Wingate?" the officer asked.

"Yes I am," Priscilla bravely answered.

"Detectives from Manhattan are on their way to get you, so please just remain where you are until they arrive. It should only be a few minutes,"

"Yes, Officer," she answered.

"Are you okay? Have you been harmed in any way?" the officer asked.

"I'm fine. A little shaky, but otherwise fine," she answered.

"Our job is to make sure you're safe and well, the other detectives are handling your case."

There was a knock on the back door and the officer went to open it. His partner told him that everything was secure in the alley, and that he would stay there until the girl was taken into custody.

A similar scene unfolded at 23680 Madison Street. Two Bed-Stuy officers secured the front and the back of the building, and two went up to Brad's second floor apartment. The door was locked and one officer ran back to his patrol car to retrieve his ram. When he returned, the two officers battered in the door. With weapons drawn, they entered the room.

"Clear," was heard from the kitchen and bathroom, and the two headed for the bedrooms.

"Clear," was heard from John and Priscilla's room.

"I got something here," came from Melany's room.

Melany lay diagonally across the bed, half naked and comatose. One of the officers felt for a pulse and found a very weak one. They turned her over on her back and saliva was oozing from her mouth.

"Ma'am are you okay?" one of the officers asked, and there was no response.

"This looks like meth to me," the other officer said, pointing at the night stand.

The officers got her to her feet and started walking her around the room. It was too small so they walked her into the living room. Her head wobbled on her shoulders and she started to cough. She was faintly aware that she was being handled by someone.

"Come on lady, try to walk."

She mumbled incoherently and they kept her moving.

The Manhattan detectives drove up and entered the building. They saw the two officers walking Melany around the room.

"We've called for paramedics, they should be here soon," an officer said.

"Anything else going on here?" the Manhattan detective asked.

"There are mattresses and chains in the far bedroom, we found this one in that bedroom. Drug paraphernalia on the night stand and what looks like a bag of meth as well. I think she got real close to an overdose."

"Keep her moving until the EMT's arrive, I want to have a little look around," the detective said.

The detective looked around the hostage room first and saw nothing out of the ordinary other than the mattresses and chains. He took photographs and went to the other bed room. He photographed Melany's room and put on rubber gloves. He collected everything from the night stand.

He walked out into the living room and noticed that the sofa had been used as a bed. A pillow and blanket were wadded up at one end. He put the bed clothes on the chair and removed the cushions. Stuffed in one corner of the sofa he found two shipping receipts, which he bagged as evidence.

In the kitchen, he photographed and bagged everything he found, including a torn violet currency band on the floor next to the refrigerator. It was partially hidden by a kitchen chair leg.

He gathered cigarette butts, beer cans, and anything else he could find.

"Sloppy bastard," he said aloud.

Back in the living room, the officers were still walking Melany. She was starting to respond, occasionally carrying her own weight for a step of two.

"Quite a looker," one of the officers said.

"That she is," said the detective. "But let's get her wrapped up in something, okay?"

Jake and his men pulled up to the front of the building and approached the officer at the front door. He asked the officer to check with the detective to see if he could enter the building. The officer returned and motioned for Jake to go in.

"Second floor, door is open. Don't touch anything."

"Aw Jesus, is she okay?" Jake asked as he walked into the room. He was taken back by her matted hair, pasty complexion, and dark circles under her eyes. He knew it was going to be a long road back if she was going to survive.

"We think so," said one of the officers. "Paramedics are on their way."

Jake had a look of deep sadness on his face. His hatred for Brad and all the pimps like him all of a sudden came to the surface. It took everything he had to maintain control. He walked up and stood directly in front of her. She raised her head and looked at him, but there was no recognition in her eyes. She dropped her head again and the police continued to walk her around.

"Hello Detective Brady," Jake said, as calmly as possible.

The detective told Jake that this was definitely the hostage apartment and that he was sure that Brad had left enough DNA to keep an army of lab techs busy for a long time. He told Jake that they found Melany, face down on the bed, very close to an overdose.

"Her panties had been pulled down and a needleless syringe was sticking out of her anus. That indicates to me that she had help taking her last hit," the detective said.

"No good son of a bitch. I had her completely clean three weeks ago. I did it then, I'll do it again," Jake said defiantly.

Brady's partner went to the 23210 address to deal with the Wingate girl. She entered the grocery store and saw Priscilla speaking with the Bed-Stuy police.

"Are you okay, Miss Wingate?" the policewoman asked. "I'm Sergeant Anderson from Manhattan."

"I'm fine Sergeant," Priscilla said with a thin smile.

"Were you molested in any way?" the sergeant asked.

"No, not really. The bad man touched me once," Priscilla said, looking down at the floor.

The sergeant asked the young Laotian girl a few questions, wrote down everyone's name, address, and phone number and told them Priscilla's family was very thankful for helping their daughter in time of need.

"The Wingates will be contacting you soon. One family member is still a hostage, which is taking all of their energy at the moment, but they will be contacting you soon," the sergeant said. "If you're ready Miss Wingate, I'll take you to your parents."

Priscilla stood up and shook hands with Adriana's parents, thanking them for their help and then gave Adriana a big hug, thanking her for her help.

"Now I'm ready," Priscilla said, taking the sergeant's hand and saying goodbye to everyone.

Priscilla rode quietly in the back of the police car. She was very concerned about her Papa and asked the policewoman if she had any news. There was none yet. Tears started to come to her eyes. It was like the whole ordeal was hitting her all at once. She was just beginning to realize the gravity of the situation she had been in.

"My Papa has to be okay," she said to the policewoman. "He's the head of the family, and everyone needs him. I need him very much, he is very important to me."

"I'm sure everything will turn out fine and your Papa will be coming home very soon," the policewoman said, trying to comfort the distraught young girl.

When Priscilla walked into her apartment, the family rushed to her, hugged her, and kissed her. Only Jennifer held back until everyone else was finished. She stepped up to the little girl and stretched out her arms to her, bending, and hugging her very hard.

"It is so good to see you back home safely," Jennifer said.

"It's good to be back, but I'm so worried about Papa. He fought with the bad man so that I could get away. Papa looked to be very strong, but the bad man looked very strong, too," Priscilla said.

"Papa will be okay, don't you worry. I'm sure we will be hearing from him very soon," Carrie said.

Carrie took Priscilla off to her bedroom.

"Take off these smelly clothes and take a good, long hot bubble bath. Soak off the last three weeks. I'll lay some fresh clothes out for you, and when you're ready, come back and join us," Carrie said. "I'm so happy that you are back safe and sound with us. My heart ached for you, but I knew you were in good hands with Papa."

"I'm so happy to be home with you too, Mommy, I prayed every night I would see you again," Priscilla said, hugging her mother. "Papa said that it was his responsibility to get me home safely, and he did."

Carrie suddenly understood why John did what he did. He had waited until the last possible moment. The kidnapper may have killed them both, and knowing John as she did, he would not let that happen, no matter what. Now she started to worry for John's life.

34

THE LAST BAG

"**W**ell, the game just got a little more exciting," said the voice into the loudspeaker. It no longer had the eerie sound of the voice changer.

"You can say that again," Vince said.

"Alright, listen to me. This afternoon I'm going to call you and give you driving instructions again. Be on First Avenue and East Fifty Eighth Street in the far left lane and be ready to go from there at exactly four o'clock."

"We're going nowhere without a proof of life between now and then," Vince said sternly.

"I understand. Our boy John is a little beaten up, but he's alive and well. You'll get your proof within the hour," the voice said, and hung up.

Jennifer looked at JT with a concerned look.

"Alright, sit up and look alive and alert," Brad said to John. "Video time."

John sat up in the passenger's side seat as best he could as Brad propped the morning paper up on his lap.

"Okay, here we go. How are you feeling, Mr. Wingate?" Brad asked.

"I'm fine," John said with an angry look on his face.

"This is your last video, Mr. Wingate, aren't you pleased?"

"Yes," John said.

"What is the date on the paper on your lap, can you see it?"

"It's today's date," John said.

Brad scanned his watch with the camera.

"Very good, I think that's enough," Brad said and turned off his camera.

"Oh my God, look at the blood on his face," Jennifer said in horror as they all watched the proof of life video.

"There was a very short message from John. He said, I OK," JT announced.

"He certainly doesn't look okay," Jennifer said. "Oh God, please bring him home safely."

JT felt confident that John was alright. He had obviously been in a fight, but those wounds heal quickly. Vince too was convinced that John was bruised, but not beaten.

Randy and JT sat at the corner of First Avenue and East Fifty Eighth, it was exactly four PM. The phone rang exactly on time.

"Okay, go the corner of First Avenue and East Fifty Ninth and turn left. Turn right onto the bridge on-ramp and maneuver into the far right hand lane, the one outside the truss. Leave the phone on," Brad said.

Randy did as they were told.

"Are you there yet?" Brad asked.

"Yes," JT answered.

"Alright, drive slowly across the bridge and just before you get to the last stone abutment structure, throw the bag at the structure hitting it between the vertical conduit on the left, and the bottom door on the right. Be accurate, you will only get one chance at this. If you miss, John is a dead man and I'll still have four mill. Understand?"

"Yes," JT said, and he heard the phone switch off.

JT opened the sunroof and stood on the floor. Most of his upper body was outside the car and he rested the bag on the roof. He saw the last stone abutment structure up ahead and got ready to throw the bag. Randy drove as close to the rail as he could as JT lifted the bag above his head and heaved it with everything he had. The sixty-five pound bag hit the structure exactly between the conduit on the left and lower door. It was a perfect throw.

A minute later the phone rang again.

"You'll find John where the bag landed," Brad said and hung up.

Brad got John out of the car and told him to sit on the sidewalk with his back against the structure. John complied.

Brad pulled out his gun and aimed it at John's head.

"Why are you doing this, we've given you everything you have asked for?" John asked. "We kept our end of the bargain."

"You're doing this to yourself asshole. You had to be the hero and fuck things up at the end. I was going to leave you and the brat at the apartment unharmed," Brad said, aiming the pistol.

The shot rang out and John slumped to the ground. Brad jumped into his car and took off North on Vernon Boulevard, to 37th Avenue, to 21st Street, heading for the Grand Central Parkway and LaGuardia Airport. Brad couldn't let John live to see which way he headed.

He drove as fast as he legally could, and made it to the airport with time to spare. He parked the car in a one hour parking space and walked to the American Airlines check-in. He checked his one travel bag and decided to carry on the last money bag. He purchased the easy check-in package and was escorted through security to the First Class Lounge. He had an hour and twenty minutes to wait.

Randy continued on in the far right lane to the Queens Plaza South off ramp. He turned right on Twenty Eighth Street, right on Forty Second Road, left on Twenty Fourth Street, and right onto Forty Third Avenue. He took Forty Third all the way to Vernon Boulevard and turned right. They went one block and noticed a police car's flashing lights and several people at the base of the bridge abutment structure. They drove past the police car and parked on the sidewalk. JT ran toward the policemen who were standing there making an initial assessment of the scene.

JT looked at John's lifeless body, slumped over on the ground. He looked up and saw where he had thrown the bag and realized John must have been standing here waiting with the kidnapper.

"That's my uncle, John Wingate," JT said.

"What is he doing here?" the officer asked.

"He was kidnapped and my driver and I were delivering the ransom money up there on the bridge," JT said, pointing up the abutment structure. "After I threw the bag of money over the side, we drove on and got back here as fast as we could. Is it okay if I cover him up with my jacket until the medics arrive?"

"Sure, go ahead, we need to ask these people some questions. Don't you go anywhere, by the way."

JT took off his jacket, walked over to John's lifeless body, and placed it over John's blood soaked head and upper torso. The police gathered in the few bystanders remaining and asked them questions.

"Did anyone see what happened?"

"I was about half a block that way," one man said, pointing south. "I heard a shot, turned around and saw a man jump into his car. He drove in that direction," pointing north on Vernon Boulevard. "That's all I know."

"Did you get a look at him?"

"No, he was too far away."

"Did anyone else see or hear anything?" the officer asked the other three people.

They all shook their heads.

The ambulance arrived and two EMTs ran up to toward the prostrate body. They went to work immediately to see if there was a pulse or if there was anything they could do to help the man lying on the ground.

"I found a shell casing," one EMT said to the policeman.

Seconds passed, and the other EMT looked at the police officer and shook his head. They brought out a gurney and body bag and loaded John's body into the ambulance.

JT walked up to the ambulance and spoke to the driver. After introducing himself, he asked where the body would be taken. He gave the driver his business card and walked back to the policeman, who was finishing up his investigation.

"I have reason to believe that the man that shot my uncle is either at, or heading to, one of the airports right now," JT said.

"With a bag full of money, he's going to have difficulty getting through security," the officer said.

"Can you have your precinct do something to try to stop the man?" JT asked.

"Not until I've had a chance to speak with my supervisors."

"Can you do that now, please?" JT asked.

"Not until I get back to the precinct," the uniformed policeman stubbornly replied.

JT got on the phone and called Vince at his apartment.

"Vince, I've got very bad news, and I would appreciate your hearing me out before you say anything into the phone," JT began.

"Go ahead," Vince said in a somber voice.

JT quickly related the entire afternoon's experience and told Vince to come up with a story to delay telling anyone the news until he could return, and to get the police interested in checking the airports as soon as possible.

"We're on our way back now," JT said.

JT hung up the phone and Vince looked at the gathered family.

"That was JT. He told me that he's delivered the last bag successfully and is waiting for the kidnapper to call him with John's whereabouts," Vince skillfully said, keeping the family in the dark.

"Did he say when the call was supposed to come?" Jennifer asked.

"He doesn't know when the call will come, but he'll call us immediately when it happens."

The family looked around at each other, and the most worried member was Jennifer. Everyone looked at her with comforting looks, but she had to get up and temporarily leave the room.

"I'll be right back," she said as she walked out.

"Did he say anything else?" Carrie asked. "You were on the phone with him for a long time."

"He was giving me the details of the delivery. It was another bridge toss, like the last one, only this time it was at the Ed Koch Queensboro Bridge, south abutment, next to Vernon Boulevard," Vince quickly said.

A half hour later, JT walked into the apartment. He noticed that Jennifer wasn't in the room, and walked toward her bedroom. The door was closed. He rapped quietly, and Jennifer appeared at the door. She knew immediately that the news was not good. JT walked into the room, put his arms around her, and held her tightly.

"John didn't make it," he whispered in her ear.

Her body slumped as if all life had left her. JT braced himself against her weight, and sat her down on her bed where she immediately broke down sobbing and moaning.

"No, no, no, no," she cried over and over again.

The rest of the family heard the cries and rushed back to the bedroom. JT looked up at them and shook his head. Everyone understood, even little Priscilla. JT hugged Carrie and Priscilla as they both broke down. Joe and Peg comforted Jennifer and broke down themselves.

Jennifer stayed in her room as the rest of the family moved back to the living room.

"Who's going to tell Mother Priscilla?" Carrie asked.

"I will," Joe said. "She is my mother as well, and she needs to hear it from me."

Joe and Peg left the group and walked the two blocks to Mother Priscilla's apartment.

Mother Priscilla was surprised to see them.

"Hello Mom, how are you feeling?" Joe said walking through the door.

"I'm fine son, to what do I owe this nice surprise?"

Peg walked up to her, hugged her, and led her to the living room. They sat on the couch together and Joe sat in a chair across from them.

"Mom, I have some very bad news for you, I'm afraid. John was killed today."

Priscilla gasped audibly. "No, it can't be true, what happened?"

"We haven't been truthful with you for the last three weeks, Mom, because John and little Priscilla were taken by a kidnapper and we didn't want to alarm you."

Priscilla sat wide eyed, listening intently to Joe's story. Peg sat close to her with one arm around her shoulders, and the other holding her hand. Priscilla began sobbing.

"Little Priscilla managed to escape with John's help, but John was not so fortunate," Joe went on. "The kidnapper killed him in cold blood as soon as the ransom had been delivered."

"Oh my God," Mother Priscilla said. "What do we do now?"

Joe reassured her that although John's presence would be missed, everyone would stand up and take over. He told her that JT, with his and Carrie's help, would continue to run the business and that everything would remain the same.

Joe asked if she would like to move to JT's house temporarily to be near everyone and be part of the family. She said that she thought that would be very nice. The two got Mother Priscilla packed up and brought her to JT's apartment where everyone met her at the door and hugged her and made her welcome.

The six bedroom apartment had ample room for everyone with room to spare. Joe and Peg continued to sleep at their own apartment, but were with the family nearly all the day and night. The office managers had direct access to everyone, but tried not to disrupt the grieving family.

The dinner gathering was initially very somber. Little Priscilla said grace while holding her grandmother's hand. Jennifer walked in just as the prayer was finished. She had washed away her grief and looked as though she was ready for a photo shoot. JT, at the head of the table where John usually sat, stood and helped her with her chair.

35

A VERY SLOW START

"What in God's name do you mean you haven't checked the airports yet?" JT yelled into the phone. "It's been three hours, he must be gone by now."

"We did call the airport police, and we did send them ID photos, but we personally haven't been to the airports yet. It is a huge undertaking, JT, especially when we don't know which airport he's using, JFK or LaGuardia, let alone which terminal," Detective Johnson said with some guilt in his voice which JT heard loud and clear.

"You and I are going to touch bases daily, and you're going to come clean with me and keep me informed. I have resources, as you know, and I am going to get the son-of-a bitch that did this, or else," JT fired back.

"I promise to maintain my end of things, as we have all along, JT. I am still a little upset that you didn't allow us to participate in the bag deliveries," Johnson said. "But that is spilled milk. From here on in we work openly together."

"What have you got so far?" JT asked.

Detective Johnson listed all of the items that were found at the hostage apartment, including a nearly overdosed Melany Barton. He told JT that nothing out of the ordinary was found at the grocery store where Priscilla was picked up, and gave JT the address, names, and phone number.

"We also got a tip from Jake O'Malley, the owner of the Pussy Cat Club where Melany apparently worked, that Brad had visited a rifle range on 20th Avenue that we are checking out now," Johnson said.

Johnson went on to tell JT that he had been assigned the case and promised to bring justice to the family for John's death.

"Out of curiosity, what were the mailing addresses on the two shipping receipts found at the hostage apartment?" JT asked.

"They were both the same address but different dates, 117 W 23rd Street, Scottsbluff, Nebraska," Johnson said. "Looks to us like the second and third bags, or at least part of the second and third bags, were sent to that address. I'm personally going out there as soon as I can get the case number and the funding to do so."

"Very good, we we'll talk again tomorrow," JT said and hung up.

JT immediately called Trent McSpadden.

"Hello JT, so sorry to hear of John's death, my condolences to the entire family, he will be sorely missed," Trent said.

"Thank you, Trent, believe me, the road ahead is going to be a tough one," JT said. "What I'm calling about is that I want to catch the bastard who did this and it's going to take a few good men to pull it off."

"What is your plan, JT?"

JT related the details of the last deliveries, and the revelations he had just learned from the Detective Johnson.

"Apparently, on the day following my delivery of bag number two and bag number three, the kidnapper sent a sixty-five pound parcel to an address in Scottsbluff, Nebraska," JT said. "Smells strongly of an accomplice, and the police haven't yet jumped on it, or they haven't leveled with me yet. I want to get someone on it right away."

"How do you want to approach this?" Trent asked.

"I really don't know," JT said. "I hoped you might have an idea."

"If we go in, guns blazing, we risk the situation of your kidnapper going deep underground and possibly losing him. I think we should try and search the shipping address, and see what we come up with. If we find something, we can work out a plan with the police, or without them. We can make that decision at that time."

"How soon can you get someone on it?"

"Remember Jim "Jumbo" Reimer? If he's not on a gig, I can get him there tomorrow. If he's busy, I'll get up there myself by tomorrow evening."

"Let's stay in touch on a daily basis for a while, and I'll keep you posted on what the police are doing here."

"Sounds good JT, I'll call you tomorrow," Trent said and hung up.

Detective Johnson got into his office early. The lab had completed a study of all the garbage that was picked up at the hostage apartment. He read the list of items and the lab tech's comments. Three items piqued his curiosity: a travel brochure of Mexico City, one of San Jose, Costa Rica, and one to Phuket, Thailand. Detective Johnson decided to leave these three items off of the list for the time being, at least until he could have time to digest all of the items. He listed them as *UNKNOWN A, UNKNOWN B* and *UNKNOWN C.*

"Mr. McSpadden, it is good to hear from you, Sir," Jim "Jumbo" Reimer, US Navy Seal Retired, said.

"Jim, please call me Trent and let me get straight to the point. Are you on a gig right now?" Trent asked, omitting the niceties.

"No, free as a bird."

"Great. John Wingate has been killed, and his nephew, JT Wingate, called me this morning with a request to get some information, and you live very close to the source in Scottsbluff."

"Aw, I'm sorry to hear that, I really liked that man. You're right though, Scottsbluff is less than a hundred miles, about an hour and a half by car," Reimer said, keeping to business.

"I want you to get down there as quickly as you can and see if you can find anything of interest at an address I'll give you before I hang up. John was kidnapped and the ransom money, four million total, was delivered in four sixty-eight pound duffle bags. We're sure at least two have been sent to the address. We need to be very careful not to cause any alarm. We believe the kidnapper has fled the New York area, and we don't want to drive him any deeper underground," Trent said.

Reimer told him that he understood, and said that it would probably be wisest to stake out the address for a day or two before searching the property.

Trent gave Reimer the address and told him to call as soon as he learned something new.

"JT is hell bent on catching the kidnapper, and he thinks we're the team to get it done."

Jim Reimer put down the phone, packed a three day bag, and told his wife he would be gone for a few days. She knew not to ask where, and she knew he would contact her as soon as he could. She worried but didn't fret. He got in his Jeep Cherokee Laredo and drove off toward Scottsbluff. The hour and forty minute drive wound west out of Chadron on Highway 20 to Crawford; south on Highway 2, through the west end of Nebraska National Forest to Highway 71, then west and finally south to Scottsbluff. The expansive prairie lands gave Reimer a strong feeling of home, roots and wellbeing, though he remembered his years growing up in rural Nebraska wondering what lay beyond the endless grassland tracts and what the rest of the world had to offer.

Ten miles out of Scottsbluff, Reimer pulled over on the shoulder of the rural highway, got out and fixed several magnetic stickers to the doors of the Jeep that read Reimer's House Painting. There were false phone numbers and email addresses advertising free estimates.

Back on the road, Reimer entered Scottsbluff and turned left on to Highway 26. At the intersection of Highway 26 and Avenue B, he pulled in to the Hampton Inn and Suites and got a room for his three night stay. He would not be spending much time there, just long enough for cat naps, showers, and changes of clothes.

Reimer got back into his Jeep and headed south on Avenue B to West 23rd Street. He turned right on West 23rd Street and cruised past address 117, all the time looking for a good vantage point to observe the property. He found an excellent place on Avenue A across the street from his quarry. He shut down the engine and began the two day and night observation. It was difficult to conceal himself, so he moved his vehicle several times, giving himself numerous different vantage points.

There was a knock on his passenger side window that startled him. He looked over and lowered the window.

"Everything okay?" the senior citizen stranger asked.

"Everything is just fine, friend, I'm just catching up on some paperwork and getting ready to go to my next estimate," Reimer answered.

"Need any directions?" the man asked.

"No thanks, I have my trusty GPS," Reimer said, patting the Garmin nuviCam mounted on his dashboard. "Gets me there every time."

"Newfangled gadgets, you young people have everything, don't ya?" the passerby said.

"Seems so," Reimer said.

"All right then, I'll be getting along, have a nice day."

Reimer thanked the man and rolled up his heavily tinted window.

Hours ticked by with no further activity. He reached into his glovebox for his package of gum when the front door of 117 opened. An attractive woman in her late thirties or early forties dressed in tight jeans and a form-fitting sweater stepped out, locked the door, and walked to a late model, pale blue Ford Fiesta parked at the curb. She got in, made a u-turn and drove off toward Broadway and turned right in the direction of downtown. At East 16th Street, she turned left and parked in front of *The Woodpile, Restaurant and Spirits*, interestingly nestled between a small storefront Baptist Church and a Spiritual Bookstore.

Reimer watched her walk into the restaurant and parked six spaces beyond. When he walked into the restaurant, all heads, including his mark's, turned to look at his imposing frame. His six-foot-four, muscular physique commanded the room. He saw the woman at the far end of the bar sitting next to a man wearing a ball cap. He situated himself at a table, affording him clear view of her activities.

He was hungry and looked at the menu. He noticed a large selection of organic meal selections, along with the usual Nebraska offerings of steak of any type or size.

"What'll it be, Stranger?" the uniformed waitress asked him.

He ordered a twelve-ounce Ribeye steak with a baked potato and asparagus.

The man and woman at the bar were laughing and drinking beer. She seemed very interested, he appeared attentive. The bartender knew the pair by their first names. The waitress brought them napkins and silverware to eat at the bar.

"Here you are, Stranger, Ribeye rare," the waitress said. "Enjoy."

Reimer ate his meal, occasionally glancing around the room, always keeping the man and woman at the bar in his sights. He finished his meal and asked for his check. He paid in cash and left the restaurant. Outside, he went to his vehicle and waited for the couple to exit. The woman went to her car, and the man went to his pickup truck, which was parked heading in the opposite direction. The pick-up drove off first, and Reimer and the woman stayed put. Within minutes, the pick-up returned and tooted his horn as he passed the woman in the blue Ford Fiesta. Reimer slumped down as far as his six-foot-four frame would allow as both vehicles passed by him. He pulled away from the curb and followed.

The pick-up, leading the procession, drove northwest out of town into the rural countryside. Reimer had to lag far behind on the straight, flat road to avoid detection. As he drove past one of the several gravel off-shoot roads, he noticed the pick-up and the blue Ford Fiesta pull up in front of a forties era farm house, a dust plume settling in their headlights. He kept driving out the rural road. Two miles further he u-turned and back-tracked to town. He noticed the two cars still in the gravel driveway illuminated by a bare porch light.

Reimer decided to go back to his motel and wait an hour or two before going back to check on the couple. When he returned to the farm house, he noticed that the Ford Fiesta was gone but the pick-up remained. *A quickie,* Reimer remarked to himself as he drove back to 117 W 23rd Street.

The blue Ford Fiesta was parked in front of the house where it had been earlier in the day. There was a single light on in the rear of the house and Reimer decided to have a look. He parked his Jeep around the corner and walked back up an alley toward 117. The light was still on as he crept up to the window and looked in. The woman had just gotten out of her shower, and she stood naked in front of her full length mirror, looking at herself up and down, smiling and brushing her hair.

Reimer walked back to his Jeep and decided to wait to see what would happen next. One hour later the bedroom light went out, and there was no further activity at 117. Reimer drove back to his motel and went directly to bed. It had been a long, dreary day.

The next morning Reimer woke at six AM. He went for a two mile run, showered, ate breakfast and drove directly to 117 to continue the surveillance. The Thursday morning air was crisp and clean, smelling of prairie grass. At eight thirty the woman, wearing a business-like dress, sweater, and sensible high heel shoes walked out of the house, locked the door behind her and got into her blue Ford Fiesta. She drove in the same direction she had driven the previous evening. She pulled into a parking lot next to the Platte River Bank, got out, and walked energetically to the front door.

Reimer waited fifteen minutes and walked into the bank. He noticed the woman sitting alone in one of the small private offices with a sign on the glass partition saying Loan Officer, Sharon Blanchet.

Reimer stood in the teller line until a position opened up. He walked up and handed the teller a one hundred dollar bill.

"Could you give me four twenties and two tens please?" He asked.

The teller checked the bill for authenticity and opened her cash drawer.

"Twenty, forty, sixty, eighty, ninety, one hundred," the teller said, looking up at him with a smile.

"Thank you, miss," Reimer said and turned to walk out.

Loan Officer, Sharon Blanchet had left her office and was walking in his direction. She did a double take as she looked at him on her way to the teller counter.

"Didn't I see you last night at the Woodpile?" the woman asked cordially and with a big smile.

"You might have ma'am, I had a nice dinner there last night."

"I never forget a face," she said. "And you managed to turn a few heads when you walked in. Are you from around here? I've never seen you before," she asked.

"No ma'am, I'm in from Omaha for two or three days to do a little business, then I'm headed home again."

"Well, if there's anything we can help you with bank-wise, please let me know," she handed him her card, smiled, and walked off.

"Thanks," Reimer answered and left the bank.

Reimer wasn't sure if this was just a very friendly bank or if he was being hit on, but the vision of Sharon Blanchet, naked in front of her bedroom mirror, flashed into his consciousness.

That evening, Reimer sat surveillance until ten PM, when he saw Sharon Blanchet's bedroom light go out. He decided that the next morning he would park in the back of the bank parking lot and wait for her, then go search her house while she was at work.

She arrived at exactly eight thirty-five and he noticed that she was wearing tight jeans, a cowboy shirt, and boots. *Casual Friday*, he thought.

He started his Jeep and rolled slowly out of the parking lot. He decided to park in front of 117 and pick the front door lock. Within seconds, he was inside and beginning his search. He used gloves and was careful to see that everything he touched went back into its original position. Finished with the living room and dining area, he searched the kitchen. Nothing. He moved on through the single story house to the bedrooms and bathroom. Nothing. He had been there two hours and found nothing. He sat on the edge of Sharon's unmade bed and scratched his head. He noticed a ceiling panel in the hallway.

He reached up easily and pulled down the Werner 8 Ft. attic ladder. Carefully he climbed to the top and looked into the attic. Neatly stacked, within arm's reach, were four duffle bags with the Double O logo clearly stenciled on the sides and ends. He decided not to risk an accident by walking in the attic with his two hundred and thirty pound frame. He took several photos with his cell phone, climbed back down and returned the ladder to its original position.

He looked around to see if he had caused any dust, dirt, or other foreign particles to fall on the floor around where the ladder had stood. He noticed some dust beside the hall runner carpet and wiped it up with some damp toilet paper and put the paper in his pocket. He went to the front door to leave and something told him to look out the peep hole. Sharon was walking up the entrance walk, looking back at Reimer's Jeep.

"Shit," Reimer said, quickly locking the front door.

He hurried to the back and quietly let himself out. He couldn't lock the back door and ran as fast as he could down the alley toward the far side of the neighboring house. He quickly walked over to the church on W 23rd Street and walked in. He sat in a pew and waited.

"That's strange," Sharon said aloud. "I could swear that I locked that door this morning after I brought the garbage out."

She locked the door and jiggled the handle to make sure it was locked. She looked up at the attic ladder, out of curiosity, satisfied herself that it hadn't been moved and walked out into her living room. She found the book she had come home to retrieve and walked to the front door. She locked the front door and double checked it to make sure. Walking back to her car, she noticed Reimer's Jeep and wondered who was having their house painted. She shrugged her shoulders and got into her car, then drove back to the bank.

36

THAT WAS CLOSE

Reimer walked to the front of the church and opened the door enough to look down the block toward 117. He noticed that the blue Ford Fiesta was gone. He walked out the entrance and the big oak church door closed heavily behind him. He walked to his Jeep and got behind the wheel. He drove off slowly and breathed a sigh of relief. That was too close.

He parked two blocks away and made his phone calls, the first of which was to Trent McSpadden.

"I just sent you a picture of the bags I saw in the woman's attic. Her name is Sharon Blanchet, she's a loan officer at the Platte River Bank here in Scottsbluff. She's an attractive woman in her late thirties or early forties and lives alone, but has at least one boyfriend that she's intimate with," Reimer reported.

"Stick around one more night Jim. I'll call Wingate and see what he wants to do next and get back to you as soon as I find out," McSpadden said. "Good work, by the way."

Reimer drove back to the Platte River Bank and took up a position as far away as he could and still keep his eye on the blue Ford Fiesta. It was three PM, and the bank would be open for two more hours.

"JT, this is Trent McSpadden,"

"How are you, Trent?" JT asked. "Anything to report yet?"

"Quite a bit," Trent said and went on, telling JT everything that Jim Reimer had told him.

"Wow, he's learned a lot in a very short period of time," JT remarked.

"I've told him to stay on in Scottsbluff until I had a chance to talk with you and find out where you want to go from here."

"We now know where the money is, we know that the woman Sharon Blanchet is the accomplice, and we know that the kidnapper is going to be calling for it soon," JT said.

"How do you feel about tapping her phone?" Trent asked. "Reimer knows how to do that, could have it done by tomorrow afternoon."

"If we do that, I'm going to have to let the police know what we are doing, and we don't want them going in guns blazing and scaring the hell out of everybody."

"It's probably a good idea to tell them anyway," Trent said.

"Okay Trent, get Reimer going on the tap, and I'll talk with the police."

"Detective Johnson, this is JT Wingate. I have a few things I need to tell you, shall we do it over the phone, or do you want to get together?"

"Let's get together this afternoon, I can come to your office," Johnson offered.

"How about three o'clock?"

"I'll be there," Johnson said, and the two men hung up.

"JT, how are you, Sir?" Detective Johnson asked, offering his hand.

"As well as can be expected, I suppose. The funeral is this weekend, and I dread the day. My uncle was the mainstay of the family, the spirit of our business, and the man I looked to on almost a daily basis," JT said, looking out his office window.

"I can imagine your anguish," Johnson said. "I felt the same way about my father, and his death caused me years of anguish. I'm at peace with everything now, but those years were tough."

The two men commiserated a little longer and sat down at JT's magnificent desk.

"Detective, I've sent a man, a US Navy Seal, Retired, to the Scottsbluff address you gave me, and he confirms that four Double O duffle bags are stacked in the attic," JT announced, pushing Reimer's photograph across the desk to Johnson.

"Did he open the bags and confirm that the money was in fact in there?" the detective asked.

"He is six-foot-four and weighs in at around two hundred and forty pounds. He was concerned about the attic ladder and the attic itself, and decided not to go all the way up. He took the picture instead."

"Sure looks like the right bags, most likely they are," Johnson said.

"I'm convinced," JT answered. "We have also placed a tap on the occupant's phone."

"That could be an issue for us going forward," Johnson stated. "We typically require warrants for that sort of thing. We'll cross that bridge when we get to it."

JT continued to tell Detective Johnson all of the information Reimer was able to learn in his short stay so far. The detective wrote furiously in his notebook, not wanting to miss anything.

"How are you coming on your end?" JT asked.

"We've been given a tight budget to send one man to Scottsbluff, but I think we'll hold off on that for the time being, and use your man's information, if that is okay with you."

JT nodded.

"I have a confession to make, however. There were three items that we found at the kidnapper's apartment that I didn't tell you about. They were travel brochures for Mexico City; San Jose, Costa Rica; and Phuket, Thailand, three of the easiest cities for a white expatriate to get lost in. There are many other similar cities that would work as well, and he may have left these behind to throw us off the track," Johnson said. "Just in case, we're contacting Interpol and city police for each of the three cities asking them to be on the lookout and apprehend. I don't hold out too much hope, however."

JT was not visibly upset by the detective's confession, but he did catalogue it for future use. Both were doing things the other didn't know about. JT knew he would have to develop a method to keep the detective as forthright as possible, and probably the only way he was going to do that was to be forthright with him.

"I'm going to keep my man in Scottsbluff for a while. Here's his cell phone number, I'll let him know you may be calling. Feel free to have him help you in any way he can."

Detective Johnson got up to leave and shook JT's hand across the desk. The two men thanked each other and the detective left the office.

"Jim, this is JT."

"Yes, Mr. Wingate, how can I help you?"

JT told Reimer of his conversation with the police and told him to be as helpful to the police as he could. He also told him about the three travel brochures the police had found and asked him to keep an ear out for any conversations the woman might have regarding the three cities.

"What did the detective say when you told him we had a tap going?" Reimer asked.

"He was concerned, but he thought he had some ideas as to how to overcome the warrant problem."

JT wanted Reimer to stay on in Scottsbluff and asked if it was going to be a problem. Reimer said that he had thought his stay might get extended and that there was no problem doing that. JT thanked him for his dedication, and told him it shouldn't be too long now before the kidnapper surfaced. He asked Reimer to be vigilant.

"Trent, I've been in contact with Jim Reimer, and I asked him to stay on in Scottsbluff for a while, if that is okay with you?" JT said.

"It's fine, JT," Trent answered.

"Great. Trent, I'd like you to come by the office and spend some time going through some 'what ifs' with me, can you do that?"

"I just happen to be in New York this week, and would be happy to stop by. What's a good time for you?" Trent said.

"I'm open for the entire afternoon today. What about having lunch with me at Henri's?" JT asked.

"That would be fine, one o'clock?"

The two men met at exactly one PM and sat at JT's regular table.

"This is really Déjà Vu, all over again," Trent said with a smile, offering his hand to JT.

"You can say that again," JT remarked, pun intended.

"I had so many wonderful meals here with your uncle. Sitting here makes me miss him very much," Trent said.

"I know what you mean, Trent. I learned most of what I know about the shipping business across this table from John," JT said, a sudden sense of sorrow and longing gripping him.

The two men shared their experiences of John in a way that men of mutual respect for another often do. They spoke in reverence of a man they both held in very high esteem. They each listened assiduously, wanting the experiences of the other.

"Trent, as you know, we tracked down the money, or rather eighty percent of it, and what you don't know is that there were three travel brochures found in the trash at the kidnapper's apartment. The subjects were Mexico City; San Jose, Costa Rica; and Phuket, Thailand," JT began.

"All three marvelous places to hide," Trent remarked.

"Detective Johnson commented that leaving the brochures in the trash could have been a ruse to throw us off," JT said. "But the fact remains that he went somewhere, and I'm guessing it's out of the country. My question is, what do you think will be our best plan to get him back to stand trial for his crimes?"

Trent looked down at his Butternut Squash soup for a moment, then looked back up at JT. He was hesitant to speak too quickly, but if the kidnapper was in any one of the three places JT named, red tape and international intrigue would severely cloud the issue and a return might never occur.

"Your uncle and I were confronted with the exact same situation, as you know, and I'm afraid that the only quick solution would be a similar snatch and grab," Trent said.

"That was the first thing that crossed my mind, but as I thought about it, the list of negatives grew and grew. What if we're caught? How could the police turn a blind eye to such an action? If he gets a jury trial, what are the legalities and pitfalls there? It goes on and on," JT said with some frustration in his voice.

"I hear your concerns JT, and frankly I don't have the answers on the tip of my tongue."

"I'm apprehensive as well, but mark my words, one way or another, that bastard is going to pay for his crime."

The two men finished their lunch and walked back to JT's office to continue their discussions.

"JT, there is a Mr. Reimer for you on line one," JT's assistant said into the intercom.

37

A FEW GOOD MEN

"Hello Jim, I have you on speaker phone, Trent is here with me," JT began.

"Hello boss, hi JT, I've got some news for you," Reimer said. "I listened in on a call from the kidnapper and I think I know where he might be. It was a short call, letting the sister know that he's looking for a place to settle and he will call in a few days to give her instructions on sending the duffle bags."

"So where do you think he is?" Trent asked.

"The whole time he was on the phone, I heard Mariachi music in the background," Reimer said.

"So you're guessing he's in Mexico City?" JT asked.

"Right," Reimer said.

"I've heard some of the greatest Mariachi music in Phuket bars," Trent said. "And Mariachi is no stranger to San Jose, Costa Rica."

"Yes, but he also said that his flight took him a little over seven hours," Reimer said.

"That eliminates Phuket, that's a twenty-two to twenty-three hour flight. However, Mexico City and San Jose, Costa Rica are about the same air distance and time from here, between seven and seven and a half hours," Trent said." I think we narrowed it down to those two, but we're still up in the air."

The three men talked for a short while longer and it was decided that Jim should stay put in Scottsbluff, at least until the next phone call, and then a plan could be put in place.

"Jim, what do you think it would take to snatch that bastard from either Mexico City or San Jose?" JT asked.

Reimer told the two men that he had been in on a raid in Mexico City once and that it was accessible by helicopter from Brownsville, Texas. He said it was a 900 mile round trip, and would require a 1000 plus mile range capacity. Reimer mentioned that the San Jose logistics were much worse and doubted if the city could be reached by helicopter from the United States.

"What if we put a helicopter on one of our RO RO ships in international waters off the Mexican or the Costa Rican coast?" JT inquired.

"That would solve logistical problems completely, and the helicopter is definitely the proper extraction tool," Trent said.

"Do you have a computer with you, Jim?" JT asked.

"I don't," was Jim's reply.

"Get one locally and work out various scenarios for an extraction by helicopter. I have a nautical chart in front of me that says the nearest Gulf Coast pick up point is approximately 155 to 160 miles from the center of Mexico City, and 80 to 85 miles from central San Jose. The company owns a Bell 206L4 Helicopter that I am licensed to fly and we could get it and a RO RO in place in less than a week. The Bell has a range of 380 miles at cruising speed, and has a payload of 2,100 pounds."

"I'll work around those numbers and see what I can come up with. I assume that this will be a clandestine effort, correct?" Reimer asked.

"For now, that is correct," McSpadden said. "No discussions with the police."

"Anything new to report about the woman?" JT asked.

"Not really, but she is active. She sees her boyfriend every other night, she works late at the bank often, she jogs in the evenings sometimes when she gets home. I have to make sure she doesn't spot me when she runs by. She seems like a pretty good citizen," Reimer reported.

"Yeah, a good citizen with four million dollars in ransom money in her attic," Trent said.

The three men talked on for another five minutes and hung up.

The following night, Jim Reimer called JT again. He had worked out three scenarios and laid each one out for both JT and Trent, who was on a conference line. Reimer felt that the optimum plan required three men and a pilot. He wasn't sure how much surveillance would be required, but three eight hour shifts would be required for at least a night or two, maybe more, until they learned the kidnapper's patterns.

"I think the pick-up should be out of town, if he's living in town," Reimer said, "It might be difficult getting the helicopter into a heavily inhabited area."

"Five million dollars goes a long way in Mexico and Costa Rica. There's a good chance he might get a place out, away from the hustle and bustle," JT said.

"OK, I think we are set with the basics," Trent interrupted. "Now all we have to do is wait for that phone call."

"What if the kidnapper doesn't have the bundles sent to his home? What if he has them sent to a PO Box?" JT questioned. "I think that is what I would do."

"We'll get someone down there the day after the phone call and stake out the PO Box. When someone looking like our guy comes in, we tail him and find out where he lives, or just take him right then and there."

"Jim, round up two more Seals and get them on the payroll. Make sure they have their passports," JT said. "Have you got your passport with you?"

"I don't, I'll have to have my wife overnight it to me at the hotel," Reimer answered.

Jim Reimer called his friends and fellow Seals Bob "Butcher" Malfanti and Charles "Chunk" Farrington in South Carolina. Both were free and more than willing to join the effort.

"Aw man, I'm really sorry to hear about John Wingate, I had a lot of time for that man," Charles said.

Both Bob and Charles agreed to be in Gering, a small town just south of Scottsbluff, by the following evening.

Reimer told them there was a shuttle to the Monument Inn Hotel and Suites from Western Nebraska Regional. He instructed them to bring passports and be prepared for anywhere up to a month's effort. Bring a knife and a gun, and plan to be in civvies for the entire gig, nothing fancy. They want to blend in with the expatriate community.

JT got on the phone with Trent and asked him to take the lead with the three Seals and make sure they had everything they needed to pull off the plan.

"Weapons, clothing, phones, communications gear, air tickets, hotel rooms, the works. We are only going to get one chance at this bastard, so we had best get it right," JT said.

"I understand that Bob Malfanti and Charles Farrington will be in Scottsbluff tomorrow evening. I'll get with them and make sure they get their planning completed," Trent promised.

"Trent, I have a RO RO in Galveston, Texas that has a heli-pad. I'm going to keep it there for the time being. As soon as you give me the word, I can have the 206L4 there in half a day, and from there it is a day and a half to Mexico and a little over three and a half days to Costa Rica," JT said, "So I'm two to four days away, maximum."

The next night, Trent set up a three way conference call with JT and Reimer. It was 9:30 PM in New York, 7:30 PM in Scottsbluff/Gering and 8:30 PM in Fort Worth, Texas. Bob and Charles gave their condolences to JT as the conference began.

"Thank you, fellas. John's passing has hit us all here pretty hard," JT said. "I don't have to tell you we're not going to let the bastard go unpunished."

"We're putting the finishing touches on our plans, and will be ready to go at a moment's notice," Reimer reported.

Reimer offered the details of the plan to the group. As soon as the kidnappers call is intercepted, the Seals will visit Sharon Blanchet and take her into custody before she can ship the money or warn or communicate with anyone. The Seals will take her and the duffle bags to the holding place and then to the airport, where a chartered flight will be waiting to take the Seals to the kidnapper's location.

The Seals will then orient themselves and find a place to stay. The Seals then stake out the delivery address and either apprehend the kidnapper immediately or wait for him to show up for the delivery and follow him to his residence.

"I have a few questions so far," JT interrupted.

"Yes, Sir," Reimer said.

"Where is the holding area and who is doing the holding?"

"My wife is a retired Naval Officer with special training," Reimer said, "She will be able to handle everything until we complete our mission. She'll meet us at the airport."

"What if the kidnapper is planning to have someone rather than himself pick up the duffle bags?" JT asked. "Or what if he has them sent to several places before he finally shows up. What if he's not in either place we think he will be, and leapfrogs the duffle bags a few times before he finally picks them up?"

"Excellent questions, Sir," Reimer said. "We hadn't considered all those possibilities."

"I'll tell you what I think," JT offered. "I think we should have at least one more, three-man back-up team that could respond to whatever might arise. I think that the first part of your plan is great and should go down the way you have planned it, but a plan B and

C are a must. We only have one shot at this guy before he goes deep underground."

"That means we need to be prepared to actually ship the bags," Trent said. "We'll need to get four more and fill them with fake bills or some other equivalent-weight material. The kidnapper knows how much the bags weigh and will be looking closely at the gross weights."

"I'll get four more bags to you by special courier tomorrow, and you should use the originals for the actual shipment. He may have marked the bags somehow for his own secret identification," JT said.

Trent and the Seals remembered how John Wingate had the same uncanny ability to find holes in plans, and they were impressed with JT's competence. He was obviously following in John's footsteps. The men would have to do a little scrambling over the next several days to catch up.

"JT, we moved to a new hotel in Gering, a small town just south of Scottsbluff. The woman has met me, and I don't want to accidentally run into her. I told her I was only in town for a few days," Reimer said, and gave JT the address.

"Very good then, let's all get our tasks completed quickly and we'll communicate again tomorrow night," Trent said, and they all hung up.

Reimer went down his list trying to find four more Seals that could travel immediately. By the seventh name, he had filled the list. Malfanti and Farrington took on the task of creating the fake currency bundles.

Malfanti went out and bought several types of paper, three heavy-duty paper cutters, and a super-sensitive, digital, AWS Scalemate scale, accurate to .01grams. He recreated the 6.4 inch by 2.5 inch bill from several different types of bond and found that the seventy-five percent cotton bond most closely matched the one gram weight of an actual bill. The hundred, twenty, ten, five and one dollar bills are all the same size and weight, the men now had their work cut out for them, literally.

Malfanti calculated that they could create four fake bills from one sheet of paper. He calculated that it would take 56 reams of paper to create the four million dollars in fake bills. He was fortunate enough to find what he needed at the four Stationers' and one Target located in the Scottsbluff/Gering area.

Malfanti determined that it would take about seventy five man-hours to complete the cutting task, and another fifteen man-hours to bundle the fake bills. With three men, working steadily, it would take thirty hours to finish. They would have to hold their breath that the kidnapper's call came in after that. They got down to the task immediately.

38

THE FUNERAL

Saturday morning, the family arose early and prepared for their day of bereavement. The church ceremony was to be held at St. Patrick's Cathedral, and John was to be buried at First Calvary Cemetery, Queens.

Jennifer was the last to appear in the living room, along with the rest of the family including Priscilla, the elder. JT tried to comfort everyone and escorted Jennifer and his grandmother to the waiting limousines as Carrie and little Priscilla followed behind. There were easily three hundred to four hundred people at the service. When the mass was over, the motorcade proceeded to the cemetery.

At graveside, JT stood between Jennifer and Carrie, little Priscilla stood to Jennifer's right. Jennifer reached for Carrie's hand and held it tightly as the two stepped up to place their single black roses on the casket. Little Priscilla, alone, placed her pink rose on the coffin, and blew it a kiss. Three Seals who had worked closely with John and the family in Hobyo stepped up and pinned their Tridents to the coffin. JT followed with Priscilla senior on his arm. She faltered momentarily at the coffin, but composed herself quickly and moved on.

John's brother Joe and his wife Peg were the last to visit the coffin. The family, with the exception of Priscilla senior, stood together as mourners passed by, offering condolences, hugs, and handshakes.

Jake O'Malley walked up to JT and offered his condolences. Jake quickly told JT who he was and about his relationship with Melany. He offered his services and resources to JT, and told him that he was very interested in seeing justice done after what had happened to Melany.

"How is Melany doing, by the way?" JT asked the club owner.

"She is back in rehab, and they tell me it will be several more weeks before she can be released. She was completely clean and happy before that bastard got hold of her. She means a lot to me, and I'll continue helping her," Jake said.

"Do you have any information where Brad might be now?" JT asked.

"I don't," Jake said. "He has completely vanished. No one has seen or heard from him in weeks."

"Did you know him well enough to know where he might have gone?" JT persisted.

"I'm sorry, I have no idea," Jake said. "I really didn't know him as a friend. He was an irritant to me and Melany. I kicked the crap out of him once for physically abusing her, and I think he tried to kill me. I'm still getting over it."

"He tried to kill you?"

Jake told JT about the sniper that fired and missed his mark, hitting Jake in the buttocks instead.

"I think he was actually trying to cripple me rather than kill me. The doctors said that a few inches to the left and a few inches higher, I would have been in a wheelchair for the rest of my life."

"Jake, here's my card. Call me Monday and we can have further discussions to see how we might collaborate moving forward," JT said. "Mornings are best."

The two men shook hands and the ceremony broke up as people started to drive away from the cemetery. *That man deserves a shot at revenge,* JT thought to himself, *he needs to be part of what we do next.*

JT and Carrie hosted a get together at Henri's for family, Double O employees, and some close friends. Jennifer was holding up extremely well, and Wingate men took turns attending her. Carrie and little Priscilla kept Jennifer moving around the room, talking with everyone.

There were many words of condolence, and not a single word of disrespect. John was loved and esteemed by everyone in the room. With British stoicism, Jennifer stood erect, smiling and accepting of everyone's comments. Shaking hands, hugging, kissing cheeks, she handled herself with characteristic calm and serenity. JT watched her in near disbelief.

Two hours later, Jennifer approached JT and Carrie.

"I must go home now, to my own apartment. Thank you both very much for all you have done for me today, but I must go home and grieve," Jennifer said in a low voice.

"Certainly, Carrie will go with you to make sure everything is okay," JT said.

"That won't be necessary, Carrie darling. If you don't mind, I just want to be alone for a day or two. Please don't worry about me, I'll be fine."

Jennifer swung her legs out of the limo and walked toward her apartment where the doorman held the door. She smiled at him, walked to the elevator, and rode quietly to her floor. She opened the door and she walked directly to the master bedroom. She walked to the bed where she and John had slept only weeks before. She collapsed on the bed and hugged John's pillow to her chest, all the while clutching her favorite picture of him; a full-face, eight-by-ten, dimpled-cheeked, blue-eyed, loving, grinning attestation of his deep love for her.

"Oh my darling, darling man, why did you have to leave me?" she cried, and began to sob and moan, rolling from side to side on the bed. She continued until her stomach muscles ached and her eyes stung with redness.

She sat up on the bed and looked at the clock. It was three thirty in the morning. She stood shakily and walked to the bathroom. She stepped out of her patent leather black heels and mourning clothes and stepped into the shower. The shower's spray was as hot as she could stand, and steam began to rise and fill the room. She dropped to her knees, water hitting her back and began to sob and moan again. Minutes later she stood, brushed back her long silver hair, scrubbed her face and still taut model's body, rinsed, and then turned off the stream.

She toweled off and put on John's terrycloth robe and walked to the living room where she poured herself two fingers of John's favorite single malt Scotch and sat curled up in his easy chair. She pulled the robe's collar close around her neck, took a sip of Scotch and rolled it around on her tongue, the way John used to do.

She tilted her head back and closed her eyes and felt his arms circle her and his hands rub up and down on her back. She felt his lips kiss her ear, cheek and mouth. Another tear formed at the corner of her eye.

She opened her eyes and stared at the ceiling.

"I have loved you since the first day I met you, and I will love you till my last," she said aloud, blinking the tears from her emerald green eyes.

She sipped the Scotch and could feel her body relaxing for the first time in weeks. She leaned her head against the chair back's wing and smiled at the portrait of her and John, standing together on the altar after their wedding.

"You beautiful, beautiful man," she said, smiling.

She closed her eyes again and again felt John's arms around her, caressing her and kissing her. Her smile broadened and she moaned softly with each caress.

"I will have you this way always," she said aloud. "You will always be here with me when I need you."

Another look at the portrait and she closed her eyes again. She was at peace for the first time since John went missing.

Jennifer knew that the crying wasn't over, but she also knew that she was on her way to recovering from the terrible blow she had been delivered. She called JT Monday morning to let him know she was okay. He and Carrie had left her completely alone as a sign of respect for her wishes to grieve alone.

"JT, I want you to know that I'm fine, and that I'm going to Tiburon for a couple of weeks and then on a trip abroad to mix a little business with pleasure. I'll be on my cell phone and would appreciate a call from time to time. I want to know the outcome of your quest, but I want it face to face. Nothing more about John until I return. Please," Jennifer told JT.

"I fully understand Jennifer, is there anything that you need, or anything I can do for you while you are gone?" JT replied.

"No, I have house sitters I can lean on and I will set that up before I leave."

"When do you depart?"

"Day after tomorrow," Jennifer said.

"Do you want the company plane?" JT offered.

"No, thank you, I have a United Flight. I would like Franklin to take me to the airport, though."

"No problem, have a good trip. I'll call often," JT said and hung up his phone.

"Here are your baggage claim tags, Mrs. Wingate," Randy said.

"Thank you so much, Franklin, and I'll see you in six weeks or so," Jennifer said as she sat back in her seat at the United First Lounge. She felt a shiver of loneliness cross her body, raising the hairs on the back of her neck. She needed to be as close to John as she could get, and she knew that Tiburon would be good for her.

The limo ride from San Francisco International Airport across the Golden Gate Bridge to Tiburon took just over one hour. The driver helped Jennifer to the door with her bags. She walked into the townhouse, and with an audible sigh of relief, she knew she was home. She gave the driver a tip and closed the door. She walked to the kitchen, got a glass of red wine, and walked back to the living room. She kicked off her heels and curled up in John's favorite chair.

She rubbed her cheek against the leather cushion and felt the chair comfortably surround her, engulf her, hold her, make her safe again. It was like the week after Chabahar, safe, here, and back in John's arms.

The wine tasted like John. For an hour she sipped her Pinot Noir, glanced around the room and felt all of the tension of the last weeks, once again, drain from her muscles and tendons. She was so relaxed she wondered if she could stand again. A smile came to her face, a smile of satisfaction and well-being. She understood, at that moment, that John was inside her, surrounding her, protecting her, even in death. Her love for him was so strong she knew she could summon his presence at any time and delight in his love for her.

The next morning she decided to walk down to Paradise Cay Yacht Harbor and look at John's boat. The air was brisk, the sky was a crystal azure blue, and her mood matched the morning. She stepped on to the deck and closed the rail gate behind her. Sitting on the stern seat, she touched the wheel. She could feel John's hands on hers helping her steer the proper point of sail. She smiled.

She got up and walked to the cabin door, opened it and descended into the sloops living compartment. She went to the bow where John had installed a double bed. She crawled onto the mattress and stretched out. Everything still smelled of the two of them. His scent mingled with her perfume and made her slightly dizzy.

She heard a knock on the hatch.

"Anybody home?" called a masculine voice.

Jennifer rose and stepped up on the hatch ladder.

"Can I help you?" she asked the handsome, tanned gentleman standing on the deck.

"I was walking by and noticed the hatch was open and wanted to make sure everything was okay," the man said. He was taken with

Jennifer's beauty and immediately recognized her. "You're Jennifer Middleton, aren't you?"

Jennifer cocked her head and smiled. "Yes, I am."

The man stuck out his hand. "I'm Ray Coburn, I own Coburn's Modeling Agency in San Francisco. I would recognize you anywhere."

"Thank you, Ray, everything is fine here, I was just checking out the boat. It has been some time since my husband and I were here last," Jennifer said in a business-like tone. It was nice to be recognized, Jennifer thought, even though it was by someone in the business.

"We can't be too careful, there's been a series of break-ins recently and the yacht club has increased security and asked everyone to look out for each other," Coburn said.

"I appreciate it, thank you," Jennifer said and turned back toward the hatch.

"You're welcome, Jennifer," Coburn said and turned to leave.

"Before you go, here's my card and if you need anything, want me to check on the boat, whatever, let me know," Coburn said, and turned to leave.

"Thank you, I will," she said "And please don't think me rude, but I had a death in the family recently, and it's still with me."

"I don't think you rude, and please accept my condolences."

Jennifer locked the hatch and walked back to the townhouse. She decided to go out for dinner and called for a cab.

"Where to, ma'am?" the young cab driver asked.

"The Caprice Restaurant, please," Jennifer said.

"We'll be there shortly," the driver said, turned frontward, and drove off.

The twenty minute drive took Jennifer to the well-known restaurant where she and John had dined many times in the past. The seafood was magnificent and the views of Angel Island and the Golden Gate Bridge were inspiring. She ordered Petrale sole Almandine with brussels sprouts, jasmine and wild rice and a glass of chilled Sauvignon Blanc. As she ate, she recalled the all-day sails with John and the evenings later at the Caprice. John was with her again as she sipped her wine and smiled, gazing at the Golden Gate Bridge in the distance and the setting sun beyond.

Jennifer paid her cab driver and walked into the Townhouse. She decided to stay up until midnight when she could call the London and Paris Stores. She reclined on the chaise lounge like she and John often did, staring out at the lights on the Benicia Bridge, the Brothers Light House beyond, Richmond, and south to Berkeley Marina. The chill from the bay caught her a little off guard, and she went inside for a warmer jacket.

At midnight, she called the London and Paris stores to set the dates for her arrival. She wanted to make sure she had a full schedule at both stores and to let them know she could be available for up to two weeks at each location. Everyone was excited and surprised that she would venture out so soon after John's death.

"Very well then, I'll arrive London in four days' time. I'll be staying at the Connaught, the Library Suite," Jennifer said and rang off.

Jennifer was on her way to wellness.

39

HERE WE GO

Reimer, Malfanti, and Farrington worked diligently cutting and banding the bills and staking out the Blanchet home and tending the remote wiretap. The only calls were from Blanchet's boyfriend. He was persistent and she was coy, making for some juicy conversations that the Seals would laughingly share over dinner meals.

With the filling of the duffle bags completed, the Seals could relax a little, and get a little sleep. They ate all of their meals at the hotel, or had them delivered to their rooms. The sudden influx of hulking strangers in tiny Gering/Scottsbluff would raise eyebrows. They waited.

"Hi Sis, it's me," Brad said into the phone. Bob shot up in the seat next Jim on the stakeout. He hand-signaled that the call they had been waiting for had come in.

"Hello, Brad," was Sharon's icy reply.

"Look, Sis. Look, I'm sorry to put you through this, but you are being well paid for your services, aren't you?" Brad continued.

"I'm also aiding and abetting a criminal who has done God knows what, and the only reason I would do this is because you're my brother," Sharon said.

"It'll be over soon," Brad said.

"Can't be soon enough, as far as I am concerned."

"I'm sending you an e-mail with the address of the post office box I want you to send the bags," Brad said. "Please have the bags boxed up for shipping, and send them as soon as you can."

"My boyfriend and I are going out of town this weekend, I'll get the bags in the mail on Monday," Sharon said.

"Send them by the fastest means possible, don't mind the expense," Brad said. "Let me know what the cost is and I'll reimburse you immediately."

They talked a few minutes longer, and Brad hung up without divulging where he was over the phone. Cagey, not taking any chances.

Sharon turned out the lights and went to sleep.

The next morning, Saturday, Sharon rose, got dressed, and put herself together. It was the day she and her boyfriend were overnight camping at Lake Minatare, north and east of Scottsbluff.

Jim Reimer, with the morning surveillance duty, watched Sharon's boyfriend drive up and park in front of 117. He rang the bell and Sharon let him in with a big smile, Daisy Duke's, and a revealing knotted blouse and what looked like a bikini bra top underneath. She gave him a big kiss on the mouth, and closed the door behind him.

"The food is in the Igloo Chest along with drinks. Our favorite Bud Light beer is in the cooler as well. Did you stop for ice?" Sharon asked.

"I did, and I got us some Tequila and limes too. I'll start loading this stuff in the truck. Is this everything you want to bring?"

"Yes," she said. "I'll lock up and be with you in a few minutes."

Jim watched the man load up the truck, and it looked very much like Sharon and her boyfriend were going on a water skiing trip for the weekend. The man loaded a food cooler, an ice chest, an air mattress and a sleeping bag. It looked like they wouldn't be back until Sunday night or Monday morning.

He slid down in the seat when he saw Sharon leave and lock the front door. She bounced happily down the walkway and jumped into the pick-up and slid over next to her boyfriend. She was obviously excited about the trip.

Jim decided to follow them for a while to see if he could figure out where they were going. The pair drove west on 23rd, then right on avenue B, left on 71 and right again on 21 North. They drove for another ten minutes and Jim noticed the boat trailer's light blinking a right turn. The sign said Lake Minatare 8.5 miles.

Jim went straight for two miles, u-turned and returned to the motel.

"Hey Bob, Sharon and her boyfriend have just left for the weekend, and I think it's a good time to switch the bags and search her computer for the address Brad gave her. You're the computer geek, so let's go," Jim said.

"I'm right behind you," Bob answered.

They drove back to 117 W 23rd and Jim noticed that the boyfriend, the pick-up and the boat and trailer were back in front of the house. They continued along, u-turned and found a vantage point to watch the goings on. Ten minutes later Sharon came out of the house again, locked the door and skipped to the pick-up. She had a grocery bag in her arms that she handed in to her boyfriend and jumped up into the seat. The boyfriend put the bag into the extended cab, turned and drove away in the same direction Jim had followed them earlier.

Reimer and Malfanti waited a full twenty minutes to make sure they wouldn't be interrupted. They went around back and entered the house with the four duffle bags. Jim went to the hallway, pulled down the attic ladder, and carefully retrieved the four real bags. He picked the Master locks on the bags and went to work. He then switched the real money for the fake bills before he locked and restacked the original bags with fake bills in the attic exactly how he had found them originally. The whole task took twenty minutes.

Malfanti was successful in hacking into Sharon's computer. She had used her address as her password, it was the third keyword Bob tried. He found the e-mail and the address he was looking for and closed down the computer. He went to help Jim finish up.

The two men were out of the house, undetected, in twenty-three minutes.

Back in the hotel room, Jim and the rest of the Seals, including new-comer Carlos "Che" Guevara, gathered around the speaker phone as Jim dialed JT's office where JT had set up a conference call. The game was on, and they had two days to get in sync.

"It's Costa Rica," Jim announced to the group.

JT interrupted the discussion as he called to his wife Carrie to get the RO RO ready to deploy from Galveston and alert the airport to have the Bell ready for him in one hour. He also instructed Carrie to have Jake O'Malley meet him at the airport as well.

"Okay fellas, where are we?" JT began.

"The woman is out with her boyfriend on an overnight camping trip about one hour from town. We can either pick her up now and take her into custody, or wait until she returns on Sunday or Monday," Jim Reimer said.

They talked about both possibilities and decided on the latter. It would be better if the boyfriend was out of the picture completely, he just represented another problem, and they didn't really need any more. JT also felt it would give him the time he needed to get the helicopter and the RO RO into position.

"I'll have my wife here Sunday midday, ready to handle the wom-an for as long as it takes for us to finish with the killer. What do you plan to do with her?" Reimer asked.

"I don't know yet, I'll have to have some words with our attorneys and think about it a little," JT answered.

It was decided that Malfanti and Carlos would head for San Jose, Costa Rica immediately, and that Farrington and two Seals would deploy there after they dealt with Sharon Blanchet on Sunday. McSpadden said that he would have two charter jets ready to go im-mediately at Western Nebraska Regional Airport.

Malfanti and Carlos packed their belongings and headed for the airport. Reimer and his wife drove out to Lake Minatare to keep an eye on Sharon and her boyfriend. Charles Farrington and one Seal were already out at 117 W 23rd Street, keeping an eye on Sharon's house.

JT was soon on his way to Galveston in the company helicopter. It would take him over fourteen hours to get to the RO RO stopping three times to refuel. It would then take another ninety hours to get the RO RO into position off the Costa Rican coast.

At Nebraska Regional, Malfanti contacted the charter company that was based in Omaha. He was told that the aircraft would be in Scottsbluff within the hour, and gave him the itinerary.

All they could do now was get in position and wait.

40

ESCAZU

Malfanti and Carlos arrived at Juan Santamaria Airport, ten miles northwest of San Jose City Center. The Seals rented a car and drove to the Wyndham Garden Hotel located near the Escazu district. After checking in, they drove to the Escazu Post Office, Correos de Costa Rica, located at the corner of Av 28 and Calle 134.

The men parked across the street from the post office to observe the area. It would be easy to watch the building that they determined was open weekdays only from 8 AM to 5 PM from this vantage point. They walked across the street and into the building to see if they could figure out where the packages would arrive and how they were processed.

Inside the building, they noticed a waiting area with several seats.

"The waiting area looks promising. We can change off sitting here during the day and cover the place from inside and out, front and back," Malfanti said.

"When will the bags get shipped?" Carlos asked.

"Reimer said that the plan was to apprehend the woman as soon as her boyfriend dropped her off from the lake, and ship the parcels first thing Monday morning," Malfanti answered.

"Here they come now," Reimer said to his wife, sitting next to him across the street from 117 W 23rd Street. The two slumped down in their seats.

Sharon and her boyfriend drove up and parked in front of the house. They got out and began unloading the items Sharon had brought along for the weekend outing. When the work was done, the two stood on the front stoop and hugged.

"I had a great time, Sharon," the boyfriend said.

"Me too," Sharon answered. "I'll call you tomorrow."

The boyfriend walked back to his truck, and Sharon smiled and waved as he drove off. She walked into the house and closed the door. Reimer and his wife walked up to the front door and knocked.

"Forget something, darling? Oh, I'm sorry," Sharon said as Reimer walked in and subdued her in her surprised state.

"I know you. You're the guy from the restaurant and the bank. What the hell are you doing?" a scared and angry Sharon asked.

"I think you know why we're here," Reimer said. "A little problem of four million dollars."

"What four million dollars?" Sharon scoffed.

"The four million dollars you have in your attic," Reimer answered.

Sharon's mouth gaped open as she realized she had been found out. She looked down and shook her head in disgust. She knew that her no-good brother had brought this down on her, and she was upset with herself for being taken in by her own greed.

"Am I under arrest?" Sharon asked.

"That is entirely up to you," Reimer answered, "If you cooperate with us, the answer is no. If not, you will be charged with abetting a criminal and booked into jail by tomorrow morning."

Sharon sat down on her sofa and put her head in her hands. She did not want to go to jail, yet she was at odds with ratting on her brother. She began to cry. Reimer and his wife sat in chairs opposite her and waited for her to come to her senses, which was slow in coming.

"We've been watching you since the day before we met. We've been listening in on all your calls and watching your every movement. We are not the police, but we are very interested in bringing your brother back to face charges for the reprehensible acts he has wrought on our client and his family."

"What has he done?" Sharon asked.

"Kidnapped my client's daughter and uncle, extorted five million dollars from his family, and brutally murdered four people in the process. If you are charged as an accomplice, you could go away for a very long time," Reimer answered.

Sharon sat stunned and speechless.

"I had nothing to do with any of this. He shipped me the bags; which I presume hold the money, against my will. He paid me, and I have not spent a penny of it, and will return it all," she said, beginning to cry.

"That isn't enough. We need your help to apprehend him."

"What do you want me to do?" she asked, resigned.

Reimer explained their plan and Sharon agreed to cooperate.

Brad opened his e-mail.

> Tried to ship your boxes today and got bad news. All packages are subject to customs inspection. There are companies that will fly the boxes in under the radar. Very expensive. $15,000 per package. Advise.

Brad chuckled and e-mailed back.

> Cost is not an issue. How do they handle the boxes?

Sharon replied.

> They helicopter them in to a remote location. You will have to meet it personally to pick up the packages.

There is a small town called Estrada about 60 miles east of San Jose, on the road to Limón. 7 miles out of town, you will come to a house number 17806. The packages will be there in five days. You pay them there, cash.

Brad's final reply.

Thank you, I'll deal with it from here.

Malfanti got a call from Reimer telling him about the revelation. JT had to trick Brad into picking up the parcels near Limón.

"What a great idea. That way we won't have to deal with him in the city, much better way of doing it," Malfanti said.

"You need to get to Estrada and check it out. You'll need to be careful, the killer will probably be doing the same thing, and would easily recognize an expatriate. There are hotels in Limón, so you and your men can set up there today," Reimer said.

Malfanti and Carlos moved out of their hotel in San Jose, and traveled to Limón that afternoon. They moved into the Park Hotel in Limón, a resort-style, beachside hotel with ocean views and outdoor bars. The hotel was mainly for international visitors and they fit right in. Malfanti had several pictures of Brad which he and his men studied with diligence. They were aware of Brad's limp and the tattoo on the nape of his neck. They were on constant alert, watching for him.

The next morning, they drove up to Estrada and looked for the 17806 house number along the Calle Estrada. They stood out among the locals, and Malfanti felt uncomfortable. He decided to move a few miles down the road and rethink his approach to the recon in this rural farm community. He decided to go back to Limón and see if he could purchase some local clothing to look a little less conspicuous. The hotel clerk told him of a nearby shop that sold work clothes.

That afternoon, they went back to Estrada with its vast banana and pineapple fields. Malfanti and one Seal got out and walked around the area, looking like itinerants seeking work. The other Seal stayed with the vehicle. The building at 17806 Calle Estrada was the main packing facility for the largest pineapple producer in the area. Carlos, the Seal with Malfanti, engaged one of the workers in fluent Spanish. He was able to learn that there were no jobs available yet but thought there would be in another *dos, tres semanas*.

Malfanti noticed a high spot across and down the gravel road that he thought they might be able to watch the goings on at 17806. The long wait and observation began.

JT's RO RO was making good time and was just rounding the Honduras/Nicaragua bulge approximately 250 miles north of Limón. They would arrive in Limón in fourteen hours. Once he cleared customs, he would join up with Malfanti at their hotel and complete their plan for Brad's abduction.

"Stroke of genius you had, Mr. Wingate," Malfanti said.

"That assumes that the bastard will take the bait," JT said. "And please, call me JT."

The two men shared all the information they had, and JT sat pondering their next move.

"Is there an open spot there where I can put the helicopter down?" JT asked.

"There are several, and we can bring you in with a flashlight and the GPS," Malfanti said.

"How would you rather work this, day or night?" JT asked.

The men explained that it really didn't matter to them, they were experienced at both. Malfanti thought that night would give them the most time before detection. JT explained that his company agent in Limón had located the 17806 address, belonging to a businessman,

Armando Bedoya, who had been shipping his goods with Double O for years. He was willing to help out and would work with them on the day of the abduction.

"Carlos speaks fluent Spanish. Can we get him inside the building with Mr. Bedoya?" Malfanti asked.

"I'm sure we can," JT said. "I'll contact him in the morning and set it up. Brad is supposed to contact Bedoya tomorrow to arrange for pickup of the ransom money."

"We have a feeling Brad is here in Limón now. We've been looking for him, but haven't spotted him," Malfanti said. "Probably still keeping a very low profile."

"Alright men, I think we are all on the same page, so I'll say goodnight to you and I'll meet you here for breakfast in the morning," JT said.

The men finished their dinner and discussions, and JT went back to his stateroom on his RO RO.

"Good morning, men," JT said as he walked up to Seals seated at the breakfast table, "Meet a friend of mine, Jake O'Malley."

"Good morning Sir. Good morning Jake," the Seals responded, shaking hands all around.

"I managed to contact Armando this morning, and he's ready to meet Carlos and get ready for the abduction," JT said.

JT explained that Malfanti was to get Carlos in place no later than three PM, and that he was planning to fly in with Malfanti and the other Seal at nine PM sharp.

41

HOOK, LINE AND OOPS, A SINKER.

At six PM, the RO RO Captain pulled away from its berth at Terminal de Limón, turned north and out to sea. At six thirty PM, JT came out of his stateroom and joined Malfanti and Jake O'Malley in the galley for dinner.

"This is a nice little boat you have here, Sir," Malfanti said to JT.

"We have many more like it, all around the world," JT answered. "They are the work horses of our fleets."

The dinner conversation stayed casual, until the Captain approached JT with a radio message from NYPD Detective Johnson. He looked at the message, and then at the two men, shook his head and shoved the message across the table for them to Read.

We have tried every avenue we can, and
no one will sign off on the authorization for
you to bring Waterman back into the country.
No one wants to offend the Costa Ricans.

"What does this mean, Sir?" Malfanti asked.

"It means we go to plan B," JT said, "Right Jake?"

"I'm ready," Jake said with a smile.

The men finished their dinner and went to their quarters to prepare for the final chapter of their plan to unfold.

At eight twenty PM, on the calm moonlit night, JT met Malfanti and Jake on the helipad and climbed into the Bell 206 helicopter. JT and Malfanti got into the front cockpit and Jake got into the back cab. They fastened their seatbelts and JT began his start-up and take-off sequence. Lights, Fuel, Fuel pressure, all check. JT opened the cockpit door, leaned out and shouted 'CLEAR'.

He closed the cockpit door, flipped the ignition, and began the rotor run-up. The attendant outside the helicopter stood by with a fire extinguisher as the blades began to spin faster and faster. Finally the rotors came up to speed and the attendant pulled the battery pack connection, walked around the fuselage, and finally gave JT a thumbs up.

The helicopter rose slowly off of the helipad until it cleared the ship and quickly began its ascent. At five hundred feet, JT set a westerly course for the half-hour trip to Estrada.

At nearly the same time, Carlos and Brad walked out to the open field behind the pineapple processing plant. They stood at the middle of the field and listened for the sound of rotor blades. It was quiet and Brad watched Carlos very closely. Carlos pretended not to be concerned, as if he did this every day. He kept his distance from Brad, however.

Shortly, the helicopter's drone could be heard. Carlos switched on his flash light and shined it up into the night sky. JT saw the light immediately and turned on his search light and drenched the area in vibrating, piercing light. Carlos and Brad moved to the side of the field as JT professionally landed the aircraft.

JT and Malfanti sat still in the cockpit as Jake, wearing a three-hole balaclava, opened the door to the back cabin. He motioned for Brad and Carlos to approach the door and retrieve the bags that he had placed in the opening. Brad walked up to the helicopter and began pulling the bags to the ground, he had the fourth bag off when Carlos gave him a firm rap on the back of his head. Brad dropped like a stone.

Carlos effortlessly picked Brad up by his underarms and handed him up to Jake. Jake pulled and Carlos pushed Brad into the cabin.

Carlos climbed in and handcuffed Brad to a seat strut, got into his seat, and buckled up.

The helicopter revved the rotors and climbed quickly up out of the field. At five hundred feet, JT did a 180 degree turn and headed back toward the RO RO. Brad began to stir, and Jake, without his balaclava, put a set of earphones on his head.

"Mr. Waterman, you are on your way back to the United States to face charges of three counts of kidnapping, four counts of murder, one count of attempted murder and extortion of five million dollars, one count of child endangerment, all with weapons enhancements. What do you say to that?" JT said, with everyone listening.

"Look whoever you are, I don't know who you are or how much you are being paid to do this, but I will double the amount," Brad said hopefully.

"No dice, pal," JT said. "You're heading for a life sentence, without the possibility of parole, in Sing Sing Gen Pop."

"OK, OK, I'll triple what you're being paid," Brad pleaded.

"Nope," JT said.

The earphones went silent as JT climbed the helicopter to two thousand feet, leaving land and heading out over the Gulf. He waited for ten long minutes and got back on the radio.

"You have another option, though," JT said into the phones.

"I can't do life in jail, what's my option?" Brad asked.

No sooner had he said that than Brad realized what his option was. He laid there thinking for several minutes and said, "I'll take the option."

Jake reached down and unhitched Brad's handcuffs from the seat strut. He reset the cuffs behind Brad's back, and reached to open the cabin door. He removed Brad's earphones. The wind from the rotors rushed in the door as Brad inched forward on his knees. At the doorway, he stopped for a moment and looked up.

"I can't do this," Brad cried, looking back at the men in the cabin. For the first time he noticed Jake sitting there with a big grin on his face.

"Sure you can asshole," Jake said as he stood and squarely planted his boot between Brad's shoulder blades, launching him out of the helicopter to begin his two thousand foot drop to the ocean below. Jake reached out and shut the cabin door.

"That should do it," Jake said.

"Good work men, we'll be back on board the RO RO in fifteen minutes," JT announced from the cockpit.

"What happened out there, JT?" Detective Johnson asked JT.

"You won't believe it, but we had him in our sights but he spotted us before we could grab him. I'll bet he goes deep underground now. Good thing is, he only has a million of my money. He'll have to be a little more conservative in his spending habits."

"We'll continue to petition the Costa Rican authorities to try and locate him and bring him back," Johnson said. "One million dollars, four deaths, and kidnappings add up to a lifetime behind bars."

"You're welcome to do that Detective, but I don't think you are going to get very far. As far as the Wingate's are concerned, it's 'case closed'".

Jim Reimer called JT to find out what he wanted done with Brad's sister.

"Jim, I think that her involvement in this was unfortunate. I don't think she had anything to do with it before the fact, and she was just being loyal to a family member. I think that she has probably suffered enough. Drop her off at home, make sure you recover any monies she may have, and let her off with a warning."

"I agree, JT," Reimer answered. "She's not an evil person."

JT met Jennifer at JFK Airport and drove her back to the city. He was very happy to see her, and she looked well and rested. After the small talk, he waited for the right moment to tell Jennifer of his efforts to bring John's killer to justice.

"Jennifer, I'm not going to cloud you with the details, but suffice to say the matter of Brad Waterman has been dealt with. There will be no more problems from that man," JT said, reaching over and patting her gloved hand.

"I am very happy to hear that, and I have something to tell you as well," she said. "I have decided to franchise the New York store, and I am moving back to England and set my base from there. The other two stores have signed off, and I think it is time to get out of the rat race."

"I'm sorry to hear that Jennifer, we will deeply miss you," JT said.

"I want to keep the Tiburon property, along with John's boat and plane," she said. "I'll keep the apartment here, as well, for when I come to visit you and the family, which I hope will be often. I want to be a part of Priscilla's growth."

"Whatever you want to do is fine with us, but you know you have a place with us anytime you come, for any reason," JT said, reaching for her hand.

She explained to JT that she had come to grips with John's passing and wanted to start fresh again. She wanted to remain a part of the family, but wanted to do that from a distance. JT understood her needs and assured her that he respected her decision and would do whatever it took to see that she found what she was looking for. She squeezed his hand and smiled at him through glistening eyes.

"I would like to have Priscilla visit me from time to time and stay with me for short periods of time," she said. "We can do some traveling together, and that way I can stay current with her."

"She will love that, and Carrie and I would be extremely happy for you to continue to be a large part of her life. She adores you, looks up to you, and talks about you constantly," JT said. "There would be a huge void if you stepped out of her life completely."

At her apartment, the doorman opened her door, and helped Jennifer with her bags.

"Will you have dinner with us this evening?" JT called out.

"Certainly. When and where?" she answered, standing in her doorway.

"I'll call you from the office," JT said, waving and watching her walk inside.

JT looked down at his lap and squeezed his eyes shut, hoping to dislodge the memories of the happenings of the last month and a half. He realized that he hadn't taken the time to morn his uncle's death, and seeing Jennifer disappear down the marble hallway and into the waiting elevator gave him a sudden feeling of finality. As tears came to his eyes he realized that the entire Wingate burden was now on his shoulders. For minutes he hung his head in thought.

JT raised his head, glanced at Jennifer's building one last time, looked forward and slowly pulled away from the curb.

EPILOG

Farewell

John Wingate was an accumulation of every character trait that I admire and respect in a man. He was handsome, square jawed, dimple cheeked with an aquiline nose flanked by azurine eyes, underscored by a genuine, white toothed smile that '*charmed the pants off of every woman he met*'. I visualized my six-foot-four, white blond haired, WWII Pacific Naval Ace, cousin Evald Holmgaard, as I wrote about John; A big man, with a big heart, and a big sense of humor. When LCDR Holmgaard had a break from the war he would come to our house, pick my mother up off her feet, twirl her around and bellow, "Ma, I'm home", as John did with Priscilla in the *Chabahar Incident*. My emotional recollection of those moments are riveted.

In his youth John was a ladies man. He had a girl in every port, and as a head of a major shipping company his ports were numerous. In my career I was fortunate enough to have visited all of the spots that John had his lady friends. In the *Hobyo Affair*, he does a sort of farewell tour of all the homes of all his ladies that were the most romantic locations of all my visits. I confess that I thought of George Clooney as I wrote that section, but the locations were all mine, reflecting my observations.

John was intelligent, not intellectual. John had the marvelous gift of concentration. He thought everything through, from concept to implementation, in minute detail. As the details occurred to him, the pros and the cons naturally flowed and he was able to reach 'plan perfection', and see all the pitfalls long before anyone else. He had the type of mental capacity that always impressed his peers, yet he never belittled others who lacked the same aptitude. He always felt that it was his responsibility, and his alone, to make sure everything was right. The *Buck Stopped* with John, which eventually stopped John, as we saw in the *Manhattan Matter*.

John was generous *to a fault*. His wealth was so vast that there was never a question in his mind when it came time to pay. His foundations attested to his largess, his desire to care for little Jennifer and later adopt her mother Carrie, in the *Hobyo Affair*, clearly showed his generosity, and his 'no holds barred' approach to Carrie's and JT's extraction from captivity in Somalia, clearly showed that results overshadowed cost in John's mind.

John was emotionally selfish in his early years, but eventually saw the need to share himself and his wealth as he aged. Adopting Carrie was an easy decision for John to make. He had missed out on marriage and family, and Carrie presented him with an opportunity to experience everything he bypassed in life.

Marrying Jennifer Middleton was inevitable and both he and Jennifer knew it. Neither career oriented character could ignore their life's burdens, but both needed love, nurturing and understanding and found it in each other, knowingly and unknowingly. Not until the realization that he was not *bullet proof* did John decide to ask for Jennifer's hand. The close calls in Hobyo, and his sudden age limitation realization, were life changing for John. Jennifer was ready almost simultaneously.

I will miss John, but I knew that I had to kill him off eventually. The initial shot to John's head hit me hard, as did watching him lay there, bloody and lifeless until JT was able to cover him up with his jacket. I felt like I had lost a great friend and hero figure, and yet I knew that his time had come. Everyone has to shift for themselves now, and it is time for me to get on with new thoughts, new characters and new plots.

Farewell John, I will miss you.

Note: Pages 14 through 19 seem completely unnecessary and out of place, and they are. Those pages were edited out of *The Chabahar Affair* by an overzealous editor who didn't see the importance of character development. For some reason I really like those pages; the way they were written, worded, and what they had to say. I vowed to get them back into the Trilogy somewhere. Thanks for bearing with me.

www.ingramcontent.com/pod-product-compliance
Lightning Source LLC
Chambersburg PA
CBHW061555170626
46811CB00001B/211